SHOOTING SCRIPT

*

GAVIN LYALL

THE COMPANION BOOK CLUB
LONDON

Made and printed in Great Britain
for the Companion Book Club (Odhams Books Ltd.)
by Odhams (Watford) Limited
Watford, Herts.
S.467.UC.

THEY came at me from high on the right, out of the afternoon sun. From just where they should have been. So perhaps I should have seen them coming.

Once, I would have done. But this time I was sitting half-asleep in the driving seat of a Dove trudging at 150 knots down Route Delta to Puerto Rico and not worrying about anything more than whether my cargo of seedlings would leave the cabin with a smell that I'd have to pay to get cleaned out.

The first I knew was when they flicked across less than a hundred yards ahead; two bright silver H-shapes in the sky, suddenly there, suddenly gone.

I came awake with a thump and a terrible sick feeling of being defeated. Beaten. Then it turned quickly to anger, and I swung the nose of the Dove around the sky, searching. But there are no guns in the nose of a Dove.

I'd recognized the shapes, of course: Vampire jets. And I knew where they must have come from—the Republica Libra. I was just south of the coastline, just past Santo Bartolomeo. But I hadn't known the Republica owned any jet fighters, not even seventeen-year-old ones.

They reappeared ahead, nearly a mile away and climbing. I watched them, angrily. If they wanted to try the same joke twice, I was going to slap on full power and swing straight at them. And if they rammed each other trying to get out of my way, then hard luck and maybe somebody'll paint your names in gold on the Honour Board . . . And if *I* got rammed? Or shot out of the sky in this old unarmed crate?

This wasn't how I'd learned the game. I started looking for a cloud to hide in. Live through today—but tomorrow . . .

But they kept going in the fast shallow climb jets use

until they were out of sight eastwards, the same direction I was going. I watched them go.

An hour and three-quarters later I touched down at San Juan airport. I parked among the usual clutter of freight and private aircraft just east of the airport building, found the man who was supposed to collect my cargo, and left him and a squad of officials arguing over whether the seedlings were suffering from the Colorado Beetle or just dialectical materialism. I went on up to the Meteorological Office.

The duty officer there recognized me as a regular even if he couldn't recall my name. We said 'Hi' to each other, and then I asked if he'd heard of any good hurricanes recently.

'Bit early in the season,' he commented.

I shrugged and said: 'July, stand by,' quoting the old Jamaican tag about hurricanes; 'June, too soon; July, stand by; August, you must; September, remember; October, all over.' In a Jamaican accent, it even rhymes.

He nodded and shoved across the weather chart he'd been working on. 'Got a small circular disturbance east of Barbados.'

'What's it going to do?'

He smiled. 'I'll tell you and you tell me what'll win the three o'clock at Hileah Park on Saturday.'

'Meteorology's marvellous except when it comes to predicting the weather.'

'We've got a Coastguard flight down there. Should be a report in an hour. Which company's looking after your plane while you're here?'

I grinned, perhaps a little sideways. 'And I have a chauffeur-driven Rolls Royce meeting me outside.'

He smiled back and pulled a piece of paper out of a pile on his desk. 'Give me your name and hotel and I'll ring you if it gets within two hundred miles of here—okay?'

'Keith Carr. I'm booked in at the El Portale. Thanks.' For a meteorologist, he was almost human.

Then I noticed a *Macdonald World Air Power Guide* on

6

the shelf behind him, and asked if I could take a look. I turned up the Republica—and there, shoved in among the usual Mustangs and Thunderbolts and their 'shortage of spares' was a neat handwritten note that read just '12 Vampire F.5'.

'Where the hell did the Republica get Vampires?'

He looked up. 'Couple of weeks or so. Have you been tangling with them?'

'Two of them made a dummy pass at me this afternoon.'

'Probably the two that came in here—just over an hour ago.' He nodded eastwards, towards the National Guard base at the far end of the main runway. 'On a good-will visit. So maybe you'll meet them around town and congratulate them personally.'

'A *good-will* visit?'

'That's what it says here.' He stood up and walked to the door with me. 'Happen our circular disturbance grows up into a real hurricane, it'll be the first of the year. So we're set to call it Annette.'

'I knew a girl once——'

'Ahh.' He patted my shoulder and smiled a deep satisfied smile. I had a kind of bet with myself—that I'd get at least a dozen pilots each saying exactly that before five o'clock. You make eleven, and there's half an hour to go.' He sighed. 'Me, I've never met an Annette in my life.'

'They're all just crazy about pilots.'

He pushed me firmly out of the door.

I got my overnight case out of the Dove, rang the agency that sometimes finds me cargoes in Puerto Rico, then took a taxi into town.

San Juan has changed—grown up, perhaps—in the last few years. Mind, I never knew it when it was a quaint old Spanish-colonial town, and I haven't met anyone who did. Now it's a five-mile stretch of hotels, offices and freeways strung along the shore from the airport to the Navy airbase, all as clean and crisp as an architect's model. It's a great place if you happen to be a building or a car, but dogs and human beings are frowned on. You could call it growing up.

7

The El Portale is built in the same style, only smaller and stepped back a few hundred yards and dollars from the big hotels down on the beach. I checked in, drank a couple of cans of beer in the drugstore beside the lobby and read a paper to see if it suggested why Republica jets should have taken to jumping innocent charter flights. It didn't, of course. So I went upstairs, took a shower, and then lay down on the bed to watch the sky darken and the line of big hotels over on the beach start lighting up like Christmas trees.

The phone woke me.

The room was flat dark by then. I groped around for the receiver and answered it with a prehistoric grunt.

A voice said: 'Mr Keith Carr of Kingston?'

You didn't have to have heard the voice before to recognize it. You hear it all over the world, and everywhere it sounds the same. As precise and impersonal as an income-tax form, and about as welcome. The voice of authority.

The voice said: 'Agent Ellis, Federal Bureau of Investigation.'

I grunted again.

'I believe you're leaving for Kingston again tomorrow, Mr Carr, so perhaps I could have a friendly talk with you sometime this evening.'

'D'you mean I have a choice?'

'You're not an American citizen, Mr Carr. Just a friendly talk.'

I didn't say anything. He went on: 'I could come to your hotel, or perhaps you're going out somewhere. I could meet you there.'

I chewed on this for a moment. Then I thought of something. 'There's a couple of Republica Libra pilots in town. Find out where they're staying and I'll meet you there.'

There was a long official silence at his end. Then: 'That isn't exactly my job, Mr Carr.'

'All right. Where I'll be this evening is walking round the big hotels looking for them. You can come along on that if you like.'

'Hold the line, please.' There was another silence. After

8

a while he came back. 'I understand they're staying at the Sheraton. Why——'

'Then I'll see you in the roof bar there at nine—all right?'

'Why do you want to meet these pilots, Mr Carr?'

'Just a friendly talk, Mr Ellis.'

★ 2 ★

I ATE a hamburger down in the drugstore, then walked up to the Sheraton, timing it to arrive at just five past nine. The FBI would be dead on time, of course—and that made him the host.

I'd cheerfully said I'd 'see' him up in the 24th-floor bar, but I'd forgotten the lighting they went in for there: a small frosted-glass lamp parked in front of each drinker. Just enough light to make every woman look beautiful and every bar bill unreadable. A big hotel thinks of such things.

So I just stood there looking lost, until somebody stood up from one of the tables, walked across and said quietly, 'Mr Carr?'

About all I could tell in that light was that he was a little shorter than me, a little wider in the shoulders, and with lightish crew-cut hair. His age could have been anything from twenty-five to forty-five. We sat down and a waiter with radar eyes took my order for Bacardi Silver Label and bitter lemon.

Ellis said: 'You know Bacardi have got over sixty per cent of the rum market in the States and only about three per cent in Puerto Rico itself. Funny. Some people think they came in here after Castro nationalized their plant in Cuba. But they've been here since 1936. Biggest tax-payer on the island now. And the Puerto Ricans still don't drink their rum. Funny.'

FBI small-talk. If I'd ordered Scotch he'd have made me feel at home by reciting the life story of Bonny Prince Charlie.

The waiter brought my drink and Ellis managed not to

say 'Cheers' and we drank. I said: 'We now come to the main attraction of the evening: a friendly talk from the FBI.'

He leant his elbows on his knees and twiddled his glass and said: 'Let's just call it advice Mr Carr. You probably know we helped the Federal Government draw up a black list of pilots grounded for illegal flights to Cuba. Either for Castro or against. Those are all American pilots, of course; we can't pull a flying licence out from under anybody else. But—like with all these things—there's always a list of people who aren't on the list. Cuban, Mexican, Venezuelan, Colombian—and some English.'

'The grey list.'

'It's been called that.'

'A bit of trouble with the Customs whenever you land in the States. A bit more difficult to get somebody to service your plane. A bit of a problem with visas. Just enough to take the profit out of a flight. You mean *that* list?'

'I've heard it happens,' he admitted.

'I haven't been in Cuba in four years. Not even illegally.'

'Sure. And none of those things have happened to you.' He sipped his drink. 'But the list's being expanded; *that* always happens, too. The State Department's getting worried about the Republica Libra now.'

'About that earthly paradise? Just because it goes in for a little midnight beating-up, arrest-without-trial, a few basement executions?'

He shook his head slowly. 'No. Oh, sure it happens. But it always has. *We* don't like it, but . . . No. They're worried about a real blow-up. The opposition to the generals has been building up since Jiminez went back in. You knew about that?'

'I'd heard a rumour.' Jiminez was the Republica's Robin Hood—or a lousy Commie or a great liberal leader or a racketeer gangster or . . . The only thing anybody really knew about Jiminez was that he thought Jiminez would make a great next president of the Republica, and the sooner the better. The better for whom nobody would know until it was too late.

He'd been down in South America somewhere for the last

10

four years: skipped or chased out by the two generals who were currently running the Republica: Castillo of the Army, Bosco of the Air Force. The Navy was just a couple of old sub-chasers and a few PT boats, so the admiral didn't rate a part-dictatorship. The admiral, if he'd got any sense, lived in the nearest bar and was careful to keep his ships slightly unserviceable so nobody could suspect him of political ambition.

Ellis said: 'Jiminez is supposed to be up in the hills organizing things—and I mean organizing. This isn't shot-guns and machetes. Castillo's got half the army out chasing them and last week they captured a three-inch mortar. *That* didn't get into the Republica in somebody's hip pocket. Now you see where I'm going?'

As my night vision improved, I could pick out a little more about him. But still not his age. He had light, steady eyes and a knobbly face full of small muscles, frozen in the weary I've-read-the-file-on-you expression that's the first lesson taught at the FBI Academy.

He was wearing a milky-coffee-coloured lightweight suit with the jacket kept buttoned, probably because he had a gun on his belt. Shoulder holsters went out with double-breasted suits.

I saw what he was getting at, all right. But I also saw why the Republica had suddenly decided to spend good beer money on a dozen jet fighters. They didn't need them for aerial defence—one nice thing about the Caribbean is that nobody ever goes to war. They can't afford it. With every-body on his own island, a war would mean a big navy, invasion fleets, long supply lines. So they keep their troubles at home. But a properly handled squadron of jets can be a good ground-attack weapon: fast, flexible, plenty of fire-power. You won't catch a rebel by hauling a tank over mountain roads at 5 m.p.h. But a jet jumping over the hill on a couple of minutes' notice might do it.

Ellis said: 'Well Mr Carr?'

Just to annoy him, I said: 'I thought the FBI was confined to the United States and the Commonwealth of Puerto Rico. Aren't you treading on Central Intelligence Agency ground?'

11

'Screw the CIA,' he said calmly.

'If you say so. But the Republica's still CIA territory.' I gave a careful pause. 'Had you thought the CIA might have hired me?'

His head came up with a jerk, and even in that light I knew I was getting a hard, penetrating stare. Then he said slowly and quietly, 'I don't think so. We know quite a bit about you, Mr Carr. English, thirty-six years old, ten years in the RAF, mostly on fighters. You were in combat with one of our squadrons in Korea, on an officer exchange scheme. The last eight years you've been a civil pilot; the last five out here, in business for yourself. You're not married, but you're not queer and you're not a fanatic. No, I don't think you're working for them.'

'Or in other words, screw the CIA.'

'Short, back and sideways.' He leant back in his chair. 'We're getting off the point. The FBI's interest is because the arms being found in the Republica are mostly American arms. Okay, so most guns in the Caribbean are American anyway. But somebody's getting them into the Republica, and from somewhere. That could make it FBI business. Just could.'

'Well, if you can't blame it on the CIA, why not try Cuba? I haven't heard that the generals were top of any popularity polls over *there*.'

He put his hands flat on the table. 'Mr Carr, in the last five years we've blamed Cuban Communists for everything except hurricanes, and I expect the Weather Bureau's working on that. Sure, they cause trouble; they're trying to. But we've had trouble in the Caribbean since Columbus. The Negro blood hates the Spanish blood, the English and Americans are looked on as a bunch of slave-drivers, and anybody who speaks French thinks everyone else is a slob anyhow. And the military think the civilians are lazy cows and the civilians think the military are trigger-happy racketeers. And they're both damn right.'

He took a deep breath. 'In the Caribbean and Latin America we've averaged one revolution a year—the successful ones, mind, not the ones that go blooey—every year

12

for the last 150. Without the help of Communism. On top of *that* mess, Communism's just an extra pint of bat's blood in the pot.'

'You'd better not let J. Edgar Hoover hear you.' He opened his mouth, and I added quickly: 'Don't say it: it could be treason.'

After a moment he said quietly: 'I was born here in PR. This is my back yard.' He shook his head. 'We're getting off the point again. We were talking about you, Mr Carr. Where do *you* stand?'

'As far aside as I can. I'm in business here. I don't think that Castillo and Bosco are Abraham Lincoln with diamond knobs on, but I don't know that Jiminez is likely to be, either. I'm not getting involved in Republica politics.'

'That doesn't really answer the question,' he said slowly. 'It isn't politics that makes a revolution: it's money. You think the Communists put Castro up in Cuba? The hell. It was the big American companies who thought they'd get a better deal from Castro than Batista. They gave him money, bought him guns, one even gave him a private airplane. And it wasn't politicians who flew the planes for him, either. Just pilots—at two, three thousand dollars a ride. Now it's happening with Jiminez: he's getting money from somewhere —three-inch mortars don't come cheap—and somebody's getting the stuff into the Republica. Maybe boat-owners, maybe pilots—but not politicians.'

'If you've got a file on me, you know I fly a twelve-year-old Dove insured for £10,000 with one-third yet to pay.'

He dived his hand inside his jacket, and for a moment I thought I was going to get shot. But he just pulled out a notebook and pen, and started writing. 'No—we didn't know that. We're not allowed to keep a Jamaica office.' He looked up. 'You still haven't answered the big question. Could we have it just once, for the record?'

'Or I go on the grey list.'

'I've got a job to do. You know that, Mr Carr.'

I nodded slowly. 'Yes, I know that. But I'm going to sound pompous for a moment first. I don't like grey lists. I have an old-fashioned idea that law enforcement agencies should

13

stick to enforcing law. And when there's no law being broken, they shouldn't enforce anything else. Such as a grey list. That's a conviction without a charge, without a trial, without a chance of being found Not Guilty.'

'That's right.' He nodded calmly. 'That does sound pretty pompous. I do it myself sometimes. When I get to talking about people expecting cops to want to be cops without expecting them to enjoy their work. Without expecting them to get mad when they see somebody getting away with a racket just because there maybe isn't a law against it right there or then.' He smiled briefly. Or maybe it was just a flicker from the lamp on the low table between us. 'It drives my wife crazy sometimes, when I talk like that. Now let's get back to the big question.'

I stared at him through the dimness. I was beginning to think there might be more than just the Academy syllabus behind the FBI Mark I expression on his face. The thought wasn't altogether cheering.

'Just once,' he said. 'Just to justify my expense account.' He waved a hand over the empty glasses.

'I haven't flown arms to the Republica. I haven't flown for Jiminez, nor anybody connected with him—as far as I know.'

He paused, watching me. 'We'd heard—' then he shook his head. 'We haven't got a Jamaica office. Okay—so that's the record.' He stood up, and tossed a couple of notes on the table. Then we walked towards the lifts.

'Just as a matter of interest,' he said, 'why d'you want to meet these Republica pilots?'

'As I said, just a friendly talk. About why they bounced me this afternoon in their Vampires. Incidentally, where did *they* come from?'

'South America.'

'I thought there was some sort of Latin American agreement limiting the trade of major arms. Like jets.'

'There is. It works, too. Until somebody wants to sell and somebody else wants to buy. But apart from that, it works.' He stabbed a lift button and stood back to wait. 'You've just been explaining how much you don't care about what

14

happens in the Republica. If you got into a public fuss with a Republica pilot, some people might misinterpret you.'

'In other words, don't hit anybody in the Sheraton.' I smiled at him. 'You know, when nobody's looking, you're quite a good FBI man.'

'Not my business. Starting a fight in the casino of the Sheraton isn't a Federal offence.'

The lift purred open beside us. In the flare of neon light, I could see the grid of tiny grained lines across his face, the grey in his crew-cut. He was in his late forties. He'd lived in Puerto Rico, as an adult, through the bad years.

But perhaps I'd guessed that already.

I said softly: 'The casino? Thanks.'

'I took a look around before coming up here. Good luck —if you're fool enough to need it.'

* 3 *

THE casino in the Sheraton is a tall, sober, well-lit room on the ground floor where government-licensed croupiers sometimes allow you to give them your money in exchange for about as much excitement as you'd get buying a tin of supermarket beans. And without you ending up with the beans, of course.

It doesn't get any more dramatic anywhere in San Juan. There was a time when it looked like heating up a little, when some of the hard boys Castro had tossed out of the Havana casinos came in to show the ignorant natives how many aces there could be in a pack. But they'd forgotten the joker: the FBI office. Some got their feet on the ground long enough to get their faces behind bars; the rest had rebooked for Las Vegas before they were off the airliner steps.

They'd have been superfluous anyway. The San Juan hotel casinos stand a living and prosperous monument to the tourists' determination to lose enough money to feel wicked,

15

and you don't need crooked gambling for that. You don't even need a house percentage when most of your customers come in prepared to lose ten, twenty or fifty dollars—and stay there until they do, because to quit when they're ahead would be unsporting and show they weren't real ramblin' gamblin' men at all—just tourists.

One day I'll patent the idea of firing all the croupiers and scrapping all the tables and just hang up a waste-basket labelled: 'It is strictly forbidden to throw your money in here.' I'll die rich.

At nine-thirty in the off-season summer the room was a lot less than crowded. There were a few people at the two roulette tables, a handful at the blackjack, and the usual noisy group at the craps. You don't pay any entrance fee, and the tables themselves change your cash for chips, so I just walked in acting like any tourist acting like Edward G. Robinson acting like Al Capone.

That made me normal.

Nobody seemed to be in Republica Air Force uniform, but you can squeeze a small overnight bag into the cockpit of a Vampire 5, so they needn't have stayed militaristic. On a 'good-will' visit, it would have been unlikely anyway. And looking at faces wasn't much help, either. Anybody flying jets for a Caribbean air force was as likely to have been born in Warsaw or Chicago as in Santo Bartolomeo.

I was wondering how many people I could ask, 'Excuse me, but did you happen to bounce me in a jet this afternoon?' before they sent for the house doctor, when a hand suddenly shoved a couple of dice under my nose and a voice said, 'You always had more luck than you deserved, Keith matey. Breathe a bit of it into these.'

Hand and voice had come out of the small, tight group around one of the craps tables, and for a moment I couldn't see who was behind them. But I knew that Australian accent, and I knew that hand: a big, steady paw, deeply tanned, covered with fine blond hairs and the small white scars of a lifetime spent grabbing for levers and switches in unfamiliar cockpits.

16

I waved a hand over the dice and intoned: 'A mother's dying curse on these playthings of the devil.'

An American tourist glared at me, shocked. 'That, suh, is an insult to both motherhood and craps.'

There was an Australian chuckle and the dice rumbled on the table.

The stick-man chanted: 'Thu-ree. The shooter craps out.' The crowd stirred, the shooter backed out and turned round.

'Still keeping your luck to yourself, Keith?' And we looked each other over for the first time in ten years.

He hadn't changed much. Broad, stocky, steady, like the hand. A snub square face with a tanned and oddly coarse skin, pale blue eyes, short curly fair hair. And a cheerful, watchful expression of enjoying this moment and making damn sure the next one didn't creep up on him unseen.

Ned Rafter, Australian gambling man and fighter-pilot-for-hire. You find the game or the war and Ned'll find you.

He said: 'How're you doing, matey, all right?'

'All right.' We didn't shake hands; pilots don't, much—maybe it's too serious, too final.

I didn't ask how he was doing—I didn't need to. He was wearing a pearl grey silk suit of a cut you couldn't find within a thousand miles or several hundred dollars of the Caribbean. And I didn't need to ask *what* he was doing, either.

'I think we met a little earlier today,' I said. 'Next time hoot your horn before overtaking.'

He smiled slowly. 'You're getting to be a Sunday driver, Keith.' We walked round to the end of the table and he tossed a $20 bill to the croupier. 'Some chips for me mate.'

'Not me,' I said quickly. 'I came here to kick your head off; I may yet. I don't need to lose your money as well.'

'You're talking like a tourist. Nobody loses.' But he picked up the chips for himself and dumped two little piles quickly on the betting layout of the table. The croupier twitched a small smile, so perhaps Ned had made a rather subtle bet.

I'm no gambler—not on principle, but just because I never get a kick out of taking risks. Anyway, the betting at craps is too complicated for me. The rules are simple enough: on your first throw you win with a 7 or 11, lose on a 2, 3 or 12. If you throw anything else, the rules change: you then go on throwing until you've either won by throwing the same number again, or lost by throwing a 7. No other numbers count after the first roll.

But on a casino table the layout lets you bet not just on winning or losing, but every number, different ways of making that number, and everything else except the chances of a nuclear war and your grandmother getting gallstones. All at different odds, of course.

The dice rolled. Ned lost one pile, but collected a fraction more than his losses on his second pile, so probably it *had* been a rather subtle bet.

'The last I heard,' I said conversationally, 'you were out in the Congo. What happened?'

'Stuffed full of crook politics. Anyway, it was only flying T-28s and a few old B-26s. Got dull.' He settled one pile of chips on the layout.

'So why not the Far East? I hear there's quite a good war out there.'

'Yeh—I thought of it. Trouble is, the Americans are keeping it democratic. No outsiders.'

He lost the pile, immediately put another in another place.

'Did you try the other side? Maybe they're not so democratic.'

He gave me a sharp look. 'You think that's funny, matey?'

'Yes—life's one big laugh today. I don't always get bounced by a couple of jets that might be going to shoot. Sets you up wonderfully for seeing the funny side of things.'

He won on his pile; took it back, put another down. 'Ah, you've just been away from things too long, Keith.'

'*I've* been away too long?' I banged a hand on the rim of the table and got a look from the stick-man. In a quieter voice, I said: 'If I'd turned into you this afternoon, you'd still be trying to walk home on the water. Your Number Two was on the wrong side for that pass *and* much too close. If

18

you'd tried more than a rate one turn you'd have had him
flying up your back passage.'

He thought about it, staring at the table. 'Maybe . . .
maybe you're right. These boys are too proud of flying close
formation. I'll get 'em out of it. Only been there a month,
yet.'

The dice rumbled across the table, were pushed back,
rumbled again. The stick-man chanted the numbers; a
shooter lost, another stepped forward. Craps is the fastest
gambling game there is—apart from dozing at the controls
of a fighter in enemy airspace.

Ned went on betting his small piles, winning and losing.
'So,' he said, 'how d'you like flying charter work?'

'Could be worse. There's good flying weather around here.
Trouble is the airlines are getting too good. Few years and
they'll be running jets down the islands.'

'Yeh.' He rubbed his chin thoughtfully. 'I suppose I
thought you'd want something a bit more exciting—after
fighters.'

'Try paying off a mortgage on your own plane sometime.
It gets exciting enough.'

'Never owned me own plane.' The dice rolled—and
suddenly Ned had won triple his normal stack of chips. He
pushed them promptly across to the croupier. 'She'll do.
Cash me in.'

'Quit while you're ahead,' I murmured.

He looked up. 'You did it yourself, once.'

I grinned. Several tourists looked at him sneeringly, as a
man who couldn't take it—although taking it was just what
he was doing.

He got back a surprisingly large stack of dollar bills. I
hadn't expected him to be gambling low—he never had in
the past and the silk suit suggested he didn't need to now—
but that wad would still have covered two months' mortgage
and running expenses on the Dove.

He riffled quickly through it, shoved it into his pocket.
'It right we can't get a drink in the casino?'

I nodded.

He shrugged disgustedly. 'Christ—what government control does. If I collapse on the way to the bar, tell mother I died trying.'

'That, suh, is an insult to both motherhood *and* alcohol.'

* 4 *

WE walked downstairs to the outside bar by the swimming pool. I ordered two Bacardis and tonic and we fell naturally into talking of people we'd both known in Korea.

Some were dead and some were squadron leaders by now. Two of the Americans had reached lieutenant-colonel; another was in training to be shot to the moon and, it was believed in some quarters, back.

Mostly for something to say, I asked: 'What rank've you got in the Republica?'

'Colonel. Full colonel. Highest I've been yet, matey. In the Congo I was just a crummy little captain.'

I stared at him. 'Good God—are you running the whole Air Force?' I'd been thinking of him as leading a flight, or perhaps as chief instructor.

'Just the Vampires.'

'I'd have thought "major" was high enough for twelve fighters.'

He grinned. 'Ah, but those twelve are the whole of Fighter Command. So I'm C-in-C Fighters. I reckon I should be a general.'

I gave him a fast look. 'Don't say that too loud, Ned. In the Caribbean, everybody else *really* wants to be a general.'

His face went very still; then he nodded. 'Yeh. I keep forgetting. Trouble is, I never take much notice of rank.'

'You and all Australia.'

He grinned again. 'Yeh, it's the money that counts. What'd you say to 750 dollars a week, no tax, no living expenses?'

'I'd say pretty damn good—while it lasts. Is that what you're getting?'

'No, I'm getting more. But it's what I can get you.'

20

I counted it; I couldn't help counting it. Seven hundred and fifty dollars a week was $3,000 a month which was £1,000 . . . even if I only stuck it three months, I'd have the mortgage on the Dove paid off clear and clean. If I lasted six months, I'd have an extra £3,000. That and selling the Dove would give me a pretty big down payment on a new Dove 8, or Aero Commander or . . .

Ned was watching me with a gentle, slightly sardonic look. The figures must have been ringing up in my eyes as in the window of a cash register. I said softly: 'Off we go, into the long green yonder . . .'

'I've got the okay to take on another outside bloke—providing he knows the job. Right now I'm having to be squadron commander, gunnery officer and chief instructor; I'm doing four or five flights a day. You'll be my second in command and take over half of it. What do you say?'

The Aero Commander was still there, gleaming faintly on a faraway tarmac. But now a little farther, a little fainter.
'Thanks for the thought, Ned. But no.'
'You take it, matey.'
I just shook my head.
His hand slammed down on the bar. 'I'm telling you to *take* it! That's good advice!'

I looked up, surprised at the violent reaction. After a while I said: 'You mean so that I can finally become an "ace"—after all these years? Suppose there aren't any enemy aircraft, though: can I count the peasants I shoot up? And the goats and donkeys as well?'

He stared, then his face crumpled up in disgust. 'Ah, don't bleed so easy. Poor peasants, hell. We knocked over a three-inch mortar last week that was lobbing stuff on to the runway as we took off. Peasants! These boys mean business.'

'Not *my* business. I'm not getting mixed up in Republica politics.'

'Who the hell's talking about politics? You wasn't in Korea because you didn't agree with Karl Marx's theories. You was there because you're a fighter pilot, and a bloody good one. So don't get fancy ideas about books you haven't read.'

I smiled; I couldn't help it. But then I shook my head again. 'Korea was our war, Ned. And I'm still pretty sure we were on the right side. In the Republica there isn't a right side; there won't even be a winning side, whatever happens. There shouldn't even be a war. Whatever's wrong there, Vampires and three-inch mortars aren't the cure.'

'You're still talking politics. You sound like a cow playing the violin.'

'*I'm* talking politics? You think you can join in somebody else's war and *you're* not playing politics?'

Ned had his mouth open to answer when somebody did an emergency landing on his right shoulder. He spun round with his hands up, and for a moment it looked like being an exciting evening after all. But then he saw who it was, said, 'Hell, you,' and turned back to the bar.

The new recruit was a tall, dark character, very handsome in a Latin-American cigarette advertisement sort of way, and very conscious of it, in the same way. But it was his suit that you met first. It was a carefully cut item of pale turquoise Madras silk, broad-shouldered, narrow-waisted, and memorable all the way. You knew you were going to remember that suit, although perhaps not on purpose.

He went on leaning on Ned's shoulder, giving a big tooth-packed grin at nothing in particular. 'A little drink, mi Coronel?' he suggested.

Ned said: 'You smell like you had enough already.' Then he remembered his social obligations. He jerked his head left and right: 'Capitan Miranda. Keith Carr.'

The Capitan swung round on me, with an expression of slow, pleasurable surprise. 'Señor Carr? I so much hope we did not frighten you too much this afternoon.' And I got the big virile grin, straight between the eyes.

I just shrugged.

He wagged a finger. 'So now you know not to come near the Republica, yes? Next time we shoot you down.'

Ned jerked around once more, his face and voice hard. 'Just *listen*, sonny. Don't you ever tangle with Keith Carr unless you've got me there to hold your hand. He knows more about this game than you'll ever learn in five lifetimes.' He waved a hand. 'Now go away and chase indoor birds. Though you don't look like you could knock over a rag doll right now.'

Miranda instinctively straightened up and said, with slightly alcoholic dignity: 'We are on a mission of good-will, mi Coronel. I have been drinking with the American officers —not with the *rebeldes*!' And I got a hot, hard look.

Ned said: 'Get lost, you boozy twerp.'

The captain snapped to attention, said 'Si Coronel,' and strode off, stiff with outraged manhood and militarism.

There was a long silence, with just Ned clinking the ice in his glass and frowning down at it. I took a pipe out of my inside pocket, filled it from a crumpled one-ounce packet, and started the lighting-up ceremony. Ned watched, still frowning, and asked: 'What's the chimney for?'

'Trying to give up cigarettes.' Smoke seemed to be coming out of every corner of the pipe and me simultaneously. I worked on.

Ned snapped his fingers, ordered two more Bacardis. By the time they came I had the pipe, and my thoughts, fairly well under control.

'Well,' I said, 'let's have the whole story.'

'You don't want to take any notice of that playboy. We have to have him because his old man's a big landowner. You should see him on—'

'The story, Ned. The story.'

He frowned at his drink.

I said: 'I didn't ask how you knew I was in the Dove this afternoon, Ned. I just assumed you'd know all the charter pilots. But I thought the bouncing was just a private joke. Now that boy calls me a *rebelde*. The story.'

'There isn't any story. Just take the job I'm giving you.'

'I told you: I'm not getting mixed up in——'

'You're mixed up already! They think you're flying for Jiminez, for the rebels. I was *told* to bounce you this afternoon, just a kind of warning.'

I felt very cold. The FBI thought it, the Republica thought it. Maybe everybody in the Caribbean thought it. Except me.

23

Ned said: 'Take the job: you'll prove 'em wrong *and* make a bundle.'

'Is that why you offered it, Ned?'

'Just take it. You'd be good at it.'

'Do *you* think I'm flying for Jiminez?'

He shook his head impatiently. 'I don't know. You're a tricky bastard, Keith. You wouldn't be a good fighter pilot if you weren't.'

'I'm not a fighter pilot any more, Ned.'

He threw the rest of his drink down his throat, stood up, and stared down at me. After a while he said carefully: 'I've done everything except paint recruiting pictures for you. But I'll do that if you like. Because next time I could get told to shoot.'

'So? Who told you that was a guarantee you'd hit anything?'

He smiled slowly. 'Who told you you weren't still a fighter pilot?' and he walked back into the hotel.

By now my pipe had gone out. I was still trying to work out if it was suffering from water in the fuel or just a blocked carburettor when somebody slipped into the empty seat beside me.

I looked and said sourly: 'I might have guessed you wouldn't miss the big picture. Sorry it had a happy ending.'

Agent Ellis smiled and said: 'Naturally. You seem to know Colonel Rafter pretty well. Guess you must have known him a long time.'

I put the pipe down on the counter. 'Give me a cigarette and I'll tell you.' He produced a Chesterfield and lit it for me.

'Thanks. It was in Korea. He was in 77 squadron, Royal Australian. They came out in Meteor 8s, to try and take on Migs. Turned out the Mig could out-climb them, out-dive them, out-turn them and was faster on the level. I won't say they took a hammering, but they damn sure didn't take a holiday. After that they were pulled back to ground-attack work. I was attached to a squadron of Sabres that used to fly high cover for them; I went to them as liaison officer for

24

a time, me being British and all that. After that, I met Ned a couple of years later in London, just after he'd left the RAAF.'

'And now he's a colonel in the *Fuerza Aerea Republicana*. What's he been doing between then and now?'

I gave him a look which I hoped he interpreted as chilly. 'Probably knitting bedsocks for an Old Folks' Home.'

Ellis looked pained. 'Just a friendly question.'

'And a friendly answer. If you want to put him on one of your little lists, do the hard work yourself. One cigarette doesn't make me an FBI informer—not after being offered a job at $750 a week.'

There was a silence while he looked thoughtful and I tried to work out why the hell I'd said that. The Sheraton must have been giving me bigger measures of Bacardi than I'd credited them for.

Then he said quietly: 'Seven-hundred and fifty, heh? Did you take it?'

'No. But it's always nice to know somebody cares that much.'

'You'd screw yourself up all over the Caribbean. No place'd let you land there—not after playing games in the Republica.'

'I know. That's why I'm not working for Jiminez, either.'

'Of course.' He nodded wisely. 'Perhaps you have that lettered on a little sign on the dashboard of your plane? *It'd screw me up all over the Caribbean.*'

I said: 'No, I don't have.'

'I'll get you one made.' He smiled. 'It'd be silly to make a mistake that size just because you happened to forget.'

And he went away.

★ 5 ★

THE next day I got a charter for a bunch of non-cost-conscious fishermen down to St. Kitts, and when I got back to San Juan Ned and the Vampires had gone. I flew out for Jamaica in the late afternoon, staying well south of the

Republica coastline and using the fair-weather cumulus that builds up after midday for cover.

I wasn't worried about radar. I didn't think they had any, and even if they had, I didn't believe they'd know how to use it properly yet. Ned had probably caught me the day before just by following the position reports I'd been dutifully radioing out. On this trip I kept shut up.

It was a long drag against some rare west winds and without the Republica as a refuelling stop. In fact, things were getting pretty thin all round at this end of the Caribbean. Cuba was out; only Pan American could get any sense or fuel out of Port-au-Prince in Haiti, and that only by damn near buying up the whole airport; now the Republica was out. Apart from trips inside Jamaica, short hops to the Grand Cayman and an occasional long slog up to Nassau or out to Puerto Rico, it looked like being a long quiet summer. The next day proved it.

I was living in a two-room flat over a night club in Kingston's East Street, which made for free calypsos while I was trying to get to sleep. I staggered out of bed around eight, flying strictly blind, set the coffee going, and spent ten minutes searching every pocket and drawer I owned in case I'd left a cigarette around. I hadn't. So I lit the first pipe of the day, which tasted like a fire in an old clothes warehouse, and sat around gulping coffee and promising myself that next week I'd find a nice quiet place over in Port Royal, where the airline crews lived.

That made the day normal so far.

By nine I was more or less shaved and dressed in more or less clean khaki drill shirt and trousers and down getting pushed off the pavement by the Kingston crowd. I put the rotor arm back on the jeep, wondered for the several-hundredth time whether anything in such a state was really a good advertisement and if I shouldn't scrape the *Keith Carr, Charter Pilot for Hire, Twin-engined Plane* off the side. I decided, as usual, to do it when I moved to Port Royal, and drove off to start getting pushed off the road by the Kingston traffic.

Palisadoes airport lies halfway around a curving spit of land enclosing Kingston harbour, with Port Royal on the far end, about five miles on. I reached the airport at nine-twenty and sat down in my daytime office—a canvas stool on the shade side of the Dove—and lit the second pipe of the day. That only tasted like a leaking exhaust, so things were improving.

Still a normal day.

I spent a little time wondering if I should be tracking down a leak in one of the air-pressure systems which was feeding out air at about the same rate that the engine compressor was feeding it in. The Dove lives on air pressure—for the undercarriage, flaps, brakes—so I'd have to do something about it eventually. But meanwhile I had a duplicate system *and* an emergency undercarriage lowering bottle in working order, so I decided to let it wait until it got bad enough to spot more easily. Anyway, I had an appointment for ten o'clock and it's poor sales psychology to let the customer find the plane with its inspection panels off and wires dangling.

For once the customer was on time: the Canadian High Commissioner and a Canadian trade delegation wanting to take a fast look at a bauxite mine in the hills. The H.C. himself had obviously heard enough about me to have preferred doing the trip in his air-conditioned Buick, but he wasn't going to let down the morale of the party, so he just scratched his moustache and remarked that both engines still had propellers and off we went.

It was only a half-hour trip on to the mine's airstrip, and the delegation couldn't take more than an hour of breathing raw bauxite dust, so we were home again soon after midday.

I was drinking a beer in the Horizon Bar of the terminal building and thinking about going out on to the 'waving gallery' to buy a hamburger when I got customer number two, Mr Peterson, who was the managing something of an hotel chain on the north coast. Dressed in the local uniform of dark trousers, white short-sleeved shirt, he was big, enthusiastic and Negro—which was a rare thing in the hotel trade; it isn't famous for promoting Jamaicans to responsible jobs.

27

And he had an idea. 'Mr Carr—you know we can't really buy good beef on the island. So we want you to fly it in, frozen, from South America for us.'

I frowned and said: 'Exactly where from?'

'Venezuela. We reckon it wouldn't melt in the time you took. It's been done before.' It had, too: somebody had started running beef up to Miami, with a refuelling stop here, in a converted bomber. But he'd had a bad brake fire, sold off the aircraft, and the idea seemed to have died away.

I asked: 'How much does a side of beef weigh?'

He waved a big pink hand. 'I'd say around three hundred pounds.'

'Caracas is 800 nautical miles. I could just about scrape out with 1,500 pounds of payload—say five sides. But——'

His face exploded into a grin. 'Man, that's wonderful. I'll just——'

'*But*,' I said firmly. I hated to kick that grin in the teeth. 'But Caracas means a ten-hour round trip. I'll shave my profit for a regular long job—but I can't shave my costs. I'd have to charge you about £235 per trip.'

The grin vanished, all right. 'But—but that's about—about nearly fifty pound a side on just transportation.'

I nodded.

He stared at me suspiciously, then shook his head. 'Man—I thought the hotel trade had fierce costs, but *flying* . . .'

'You're playing my song.'

'You couldn't bring it down just a bit?'

'I know the words. I just can't remember the tune.'

He smiled briefly—on and off like a light switch. Then he said, sadly: 'You don't want our business, Mr Carr?'

'Your business is what any charter pilot dreams of: regular, dependable work. But it still costs me £22 4s. an hour to keep that Dove in the air. I'm charging you just over £1 an hour for myself. And a check four coming up.'

'A what?'

'Check four: happens every 1,800 flying hours. A bunch of engineers tear the whole plane apart, tell you it's in fine shape and stick it together again. Costs you up to £3,000. Then you're all licensed to fly again.'

He smiled again, this time a little more sincerely. 'Man, you really *have* got costs. Well, I'll put it to my board, but . . . I suppose the trouble is we'd be paying you for going out there empty. Right?'

'Right. Just find me a regular cargo for Caracas and it'll halve your cost.'

He nodded wearily. That's the real problem with the Caribbean: it's really just a string of suburbs. If you're travelling anywhere on business or pleasure, you don't go to another suburb, you go into town—Miami, New York, London, Paris, Amsterdam. The islands just don't want to know about each other.

That's why the idea of federating Jamaica and Trinidad sprang a leak: Jamaicans and Trinidadians never met except in London and didn't much like each other there. Why not federate Malta and the Channel Isles?—they speak just as much English and they aren't any farther apart than Jamaica and Trinidad.

Mr Peterson climbed off his stool. 'Well, I *said* I'd put it to the board of directors.' He looked at me and shook his head. 'I'm sorry.' And went away.

I looked at my watch, decided I hadn't quite got time for another beer, then ordered one anyway.

It was a mistake. The fuelling supervisor came out of the dining room where most of the airport senior staff eat, saw me, and came over.

He asked me how it was going and I said so-so and he said he was sorry and I said so was I but more so and he said he doubted it.

'Because,' he said, 'you owe us £165. We've just sent off our final demand.'

'I'll let you have a hundred by the end of the week.'

He smiled. At any rate, he showed me his teeth. 'I'm sorry. The whole amount—or we stop serving you. You must have something tucked away.'

'Something—and a check four coming up.'

'Oh-ho. I'd hate to see you squander it on a major over-haul when you really owe it to us.'

'Squander it?' I glared at him. 'I'll make it a hundred

this week and another hundred in two weeks' time.'

'Keith—you're taking £60-worth of fuel off us *a week.*'

'So just let me run up a bill until I know how much the check's going to cost.'

He shook his head. 'Keith, I like you, and I like your business. But most of all I like your money. Anyhow, I've already got you and your business.'

I groaned. 'They're issuing joke books to fuelling supervisors, yet.'

He gave me another quick look at his teeth. '£165. Within a week. Good luck, Keith.' And he went off downstairs.

It was still a normal day.

★ 6 ★

I ATE a couple of hot dogs on the gallery and was back at the Dove by two. Now the day was really coming to the boil. On the airport it was just plain hot, but across the bay in Kingston, sitting in its bowl between the hills, the air in the narrow streets would be like breathing under a sweaty electric blanket. Out in the box-top shacks of the nameless town built on the city dump up by the oil refinery, there would be sudden, vicious fights over a choice piece of rubbish. And up in the rich suburbs beyond Half Way Tree, dignified elderly gardeners would move listlessly among the mangoes, feeling the long sharp edges of their machetes and thinking of the owner's wife asleep in the air-conditioned room upstairs.

Kingston, the perfect natural harbour—except that it's on the south coast and the cool summer breeze comes from the north. So it only blows—no, it doesn't blow, just breathes politely—on the private beaches and modern houses and big hotels of the north coast. So move up there, man; nobody's stopping you. All you need is the money. And you think you're going to get rich in Kingston? Haul your rice, man; emigrate. Maybe London isn't paved with gold, but it's cool, man. Yes, you'll find out how cool.

Perhaps the heat was getting at me, too. The Dove was too hot to touch without gloves and there was a faint haze over the fuel tank vents, so I was wasting petrol by evaporation. Well, I hadn't paid for it, anyway.

Customer number three was late. He always was, but he was still the only regular income I had. A young Venezuelan businessman named Diego Ingles who'd got the idea that his company would buy him a brand-new twin-engined airplane the moment he'd qualified to fly it. He hired me twice a week for twin-engine instruction.

Personally I had my doubts that his company could go crazy enough to hand him a £35,000 airplane, but perhaps it could happen. He obviously came of a genuine aged-in-the-money family back in Caracas, and that counts for a lot in Venezuelan business circles. Anyway, it was his money and my pocket.

All that apart, he was a nice young lad: in his early twenties, shortish and slightly tubby, with a flat cheerful face, a bush of dark hair and the politely rakish manner of an old Spanish family upbringing.

He finally appeared at twenty past, with a long graceful apology which boiled down to the fact that he'd only just got out of bed, and not even his own.

With the heat and the tall thunderclouds building up on the Blue Mountains I wanted to get away from the airport, so we skipped the circuits-and-landings and I gave him a dead-reckoning navigation exercise out to the Pedro Cays, about eighty miles to the south-west. No radio to be used: he had to do it on maps and weather reports alone.

It wasn't his favourite type of flying: quiet, steady, accurate. Like most of Latin America he believed that aviation was a branch of sports-car racing. I'd had to keep taunting him about becoming a 'fair-weather pilot' to keep him looking at—and believing—his instruments, maps and forecasts. This time I was feeling irritable enough to taunt him into making a near-perfect landfall over North-east Cay within a minute of his ETA.

I remembered to tell him I'd noticed.

He smiled very charmingly and asked: 'So perhaps you think I am good enough?'

I looked at him. 'For what? You could probably get your licence up-rated to a "B", so you could fly this size of thing privately. That's if you've been doing any book-work. D'you want me to arrange a test?'

'Not quite that, Señor. I mean—do *you* believe in me? Can I use an airplane like this—anywhere—at any time?'

'Nobody can. You still think an airplane's a miracle with a starter button. Some weather, even the birds are walking.'

'I understand there may be risks, Señor, but . . .' He took his right hand off the wheel and fluttered it delicately.

'Just try and remember,' I said slowly, 'that if God had intended men to fly He'd have given us wings. So all flying is flying in the face of nature. It's unnatural, wicked and stuffed with risks all the time. The secret of flying is learning to minimize the risks.'

'Or perhaps—the secret of life is to choose your risks?' He smiled disarmingly. 'But I think you were a fighter pilot, and yet you talk of minimizing risks?'

'That's where I learnt it. Don't fall for the King-Arthur-of-the-air stuff about fighter pilots. Clean knightly combats and all that. It's the one trade where the whole point is to catch a man by surprise and shoot him in the back. That's how the top men made their scores. And if they *couldn't* catch a man like that, they didn't tangle with him.'

'Ah, now I know, Señor.' He ducked his head gracefully. 'So I should catch the weather by surprise and shoot it in the back. And also I see why the unromantic English make such good pilots.'

He was laughing at me, but as long as he remembered . . . I said: 'So what about a licence test?'

'I will talk to Caracas about it. But the important thing is that *you* believe I am good enough. That is my true examination.' It takes generations of high Spanish blood to laugh at a man so courteously.

I put my pipe in my mouth and said: 'You may still find a licence is useful. In fact, licences are useful in all walks of life.'

'Señor?'

'Just an old saying the unromantic RAF had: only birds can fornicate *and* fly. And birds don't booze.'

The thunderclouds had finally, mercifully, split and drenched Kingston for half an hour by the time we got back over Palisadoes. Steam was rising gently off the suburbs behind the town: even the air in the cockpit felt fresh and green.

We tried three landings, including one with an engine stopped and abandoning the approach at 200 feet and going round again. He handled it pretty well; he wasn't going to get killed in an emergency—that was his best time. It would be the small things that killed him: a bit of fluff in a carburettor and a slipped connection in a radio and a twenty-degree shift in wind—incredible coincidences of bad luck like that, in a time when the millions of flights every year make a million-to-one chance a tenfold statistical certainty.

He would die in a clear, still blue sky—because he still believed that he had a *right* to be there. Because he wouldn't believe he was a trespasser who had to keep awake and alert every single damn minute.

I was wrong, of course, as I usually am about people. But only in a way.

We landed finally around half-past four and I charged him for two hours—and he paid me cash on the nail, which was a Spanish courtesy I appreciated. He also offered to drive me back to Kingston in his Jaguar E-type, which was a Spanish courtesy I turned down fast. Anyway, it was about time I filled in my log-books.

I parked myself in the rearmost passenger seat, closest to the open door, and started the paperwork. It should have been easy, just the San Juan trip, the St Kitts trip, and today's flights. Easy—except for that check four, creeping closer flying hour by flying hour.

Well, that was easy, too: clip ten minutes in the hour off the San Juan flight—would the Air Registration Board ever cross-check Kingston tower's times against San Juan's?

Would they even get to hear of the St Kitt's side-trip at all? Hell, I could save nearly four hours, in all.

In all three logs: one for the airplane, one for each engine, because an engine can move around in its lifetime. You hand in an engine for overhaul and get a reconditioned one in exchange—and the logbook with it. And you just hope the previous pilot hasn't done something that doesn't show in the log: pushed the throttle through the gate too often, run at high boost and low revs . . . faked the hours.

Reluctantly, I wrote down both the San Juan and St Kitt's trips—clipping just ten minutes in the hour off each.

Then I counted the day's takings. It came exactly to £75—three hours' work. Leaving a profit of £8 8s.—until you counted my East Street rent, a little food and booze, and keeping the jeep in near-running order. And remembered the other days with the Dove grounded through lack of spares, weather or just work.

It was still a normal day in the gay, glamorous life of a free-lance pilot roaming the blue skies of the sun-kissed Caribbean. Or of a shoestring operator selling a luxury product that most people didn't need, didn't even want and certainly couldn't afford. A street-corner match-seller with a tray full of diamond-studded matchboxes.

It depends on your point of view. Right now, my view was that it was the cocktail hour.

I was in the bar of the Myrtle Bank Hotel just before six. It's an old hotel—by Jamaican standards—and planted right down in the business quarter on the waterfront, so that freighters dock on either side of the back garden. And with the bar an open-sided affair out there in the garden instead of inside and sunk in total gloom as per the New York ideals of the latest hotels.

The barman handed me a Red Stripe beer and a message without being asked for either. This year, the Myrtle Bank bar was as close to an office as I could afford, and him as close to a secretary. The beer was cold and the message wasn't much warmer: I was to call on J. B. Penrose the next morning at eleven a.m. sharp.

I didn't know J. B. Penrose from the cat's stepmother and my first idea was that I didn't want to. Even in the barman's thick, laboured scrawl the tone came over as clear as across a frosty parade ground: call on—not just call—J. B. Penrose in Apartment C, the Shaw Park Beach Club, at eleven.

Only fifty miles off, right across the island on the north coast.

I drank my beer and thought about ringing Penrose and telling him to spend the morning swimming outside the reef with the other sharks. Then I started on my second beer and thought about Shaw Park.

The 'Club' bit is deceptive. It started life that way, when the north coast was strictly for winter residents, with no hotels or tourist trash like bank presidents. But when the tourists started coming anyway, the Shaw Park remembered it owned the best beach on the island, and ran up a couple of blocks of rooms and two more of the de luxe apartments. I'd visited one of these apartments before: if J. B. Penrose was staying in one of them, he liked diamond-studded matchboxes.

* 7 *

I LANDED on the north coast at a quarter to eleven the next morning.

Some pretty inventive writers have lived within a few miles of Boscobel airstrip, Ian Fleming and Noel Coward among them, but none of them in the same class as the man who thought up the sign on the Jamaican Air Service hut there. It says WELCOME TO OCHO RIOS AIRPORT.

Point one: it isn't at Ocho Rios, which is where most of the big hotels are, but twelve miles east at Oracabessa. Point two: it isn't an airport. It's a 3,000-foot tarmac strip wedged in between the sea and the hills, and you couldn't even operate a Dakota off that. Mostly it's used by the crop-spray planes working over the banana plantations on the slopes.

I was standing there admiring the sign while the clerk in the hut phoned various millionaires who drive taxis in those parts, when one of the crop-spray pilots walked up and thumped me on the back. He'd probably just finished his day's work: they fly from first light until the sun starts up too many updrafts off the plantation slopes.

'What's the big twin-engined boy doing down in the jungle—slumming?'

'Clients at Shaw Park. I hope.'

'The film people?'

I looked puzzled. 'Not another film?'

'Of course. Don't you read your *Daily Gleaner*? Ruddy Hollywood up here, boy.' And he was about right; they were always shooting some Technicolor epic on this part of the north coast. It was great film country: sun, palm trees, hills, beaches—and half a dozen luxury hotels just up the road. Sometimes they turned it into a Pacific island, sometimes Darkest Africa; twice they forgot where they were and shot films about Jamaica, but probably somebody got fired for that.

'Where are we this time?' I asked.

'Headwaters of the Amazon, I think. South America, anyway. Makes a change from the Congo.' He wiped the sweat off his forehead with the back of his hand, leaving a long streak of oil in its place. 'So when are you going to drop this fancy air-taxi stuff and come and do some real work with us?'

'Tomorrow, if they keep pushing on my fuel bill.'

'See you at five in the morning, then.'

'Make it nine; I'm getting old.'

He grinned. 'You'll get used to it. The only trouble is getting a whole evening's drinking done at lunchtime. Think of it as a dawn patrol—you should know all about that, after fighters.'

I said slowly: 'Everybody keeps remembering I flew fighters. These days I'm a Dove driver.'

He grinned, thumped my shoulder again, and started towards the hut. 'Still, must be nice to know you've got something to fall back on.'

36

'Like the Blue Mountains?' I called after him. He laughed over his shoulder and went on out.

To me, it wasn't all that funny. He was making money—probably £7,000 a year—but he was earning it, too. I knew he'd smashed up once already, spraying from twenty feet up and finding himself flying up a blind gully with a sheer slope ahead. They wrote off a plane a year, on average.

Perhaps I really *was* getting old.

I reached Shaw Park just after eleven and saved a couple of minutes by taking a short cut through the walled car park instead of going round through the lobby. That put me right opposite the front door to Apartment C.

The apartments were built in two-storey blocks—two up, two down—that looked oddly like English suburban houses, transplanted 4,000 miles and slightly overgrown under the tropical sun. I pressed the doorbell and waited.

No answer. I tried again; still no answer. So? All right, I admit I was a few minutes late, but in Jamaican terms that's early. But maybe J. B. Penrose hadn't got fully acclimatized yet; maybe he still thought eleven meant eleven and at two minutes past he had a date to fly to New York and buy the Rockefeller Plaza.

Damn. I was beginning to think I'd wasted a morning and several gallons of fuel.

As a last chance, I tried the door and it opened. I thought about that for a moment, then decided the least I could do was find out if Penrose had packed and gone. I walked in down a shadowy corridor and out into the dining room.

From the inside, you forgot all about the English suburban look. It was a big, cool room with one wall of sliding glass doors looking out across a private walled patio to the glare of the beach and sea beyond. Almost everything in the room was white: the walls, the small coffee-table, the sideboards, the Spanish metalwork of the chairs and the round glass-topped table, the four desk lamps. It was a very nice room; the only thing wrong with it was that there was nobody there except a small dark lizard.

He was clinging to the wall by some private theory of

37

anti-gravity, his head cocked and giving me a bright suspicious stare. I nodded to him and walked over to the open
glass doors and looked out. The patio had a clutter of alloy
and plastic beach chairs, but nothing else. A few people
were swimming near the shore, and a couple of metal
dinghies with bright sails were staggering around between
the stone piers. But all very quietly. Shaw Park clients don't
laugh out loud.

I turned back into the room. The lizard had his head
screwed round 180 degrees, still watching me, so I asked:
'You don't happen to know a J. B. Penrose who's supposed
to be staying here?' He went on watching. 'In fact, you don't
happen to *be* J. B. Penrose, do you?'

That did it; he flickered across the wall and out of sight
behind a hanging picture. Residents hate being mistaken for
tourists. I shrugged and started for the bedroom door, then
thought to check the sideboard first.

That was definitely progress. The sideboard held three
near-full bottles of gin, white Cinzano and Canadian Club,
a few clean glasses and two leather-bound volumes on
American contract law. Penrose might have walked out on
the bottles—from the amount in them he didn't seem to be
a serious drinking man—but if the law-books were worth
bringing they were worth taking home again. For me, at
ten past eleven in the morning, that wasn't a bad bit of
deduction.

I found that while I'd been deducing, I'd poured myself
a glass of straight Canadian Club, which perhaps wasn't so
good for ten past eleven, but by then I couldn't do much
but drink it. I had the glass halfway to my face when a voice
said: 'And who the hell are you and what the hell are you
doing?'

She was standing just outside the sliding doors, wearing a
simple black-and-white bathing dress, big black sunglasses,
dripping sea-water—and carrying an overstuffed black briefcase.

I said: 'I'm Keith Carr, waiting for a Mr J. B. Penrose
and availing myself of some of the hospitality he'd have
lavished on me if he'd remembered to be here himself.'

She came in, tossed the case on the sofa and said: 'You're late, Carr.' I just stood there with my mouth slightly open and looked at her. She was a bit short and a bit slim—not flat-chested, but it wouldn't be insured for a million, either. She had long fine hair that might once have been mousy but now streaked with the sun and touched up with every colour from chestnut to silver blonde and tied up in a careful-casual knot around the back. Her legs were long, rather thin, and covered with golden sand broken by zigzag trickles of water. For some reason I like watching girls' legs covered with sand; psychologists probably have a long word for it. I have a short one.

I said slowly: '*I'm* late? What happened to the well-known J. B. Penrose?'

'I'm Penrose. Most people call me J.B. You call me Miss Penrose. I waited until five past eleven; then I went for a swim.' She walked out into the bedroom. I finally took my first taste of the whisky.

But she was back in a few seconds, without the sunglasses and rubbing herself here and there with a small hand towel. 'Aren't you starting drinking a little early for a pilot?'

I nodded. 'You might have a reasonable grievance there —once I'm on the payroll.'

She looked at me thoughtfully. Without the sunglasses, she had a sharp-edged face, with a small pointed chin, a nose a bit too thin, a mouth a lot too wide, and quick-moving blue eyes. A flexible face; one that could go from a suspicious stare to megaton grin, and neither expression looking out of place and it all remaining the same face all the time.

'All right.' She dipped her head quickly. 'I'll have a Cinzano and ice—there should be some ice in the refrigerator in the kitchen.'

I went back down the hall, found the kitchen and refrigerator and the ice and hauled it back, stopping only long enough to finish my own glass *en route*. I had a feeling I was going to need something in my blood besides blood.

She was sitting on the sofa beside her briefcase, scratching herself idly between her thighs with the towel and staring at

39

a piece of paper. I poured her drink, my second one, and handed hers across. Then I got out my pipe and sat down at the table.

After a while she said: 'They say you're the best multi-engined independent pilot on the island—that right?'

I liked her use of 'on the island'; she'd picked up the local phraseology quickly. 'Since there isn't anybody else, I imagine I'm the best.'

'Hmm.' She handed across the piece of paper. 'Is that an accurate breakdown of your costs?'

It was. It had even got the insurance and depreciation figures right, which meant she must have known how much I'd paid for the Dove in the first place. Still, that wouldn't be much of a secret around Palisadoes.

'It's near enough,' I admitted.

'Good. Ever done any film work before?'

'I've flown a few film people around. The place is crawling with them every summer. They pay promptly, but always in the wrong currency.'

That didn't advance my cause much. She said coldly: 'I mean *real* film work. We may want you to fly a camera plane for us.'

I frowned and puffed a tired bit of smoke that had managed to crawl down the pipe-stem into my mouth and said: 'Let's go back to the beginning: who is "we"?'

She stared. 'My God, I thought you'd know *that*.'

'I'm an unworldly character, Miss Penrose. Just start at the beginning.'

'Well, you've heard of Walt Whitmore?'

At least I had that. He must have been a little younger than the John Wayne-Gary Cooper generation, but he'd started in Hollywood when half the actors were still horses. And he'd stayed in the saddle come the time when a lot of old-timers had climbed down to act bedroom scenes—and been professionally dead before they'd had time to change the sheets. The critics had tried nicknaming him everything from One-Expression Whitmore to The Original Council Bluff, but they'd gone on getting him twice a year for the past thirty. In a country where they elect politicians for looking good on horses, a man whose whole profession is looking good on a horse can't lose.

I nodded. 'I know who you mean.'

'He's independent these days. He runs his own company, puts his own money into his pictures, takes his pay as a percentage of the profit. He's down here shooting a film called *Bolivar Smith*. Have you heard of *that*?'

'No, but don't tell me the story; let me guess. He's an American gun-for-hire in this country called—say, Amazonia —and the dictator's tough guys push him around and he gets impressed with the nobility of an honest peasant maid and he helps them revolt and doesn't take any pay for it——'

'All *right*,' I saw from the look on her face that I'd just scripted the film for them. She growled: 'You'd go great in the movie business. We may not fit you in as a third assistant clapper boy just yet, but you'd go big as a critic.'

'Miss Penrose,' I spread my hands, 'don't get me wrong. I like Walt Whitmore. I've just seen him do this same story in Mexico, Texas and New Orleans. But it won't stop me paying to watch him do it in Amazonia.'

She looked at me, running through a silent-movie expressions catalogue of suspicion, mistrust, loathing, surprise, appreciation, delight and a few I couldn't name. 'All right,' she said finally. 'I withdraw that word "critic".'

'You haven't yet told me where you fit in,' I reminded her. 'I don't quite see you as the Amazon maid who brings him mangoes in jail nor as the fiery village dancer who——'

'I'm not an *actress*!' You couldn't mistake the expression that time: disgust. 'I'm Whitmore's lawyer; I fix the contracts for his company. If you'd quiet down for a few seconds, I might fix one for you.'

I shut up, except for the pipe which was making plumbing noises. After a while she said: 'Do you accept those figures?'

I nodded.

'Okay. I'm prepared to offer you a retainer of $20 a day for the next four weeks, just to be available on twenty-four hours' notice. When you fly for us, you get costs on this scale and $10 an hour with a minimum of $20 a day over the retainer. Do you agree?'

41

'Hold on a minute.' I was waiting for the rusty wheels in my head to catch up on a currency conversion. When I had it sorted out, it still looked pretty good: £7 a day for doing nothing plus another £7 at least and costs for flying. Then I remembered something. 'You talked about flying a camera plane: what about that?'

'Same deal without costs.'

'No.' I shook my head. 'I want half the scale costs: the Dove's costing me money just sitting on the ground when I'm not free to fly it. And what camera plane are we talking about, anyway?'

'We haven't got one yet.'

'Right—then I'll agree to that part of the deal when I see what you get.'

Her wide mouth turned into a wide smile, just a little twisted at one end. 'Are you afraid it might be a bit much for you?'

'Miss Penrose—I don't know much about film business, but I know a little about film flying. Most of it's done by professional outfits who hire or buy their own planes. You're trying to do it on the cheap by getting the plane and pilot separately. You might get the plane a little too cheap; this part of the world's full of planes like that. I'll agree to fly it when I've seen it.'

She went on looking at me for a moment, then nodded and sorted quickly through a stack of papers on the sofa. She handed one across. 'Okay. Just sign that.'

It was a printed contract form running to about eight pages, most of it about what I agreed not to sue the company for. Typed into blank spaces were my name, nationality, the rates of pay and costs. I wondered what all the other papers in the stack had been; probably versions of the same thing but with higher pay scales in case I'd forced a bargain. So probably I wasn't being too bright. I signed anyway; in the summer season I wasn't going to do better than this for the next month whatever.

She stood up and said briskly: 'Right. We'll go down to the set and get the Boss Man to sign your copy.'

I must have been looking puzzled. She said: 'Walt signs

42

all his company's contracts; and they call him Boss Man—
don't ask me why. Just the same way they call John Wayne
"Duke".'

'And they call you J.B.'

'Miss Penrose.'

I winced. 'A couple of days ago I was offered a job at
$750 a week. If I'd taken it, could I at least have called
you J?'

She stared. 'You really got offered that—and didn't take
it?'

'There was a moral question. They call me "Peaceful"
Carr.'

She went on staring at me just a little longer than the
crack seemed to deserve. Then she just said: 'Would you
bring my briefcase?'

I brought her briefcase.

★ 8 ★

SHE put on her sunglasses, a white towelling jacket and a
pair of black espadrilles, then led the way to a blood-red
space-bomb that turned out to be a Studebaker Avanti.

Perhaps she felt she'd been trampling my masculinity a
little, because she offered me the keys. I took one look at
the dashboard and shook my head. 'Not me. I don't have
an astronaut's licence.'

She drove. We went back east on the coast road for a
little less than a mile, but even in that distance we managed
to hit both verges and only just missed the sound barrier.
Just where the road swings right to avoid the White River
and it looked as if we weren't going to, she slid to a stop.

Just below the bridge on the coast road the river widens
out and runs slow and shallow through a flat, soggy coconut-
palm grove. Parked at the edge of it were a collection of
lorries, jeeps and station wagons, their drivers sitting in the
shadows and drinking Red Stripe or just dozing. We parked
alongside them and got out, although my knees would

rather have sat quietly for five minutes after that drive.

At the very edge of the trees a generator truck was chugging softly away by itself; we followed the line of cables leading forward through the grove.

The first thing we passed was a collection of small trollies, drums of rubber-covered cables and heaps of tarpaulins; seated on one heap, half a dozen men were playing cards in that private grunting language of men who've spent most of their lives playing cards together. Next, a small group of people sitting in folding canvas chairs, reading or sleeping or talking quietly; a couple of them nodded to J.B. as we went past. Finally there was just one man alone, wearing a vivid beach shirt and headphones and sitting at a small desk of electrical equipment, turning knobs and swearing softly to himself. He didn't even notice us come past. After that we were at the holy place itself.

There was a crescent ring of more people in more canvas chairs, looking a little older and spreading out of the chairs a little farther. Inside them was another crescent of tall arc lights blazing down towards the river. Somehow I hadn't thought of anybody coming to Jamaica in high summer and bringing his own light, but I suppose there was a reason. And inside them, the camera itself.

It took a moment to recognize it. It was mounted on a trolley placed on about fifteen yards of rails laid over a plank floor parallel to the river. Several people were standing around poking bits of the camera; the rest of the trolley was covered with men playing cards. For an epic, it all seemed very quiet and peaceful.

'Are you sure I'm the man you want?' I asked. 'I'm lousy at cards.'

J.B. glared at me, then turned to the nearest chair. 'Where's the Boss Man?'

The man in the chair was youngish, with limp fair hair and a pale smile. He waved towards the river. 'Over the other side. They're just going to do the crossing-the-river-under-fire scene.' He went back to staring at the wedge of yellow typescript. 'What *would* Spaniards shout while crossing a river under fire?'

44

'Caramba?' I suggested.

He looked up balefully. 'This isn't television, you know.'

The man next to him stretched his legs and said: 'How about "Thirty-five bucks a day isn't enough if I have to earn it by falling on my fanny in this goddamn river"?'

The young man said sourly: 'How does it sound in Spanish?'

'Most inspiring but rather long.' He looked up and gave me a very handsome but rather practised grin. I knew the face: he was one of the Latin lovers with a phoney-Spanish name like Luiz Montecristo or Montego or . . . yes: Monterrey. Luiz Monterrey. He'd had a few years starring in carnival-in-Rio type films just after the war, but by now the lean hatchet face was sagging a little, the neat black moustache had flecks of grey in it. He'd been playing the bandit chief or the aloof aristocrat in Whitmore films for the past several years.

This time he was wearing a frilly silk shirt that was torn and smudged, whipcord riding breeches and a cartridge bandolier slung across his chest.

A voice by the camera shouted: 'Where's the dialogue?'

The young man called hopefully: *'Viva el liberador!'*

That fell on stony ground all right. The voice said: 'We'll think up something later and dub it in. Right, let's go. Luiz!'

Luiz called: 'Here,' and didn't move. Neither did anybody else.

Another voice shouted: 'Bill says he's getting wind noise in the mike.'

'There isn't any wind. Let's go.'

'We need a scrim on that brute or you'll have too much underlight by the tree.'

'Put it up, then. Right? Let's go.'

'With that scrim you'll have to come up to five-six in the pan.'

'Okay. Let's go.'

'Bill says it must be the leaves rustling then.'

'The leaves don't rustle if there isn't any wind. Let's go.'

'This is a tracking shot ending in a pan and a tilt with a

change of focus and aperture. You want to zoom in as well and make movie history?'

'Sell it to Hitchcock. Let's *go*.'

'Bill says he thinks it must be water running.'

'If he'd come out from behind that bloody tree he'd see we're taking a shot of a bloody river! Let's GO!'

Suddenly Luiz put on a broad hat and walked down to the bank. The card players jumped off the trolley. It went very quiet.

Two people shouted: 'Quiet!'

Then the camera trolley, pushed by the card-players, started to move. A dozen men ran into the water from the far side of the river, waving rifles. Spouts of water spat up around them with gunshot sounds, and several fell down. The rest waded on and threw themselves into the cover of the first palms as the camera reached the end of its rails.

Although they'd only been some sort of waterproof fire-cracker touched off electrically, the gunshots had made me jump.

Several people shouted again, the lights went off, the dead men climbed ashore and shook themselves like wet dogs, the card-players settled down on the edge of the trolley. The river flowed quiet and peaceful.

J.B. said: 'That looked good; they probably won't want to go on that again. Let's get to the Boss Man while they're setting up the next one.' I followed her down to the camera.

You couldn't mistake Whitmore. You were just surprised, stupidly, to find he looked so much like himself. Maybe you'd read too much about five-foot Hollywood heroes riding tall in the saddle. Not this boy: he was a clear six-foot-four in low-heeled boots, with a chest like a banqueting table and a skin of tanned horse-hide. The eyes really were permanently half-closed against the sun, the mouth really was set in a grim-humorous line, his voice really could have shifted a thousand longhorns up the Chisholm trail on volume alone. Somehow, you'd expected all this to switch off with the arc lights.

Yet why? He'd been standing and talking and looking like

46

that for thirty years and it had made him several million dollars. Even if it hadn't begun that way, by now it was no more phoney than the way a bank clerk who's been at the job thirty years looks like a bank clerk.

J.B. was looking at me sideways, with a gleam of knowing amusement. 'Impressive, isn't it?' she said softly. 'I felt the same way, the first time.'

'Him and the Eiffel Tower.'

Whitmore was talking to the man who'd shouted 'Let's go', presumably the director. About fifty, stoutish, with grey hair and moustache and looking like an English colonel with strong black market connections.

They broke off as J.B. went forward. Whitmore said: 'Hi. What's new at the courthouse?'

'I've got your flying boy. All signed up.'

He looked at me, then reached out a huge blunt-fingered hand. 'Hi, fella.' We shook hands. J.B. passed him the contract and he studied it.

He was wearing a thin bush jacket, khaki drill trousers stuffed into high-laced paratroop boots, a webbing belt and army holster and a wide crumpled hat with a snakeskin band.

He cocked his head at me in a gesture I knew as well as he did. 'You were the boy out in Korea, right?'

Here we went again. 'That's right, Mr Whitmore.'

'How many d'you knock down out there?'

'Three.'

'How many d'you shoot at?'

'Three.'

He let out a big bark of laughter. 'That's good enough for me. Anybody got a pen?' He reached and tweaked the top of J.B.'s bathing dress. 'Got anything down there? No, not much.'

Several people laughed. She grinned, quickly and vividly, unembarrassed. With him, the gesture had been a simple, boyish dirty joke.

Whitmore raised his voice to Chisholm trail level. 'I'm paying three writers and I can't find a single goddamned pen!' The director gave him a pen.

47

He was about to sign when Luiz came up behind him, squelching in his wet boots and holding his damp trousers distastefully out from his legs. He looked, saw the contract, then looked at me and said sadly: 'Don't sign up with the Boss Man, my friend. You only end up with wet feet.' Then, to Whitmore, he added: 'He's Commonwealth, I trust?'

Whitmore looked at me sharply: 'You *are* a Commonwealth citizen, right?'

'Yes.' I was probably looking puzzled again.

He signed with a quick rasping scribble and gave the pen back to the director, who looked at the nib sadly and tucked it away. Whitmore handed the contract to J.B. 'Explain to him about Eady, honey.' To me, he said: 'Stick around for some chow, fella. We'll talk then.' Then he walked off with the familiar rolling stride, chatting to a distant group of raggedly-dressed actors in a voice that shivered the palm fronds.

J.B. was studying me thoughtfully. 'I think you just joined the club, Carr. The Boss Man likes that Korean stuff.' The thought didn't seem to be brightening her day much.

I said: 'It was twelve years ago, for God's sake.'

'The Boss Man's been around a long time. Come on: I'll see if we can't find a drink. They'll probably break for lunch after the next shot.' We went back through the grove to the lorry park.

By then some of the drivers and helpers were setting up a number of long trestle tables and unfolding more canvas chairs, but not moving as if they were worried about the world ending first. J.B. went over to one of the station wagons, brought out a big Thermos bucket, and produced a couple of tins of American beer. I jabbed them with a pocket screwdriver and we sat down in the shade of the car.

After a while I asked: 'What's all this Eady thing?'

'Eady plan. It's the ground rules for qualifying a picture as a British production. One—' she raised a finger '—you've got to have a British company producing it. Two, eighty per cent of your salary budget has to go to Commonwealth citizens. Three, any studio work has to be done in Britain or Ireland. Then you qualify for Eady.'

'Which is what?'

'Sort of legal kick-back. They take a levy on all movie-house seats sold in Britain and pay it back to the producer as a percentage of his gross box-office take. It's running about forty per cent, now.'

I closed my eyes and thought for a moment. 'You mean if he makes say, a hundred thousand he gets paid another forty? Two hundred thousand and he gets eighty?'

'Right.'

I stared. 'Good times are here again, aren't they?'

She looked at me coldly. 'Movies aren't a way of printing your own money, Carr, the way they were before TV.'

'I know: all that glitters isn't gold: some of it's diamonds. Who is Eady, anyway?'

'Some guy in the British Treasury, I think.'

'He knew his Bible, didn't he? "To him that hath shall be given" and so forth.'

'It works out that way. I guess it was originally supposed to help the small producers.'

I thought for another moment. 'Just explain to me how you make *this* picture an Eady one. Apart from these boys—' I nodded at the men setting up the tables '—the place isn't exactly crowded with Commonwealth citizens.'

'They're there. The crew's mostly British: director, camera, sound, lights, the grips. We got the script done in London. And you're allowed to hold out two salaries when you come to figure your eighty per cent. Naturally you make them the highest ones: we made it female lead and Luiz.'

'What about Whitmore?'

'He's not on salary. He takes a percentage of the picture.'

I nodded. 'I'm beginning to see the strategy. And to be a British company, I suppose you set one up specially in London?'

'Nassau. The Bahamas count as British.'

'So this is why you didn't bring in an American pilot. I suppose I'm really quite a help to you: if you find you're

49

running under the eighty per cent, you can put up my pay and balance it out again.'

'Don't hope too hard. If we run under eighty, I'll be fired the next day.'

'Are you really going to cart everybody across the Atlantic to do the studio stuff?'

She shook her head. 'Pictures likes this you don't do studio work if you can help it. You script it so most of it's outdoors, and when you got to have an interior you do that on location, too: with fast colour film you can do it with the lights you bring along anyway. We're only doing inside a couple of native huts and a hacienda: we'll build that in the hangar up on the airstrip.'

A larger-than-usual lizard with a light-green body, blue hips and a bronze tail scuttled out from under the car, nodded several times, belched and puffed out his throat in a bright orange sac.

J.B. frowned at him. 'Whatever he's doing, I wish he wouldn't.'

'Mating call. They call them Croakers. Belch back and you'll have a new boy-friend.'

'Another Method actor in blue jeans. Them, I can do without.'

I got out my pipe and started to pack it. 'Which reminds me—I didn't notice the feminine interest in the picture.'

'Boss Man did all her scenes first and sent her back to the States to get her picture in the papers. They didn't hit it off.'

'Don't tell me he prefers horses.'

She shrugged. 'Horses, guns, dogs, whisky, men. He's not against women; he just thinks sex and thirst are itches you scratch. You buy a whisky in a bar, a woman in a cat-house. In his time off he goes hunting with the boys—and I mean in the mountains.' She frowned down at her beer can. 'I don't know what damn business it is of yours.'

I put a match to the pipe and breathed smoke away from her. 'But he's been married, hasn't he?'

'Three times. I got him out of the last one a few months ago. He didn't exactly notice any of them; it was just the fashion. In those days it didn't matter who you laid as long as you were married. Does movie gossip really interest you?'

'He's the man I'm working for. Same as you.'

She nodded and then said slowly and thoughtfully: 'Don't get him wrong, Carr. He's a pro: he doesn't act much, but he doesn't need to. He's never got an Oscar and never will and he honestly doesn't give a damn. He knows what he's selling and he doesn't sell short: if he wasn't in pictures he'd be busting horses in rodeos and going hunting and whoring and . . .' She took a deep breath. 'Christ, I don't *approve* of the big sonofabitch, but I like him.'

I said softly: 'Perhaps just enough to want to save him from those long dull evenings in the cat-house?'

Her head came round with a snap and her face was a hard, glittering glare. For a moment it looked as if I was going to be smoking my pipe from somewhere around my tonsils.

Then she suddenly flashed a wide grin. 'Maybe. Maybe—once. Women are suckers for wanting to save men from a man's world. Never works. I'm not too particular about wedding rings, but I'm damned if I'll settle for a brand on the backside.'

'I'm encouraged to hear it.'

Her voice got a little colder. 'Don't puff out your throat at me, Carr.'

We ate at the stars' table, which meant that the food got brought to us instead of queueing up for it. It was the same food; peas and rice with chicken, which is about as close to a Jamaican national dish as you'll get, apart from salt cod and ackee. Whitmore, Luiz, the director, J.B., four others and me.

Whitmore said. 'We got to get somebody in to do the Spanish for us. You heard what that slob of a writer asked the boys to shout about just now?—"*Viva el liberador*", for Chrissake.' He looked at Luiz. 'You heard that?'

Luiz shrugged elegantly. 'To me, it seemed reasonably appropriate. Those of Spanish blood who rush across rivers under fire often shout the most naïve things.'

Whitmore grunted. 'Well, we got to get somebody.' He turned to me. 'Anybody you know speak Spanish, fella?'

'I know one man. I don't know if he'd be free, though.'

'We can try him. Tell J.B.'

So I gave her Diego Ingles' name and a telephone number where you could sometimes catch him between beds.

Another man, who seemed to be head of the camera team, suddenly asked me: 'Have you ever flown a camera plane before?' His accent was English English, so I seemed to have struck another part of the eighty per cent.

I shook my head. 'I haven't agreed to fly this one, yet.'

J.B. said: 'He's worried about what we might get for him.'

The cameraman looked a little contemptuous. 'It'll be my neck up there, too, you know. So if I don't mind—'

'That's splendid,' I said, 'as long as your neck's as good as mine at recognizing a cracked mainspar.'

Whitmore said calmly: 'What kind of plane d'you want, fella?'

'I'd've thought a helicopter was the most versatile. But I'm no helicopter pilot.'

J.B. said: 'Choppers are out. You know what they cost an hour?'

The cameraman said: 'Vibration.'

The director pushed away his plate and started fitting a cigarette into a stubby holder. 'We can do without the aerials, Walt.'

'Sure—you can cut any picture to the bone. So who pays to see dry bones?'

I said: 'There's a Harvard—what you'd call a Texan—on the Boscobel strip. A film company used it as a Jap bomber last year.'

The cameraman said impatiently: 'We're not looking for Jap bombers. And you can't do good aerials from a single-engined plane: it has to be hand-held stuff and you don't get the down-ahead tracking shots.'

Whitmore nodded, planted his elbows solidly on the table, and started to peel an orange in big tearing, sweeping strokes. 'Okay, fella. So what do you figure we should get?'

I said carefully: 'If you want to shoot down and ahead you need twin engines—and a glass nose. That wipes out my Dove. You'd better try and pick up an old bomber—B-25 or a B-26—with a bomb-aimer's position in the nose. There's still a lot of them around, in Central and South America.'

Whitmore cocked an eyebrow at the cameraman, then the director. Then said: 'Sounds good. Can you find one, J.B.?'

'I can start people looking.'

'Fine, fine.' He ate a strip of orange. 'Hell, maybe we could write it into the picture. Say instead of where the government sends a patrol on horses, they send a bomber. That's where we're walking up the river. So I have a Browning or a Thompson and I'm standing in these goddamn rapids up to my knees and shooting hell out of this bomber overhead. Could make a great scene.'

The table went very quiet. The director slowly put both hands to his head and started muttering.

But it *would* make a great scene—for Whitmore. Him standing to his knees in foaming white water, blazing defiance at the sky with a tommy-gun.

Just to be technical, a bomber doing 200 m.p.h. would be 100 yards ahead one moment and 100 yards behind two seconds later. Perhaps that's why so few bombers ever get shot down with Browning automatic rifles and Thompson sub-machine guns.

It would still be a great scene—and everybody round the table knew it.

Luiz said: 'I think I see where we all get our feet wet once more.'

Whitmore ate another piece of orange. 'Fine. Tell the dialogue boys what we want.' He looked back at me. 'Now we got another problem. We need a location. We can do all the jungle, river, tin-roof village stuff here. But just a coupla scenes, we need some real Spanish architecture. Something like those big two-peak churches you get in Mexico—you know?'

I knew. I'd seen him park his horse outside that type of church half a dozen times. It labelled the film Spanish New World faster than you could speak it aloud.

The cameraman said: 'Puerto Rico—I did a documentary there once. It's full of—'

J.B. said: '*Not* Puerto Rico. We'd be back in US labour laws. The budget'll blow to hell and we'll never make Eady.'

The director said: 'Walt—we can get Roddie down here and he'll build you one in a week.'

J.B. said: 'Roddie costs money. He's another American salary, Boss.'

'Will you let the man speak?' Whitmore roared. Everybody shut up. He nodded to me. 'You're the local boy, fella. Let's hear from you.'

'Nothing like that in Jamaica: we've been British too long.' I shut my eyes, pinned up a mental map of the Caribbean, and started touring. 'Cuba's the nearest, but . . . Mexico's seven hundred miles, the nearest point in South America's a good five hundred. There's Haiti just down the road, but I've never heard of anybody getting any work done in Haiti.'

The director said: 'Let's get Roddie down.'

'And there's the Republica Libra.'

Whitmore and Luiz looked at each other. Luiz gave another slow shrug. 'We could take a look this week-end.'

'Yeah.' Whitmore looked at the cameraman. 'You wanted to do some servicing on the cameras anyway, right? So we won't shoot Saturday and Sunday and our friend'll fly us down to the Republica. There'll be—' he counted round the table: himself, the director, Luiz, a delicately dressed young man who hadn't said anything yet, and J.B. 'There'll be six of us. Fix a hotel, will you, J.B.?'

'Hold on,' I said. Everybody looked at me. 'The Republica's having a little trouble right now. I don't know how they're reacting to strangers: they may want to keep them out, they may want to let them in just to prove everything's nice and normal. I just don't know.'

Luiz said gently: 'But we can find out.'

'Yes. But you've got an extra problem with me. They seem to have taken against me: decided I've been helping the rebels. A couple of their jets bounced me the other day. So however they take to you, they may not be too glad to see me in Bartolomeo.'

'You don't wanna go?' Whitmore asked bluntly.

'Not quite that.' It might be the best thing to go—a chance to argue it out with the Republica authorities when I could offer them solid proof that I might bring profitable trade to the country. It might put the Republica back on my map—and I certainly needed places on that map.

'Not quite that,' I said again. 'Just that they might not think I'm adding tone to your business.'

'I guess they won't put me in jail,' Whitmore said. Then his face tightened into a thin, slightly crooked smile. I knew that expression: it came when the unshaven character at the far end of the bar announces that he can't stand the smell of lawmen. 'Just stick close to me, fella. We'll manage.'

The director caught my eye and took a deep, weary breath. He knew that expression—and the scene that came after it: the bar-room brawl.

★ 9 ★

FILM companies don't seem to mind getting up at crop-spraying hours, so they were waiting for me when I put down at Boscobel at seven on Saturday morning.

They made an assorted bunch. J.B. was in a crisp blue-and-white striped linen suit and dark-blue blouse; Luiz in a dark-blue silk suit with a yellow scarf at the neck; Whitmore looking like a big-game hunter in fawn beach trousers, an army shirt and the same broad hat he wore in the film. The director just looked English in an open-necked shirt under a tweed jacket, and the art director looked very art directorish in a waisted crocodile-skin jacket, tight trousers and high boots.

I got everybody and a few suitcases on board and we took off around seven-thirty.

I'd been a little worried about how to announce our arrival to Santo Bartolomeo without issuing Ned an invitation to come and breathe jet fumes down my neck—or worse. I could just appear over the end of the runway, of course; that wouldn't be difficult. But it would also give them a reasonable cause for complaint: you're supposed to file a flight plan. So in the end I'd just sent a cable the night before saying I'd be in by noon carrying several important American businessmen, repeat important. Flight plans usually carry both less and more than that, but I could say the cable office had cocked it up.

Whitmore spent most of the trip up beside me, crammed into the co-pilot's seat and staring out through a huge pair of binoculars whenever there was anything to stare at. I held off radioing an estimated time of arrival until we were almost crossing the coast, ten minutes from landing. If Ned could scramble a section of Vamps in that time on a Saturday, he'd been working even harder than he claimed.

As I turned north to angle round the city, the dark cross of asphalt runways came up a couple of miles to our left.

Whitmore leaned across. 'That the field?'

'The military air base. The civil airport's over on the east, the other side of town.'

'Yeah?' He peered through the binoculars. 'What they got?'

'Squadron of Vampire jets, two or three DC-3s for transport, some light trainers and communications jobs. And the usual old prop fighters rotting for lack of spares.'

'Yeah. I can see the jets. All lined up.'

I could just about see them myself: a line of sparkling silver dots. I tried to count them, to make sure they were all safely on the ground, but the sparkle blurred them into each other.

Whitmore asked: 'Can we get closer?'

I thought he was overdoing the little-boy-watching-trains act a bit. 'No. They get pretty touchy about people looking over the fence on this island.' I was clear of the city by now. 'Turning starboard,' I warned him.

There was a sudden shadow over the cockpit and a thump as we rode into a blast of hot jet exhaust. Then a Vampire pulling out of its pass and climbing ahead.

Without thinking, I yanked the Dove's nose savagely around and pointed it: if there was a gunsight on the windscreen, a gun-button on the control wheel . . . There wasn't. My stomach clenched into a knot of helpless anger. *Damn you, damn you,* DAMN *you;* NOBODY *does that to me!*

56

The door behind me swung open and the art director asked: 'What was that?'

'We got bounced. Tell everybody to fasten their seat-belts.' He hesitated, then Whitmore said calmly: 'Shut the door, fella.' The door slapped shut.

I glanced across. The big man was firmly pulling his own belt tight. He caught my eye and gave a small twist of a smile. 'You're the boss here, fella.'

We were at only 2,000 feet. About a thousand feet higher, and out to the left, the Vampire was levelling out of his climbing turn and coming back past me before diving in behind for another pass.

Ned had said: 'Next time I could get orders to shoot.' And now was next time . . . But it wasn't Ned in the Vamp. His fighter pilot instinct went too deep to have allowed him to pull up ahead of me, to turn his back on another plane even if it was unarmed.

I yanked back the throttles and pushed the Dove's nose hard down. The Vampire saw it and turned in a little earlier and a little steeper than he should have. No, it wasn't Ned.

I swung hard left, into and underneath him, forcing him to tighten and steepen his turn even more if he was going to bring his guns to bear. But coming down-hill in a jet, he was going too fast. His wings swung vertical for a moment as he tried to make it, then he levelled and soared away up to start again from scratch.

'Missed, you bastard.'

Whitmore twisted around, watching the Vampire over his shoulder. 'You figure he's going to shoot?'

'I figure on keeping out of his sights.' *Was that all I figured?*

We were below 1,500 feet now and still going down in wide spirals. But the Vampire had learned something. He'd positioned himself only about five hundred feet higher this time and—as far as I could judge—he'd slowed down a lot. He circled in a gentle turn outside our spiral, waiting his moment.

Keeping an eye on the Vampire, I put my right hand down

on the flaps lever. 'Get your hand on this,' I told Whitmore. 'When I say "Flaps" I want it all the way down. But not before. Don't practise.' I felt his big paw push mine aside.

He said calmly: 'Got it.'

I waited until the sun was where it wouldn't blind the Vampire or me, turned extra steeply for a few seconds, then straightened out as if I'd spotted where I wanted to go and was heading there direct.

Come on, you bastard: try and bite me.

He bit. He flipped over and came down in the classic 'curve of pursuit', the long curling dive to end up sitting on my tail.

I turned into and under him again—but now he was expecting that. He was moving slow enough to follow me. He tightened his diving curve, holding me easily, swinging smoothly into firing range.

I levelled the Dove and pulled back the throttles. The Vampire slid behind my left shoulder, almost dead behind us. I yelled: 'Flaps down!'

The lever clicked in the silence. Then it was as if I'd stamped on the brakes: the Dove collided with a soft pillow of air and bounced soggily upwards, into the Vampire's path.

Suddenly he was on top of us.

He reared like a startled horse, jerking into a wildly tight turn. His wings blurred with mist condensing in the shattered airflow, then flicked level as he stalled out. He shuddered past a few yards to the left and I caught a glimpse of a helmeted, hunched figure in the cockpit, fighting controls that weren't controlling anything any more. His nose began to swing inexorably downwards.

A Vampire can lose over two thousand feet in a gentle stall. This one had only 1,200 feet to lose—and he was as totally stalled as I've seen an airplane. There was nothing to do now but watch him die.

To bale out of a Vampire 5 you dump the cockpit canopy, roll on your back and drop out—if you're still in control.

I put the Dove's nose down, pushed up the throttles: we were close to stalling ourselves. Below, the cockpit canopy flashed off the Vampire, so perhaps he tried at the last second to jump. Then he was a burst of flame and a swelling cloud of smoke on the harsh green countryside. From inside the Dove you couldn't even hear the bang.

We landed at Santo Bartolomeo five minutes later.

The control tower didn't throw a banquet in my honour, but hadn't got any orders to cut my throat, either. And they knew Whitmore's name when I dropped it on their toes a few times. They cleared me in with just a few nasty remarks about how to write a flight plan, but I swallowed that easily.

Nobody said anything about a crashed Vampire.

It was at least possible that nothing *would* be said. If the pilot hadn't had orders to intercept, he might not have radioed that he was doing something without orders. So he might just be written off as a training crash: Ned must be expecting crashes, even if he hadn't had them already. And I'd been investigating officer on too many RAF crashes to worry about eye-witnesses. All Ned would learn from them would be that five Boeing 707s had simultaneously burst into flames three feet above their rooftops.

Well, I'd find out. But it still wasn't the best start to what I'd hoped would be a good-will visit. I went back downstairs, got my passport stamped, and went through to join the others in the dingy-modern lobby.

They were standing round a smeared glass case showing a model of what the grand and glorious new airport terminal would look like—when the government stopped spending the taxes on American blondes and Swiss bank accounts. Even the model had several years' dust on it by now.

The director and art director gave me rather white, suspicious looks; Whitmore and Luiz just nodded. J.B. marched up and whispered fiercely: 'Just what really happened back there before we landed?'

'Man made a pass at us, missed, and crashed.'

'Is that all?'

I shrugged. 'I thought you'd be used to men doing that.'

59

Her eyes glittered. 'What *made* him crash?'

'One of those rare non-habit-forming vices: stalling at twelve hundred feet.'

'And you think it's just a joke?'

'You'd have preferred a serious ending? Like him shooting us down?'

'You can't be sure——'

'This way, I can.'

She stared at me a few moments more, sizzling quietly, her face in hard still lines. Angry like that, she seemed oddly feminine and somehow defenceless. I started to grin, and she jammed on her sunglasses and turned away.

The lobby was beginning to fill with outbound passengers. Whitmore dropped a hand on my shoulder and said: 'Lot of artillery around, fella.'

There was. About half a dozen of the passengers—all of them a little fatter or better dressed than the average—were shoving through the crowd with revolvers jammed in their hip pockets or slung on wide, fancy cowboy belts.

I nodded. 'They're government employees. Above a certain rank in the civil service, you get the right to carry a gun. And as it's a status-symbol and a sex-symbol *and* they think it makes them look like Walt Whitmore, they carry it. It's the same idea as the old British Army one of selling its commissions.'

He shook his head slowly. 'How's that again?'

'A hundred years ago and more, when you were getting army revolutions all over Europe, they reckoned if you sold commissions, you'd have the Army run by rich men—and rich men don't want to change a system that keeps them rich. Same here: with everything run by bribery, the civil service is one of the best-paid jobs. *They* don't want a change. So you arm them and you've got a standing counter-revolutionary force.

'I get it.' He nodded thoughtfully, probably working out where the idea would fit into *Bolivar Smith*. Apparently it wouldn't, because then he swung round and made a sweeping git-along-little-dogies gesture. 'Come on, kids, let's roll.'

60

We rolled in two taxis: Whitmore, Luiz and J.B. in one, me and the two directors behind. They were still suspicious of me and still shaken by the flight, so it was a quiet ride.

We went too fast down a narrow concrete highway between overgrown plantations and tin-shack farmhouses for fifteen minutes. After that we were weaving through the shanty-town on the edge of the city itself.

Santo Bartolomeo is an old city. It's supposed to be named after Colombus's brother, who certainly wasn't a saint except by Republica standards. It's also supposed to be the gayest, wickedest city in the Caribbean. Maybe it was, in the sailing-ship days when you could get a bottle of rum, two women and three knife-fights for a silver dollar. Not any more.

Now it's just old, tired, shabby, worn out by two much politicking. The steam-ships are bigger and fewer and turn round quicker than the clippers, and banks and warehouses have replaced the brothels and inns of the waterfront. The rest of the town is a mess: 400-year-old Spanish cathedrals flanking Victorian office blocks flanking stucco split-level houses that look as new as tomorrow for three months and as old as Columbus after six. But maybe after centuries of fast-changing governments, even the buildings don't want to look as if they might be talking to their neighbours.

You can count the revolutions in the avenidas. A new man takes over, carves out a new avenida lined with Royal Palms, names it after himself, and the new civil servants pocket their bribes and rush in to build the latest-style residences along it. But in five years there's a new man, a new avenida, new men building in a new style. Nobody rebuilds the oozing, crumbling houses on the narrow streets joining the avenidas. The people who live there never reach the pistol-packing ranks, so didn't take part in the last revolution and won't take part in the next. Nobody owes them anything.

The taxi stuck to the avenidas. We came in on Lincoln, turned down George Washington and up Independencia. Most of the avenidas end up with such names: heroes too long ago or far away to have any political significance, or abstract ideas like *independencia* and *libertad* that are what every revolution's about anyway. It doesn't make much difference. A new *libertad* comes every five or ten years, but there'll still be two grey soldiers with carbines and eighteen-inch truncheons on every corner to remind you that you are now really *libre*.

With the last *libertad* they'd decided the town was the new Miami Beach and had built three modern resort hotels. We drove clear through the town to the biggest and best of all, the Americana, on the western edge.

It sat at the end of a long avenue of Royal Palms: a crescent-shaped five-storey copy of the Fontainebleau at Miami Beach itself. Every room guaranteed its own balcony and air-conditioning, every bell-boy, lift-boy and floor waiter guaranteed a pimp. Maybe that made it Whitmore country. For me, it made it the week-end I caught up on my drinking.

I dumped my bag in my room and went straight down to the patio bar on the terrace and bought a beer. By then it was about half-past noon. Ten minutes later, the director came in; he saw me, wondered if he could pretend he hadn't, decided not, and came over.

'If I'd got any pesos I'd buy you a drink,' he announced.

'I've got some.'

He let me buy him a Scotch, then asked: 'How do you change money here?'

'Try the bell-boy. The official exchange rate's one peso to a dollar. It should be about a peso and a half. Don't settle for less than one-thirty-five. And remember to change any pesos back before you go out: officially you can't export currency, so no bank outside'll touch your pesos.'

'My God.' He sucked at his drink. 'We'll never be able to shoot here. They'll cheat us blind the moment we've got the full crew in and they know we're depending on them.'

'Tell Whitmore.'

'I've been telling him.' He gave me a sideways look. '*You* try telling him. You seem to be in with the Boss Man.'

I let that remark go its lonely way and started to fill my pipe.

After a decent interval, he said: 'Well, you've got a fresh viewpoint: what d'you think of the Boss Man?'

'He's tall.'

When I didn't go on, he said: 'That's all you've noticed?'

'He's broad, too.'

'All right, Carr. I see. But just let me tell you something; Don't ever think that man can't act.' Whitmore, Luiz and J.B. came into the bar. The director put the last of his Scotch down the hatch and said quickly and quietly: 'Check your contract. Mine's quite clear: I just direct.'

He slid off the stool and walked away, nodding to Whitmore.

The big man put both hands on the bar and looked up and down. 'Beer—right? Right. *Cuatro* beer!' He tossed a handful of pesos on the bar.

'You managed to change some dollars,' I remarked.

'Fella—one thing I don't need to do is change any money. I got nearly a quarter of a million dollars tied up in this island: frozen assets from every goddamned picture of mine they've shown here in twelve years. It's nice to be able to cash a cheque and spend some of it.'

I nodded and put the third match to my pipe. Experience had shown that this was the one voted most likely to succeed.

Whitmore said: 'Do you really *like* that thing?'

The match died, disillusioned. I took the pipe out of my mouth and looked at it. 'I'm told it grows on you.'

'Not only on you, fella. Would you like a butt instead?'

'If you insist.' I put the pipe down and lit one of his Chesterfields.

J.B. shook her head wearily. 'There's a boy who's got the price of cigarettes licked.'

Ned said: 'All right, Keith. You're under arrest.'

He was standing, feet spread, pointing a blunt finger like a pistol and giving me a look as friendly as a blowtorch. He obviously hadn't wasted any time: he was still in a stained lightweight flying suit, covered in zips and pockets, with a fat stubby revolver in a shoulder harness buckled over the lot. In the carefully-staged half-light of the patio bar, he looked like the scene from a Whitmore film where the hero staggers shirtless into the Southern ballroom.

The two tall air policemen in white helmets and heavy

webbing holsters didn't look as if they belonged, either. It didn't stop them moving towards me.

Then J.B. slid off her stool and said crisply: 'I'm Mr Carr's lawyer. Will you tell me the charge, please?'

Ned jerked his head round and gave her a suspicious frown. Then he said heavily: 'Yeh—I suppose I should've expected something like you. Well, we can start with murder and an act of war and see what builds up from there.'

She took off her sunglasses and looked at him as if he'd crept out of the wall. 'You are quite certain *you* have power of arrest?'

'Yeh. You sure you got the right to practise law here?'

She flicked him a brief condescending smile. 'I didn't want you to make a fool of yourself—whoever you are.'

It seemed time to make some introductions. I said: 'Coronel Ned Rafter, commanding the Republica fighter squadron. Meet Miss J. B. Penrose.' I waved a hand down the bar. 'And you'll have recognized Walt Whitmore and Luiz Monterrey, of course.'

Of course he hadn't; he'd only been looking at me. He lifted a hand slowly to his stubbly hair, scratched, and said: 'Yeh. I suppose I should've expected somebody like you, too.' He turned back to me. 'You sure pick your witnesses before you throw your punch.'

Whitmore stuck out a hand. 'Glad to meet you, Coronel. Have a beer.'

Ned looked at the hand, then shook his head. 'I've come for *him*. I'll make do with that.'

Whitmore said: 'Anything he's supposed to have done, I was there at the time.'

'Yeh. I'm beginning to get the idea.'

J.B. asked smoothly: 'What were the charges again, Coronel?'

'I want a statement from Keith in front of the General for a court of inquiry,' he growled. 'He don't move out of my sight until we've got that.'

'We're down to a subpoena for an inquiry now, are we?' she asked. 'Let's work on it a bit more. We could get your "act of war" down to a parking ticket yet.'

But that did it. Ned's faced clamped tight. 'Bring him in!'

The two guards moved for me.

I slid off the stool and stood waiting, feeling the old anger surge up inside. *Nobody does this to . . .* But you're always hitting the wrong men. The man in the Vampire hadn't bought the Vampire himself, hadn't been the one who decided I was a danger to the state. The two guards might like their work—they looked as if they did—but they were still under orders. You can never hit the men who give the orders. But maybe the time comes when you've got to hit *somebody . . .*

The decision had been made for me. The guard on my right seized my arm. Then a huge hand landed on his shoulder, twisted him as easily as I could turn a switch, and another hand thumped in just under the white helmet. The guard took a short backwards sprint and fell over a bamboo table.

The second guard was tearing at his holster, pulling a long revolver. I grabbed the gun by the cylinder and hit him in the stomach with my right. He grunted and pulled the trigger —but the cylinder couldn't turn, the gun couldn't fire. I hit him again and he started to fall, dangling from the gun in my left hand.

J.B. let out a yell. Whitmore took three strides and a swinging place-kick. The first guard's arm whipped out straight and his revolver sailed out of the bar on to the lawn.

There was a thundering bang.

Ned was still standing there, surrounded by fading wisps of smoke, his arm stretched sideways where he'd fired into the open. Then his gun swung back towards us.

'All right,' he said grimly, 'if you all won your Oscars, let's get back to where we started.'

Whitmore turned to him. Ned twitched the gun. 'I just *might* want to become famous.'

Whitmore shrugged, smiled slightly, and walked back to me. 'Turning out a better day than I expected, fella. I like the way you drop your shoulder with the punch.'

'Thank you. That was a nice piece of place-kicking.'

We grinned at each other. Luiz murmured: 'One for all

and all for one. And that was the one picture he *didn't* play in.'

Whitmore gave him a look, then said easily: 'Okay, so let's go see the General.'

J.B. said: 'Just you wait a minute, Coronel.' She was looking white and angry.

'You're in the Republica here,' Ned snapped. 'If you want to try your hand at prosecuting, you can start on me: for blowing size eleven holes in your clients *unless* they start moving right now.'

I tossed the guard's gun over the bar into a sink full of crushed ice, and we all went to see the General.

★ II ★

I'D expected a ride out to the air base or at least downtown to the Hall of Justice. Instead, we just pushed through a small crowd of tourists and hotel staff who'd come to see—from a distance—what the shot had been about, turned left in the hotel lobby and ended up in the casino room.

This was one thing they did better here than in San Juan. It was a tall, arched, elegant room decorated in the style of Louis the Fifteenth or Onassis the First or somebody. Anyway, long scarlet drapes, white paint, gold mouldings and chandeliers like crystal clouds, glowing gently—only gently. At tropical high noon, the place had the soft, seductive atmosphere of midnight. You could feel the money in your pocket fighting to be out and into the action.

The room looked pretty full for lunchtime, until I remembered it was Saturday. A white dinner jacket hurried up to us, staring horrified at Ned—perhaps more at his old flying suit than the gun in his hand. Then he recognized him.

'General Bosco,' Ned said flatly.

The white jacket nodded a smooth dark head towards the craps tables. We filed across.

Either the General didn't like rolling dice with the mob, or the mob had more sense than to roll dice with a man who's fifty per cent of a dictator. Despite the crowd, he had a whole craps table to himself, an aide-de-camp in a gold-braided uniform, a croupier and a couple of characters keeping the crowd at a distance with watchful plain-clothes expressions that were far more obvious than the bulges under their jackets.

The General had his back to us, rolling the dice across the table. But the aide caught my eye and smiled hungrily, and I knew him: Capitan Miranda.

Ned marched up and said: 'General—about that crash. I've got Carr, the pilot of the Dove.'

Bosco turned slowly and looked at him.

Perhaps he looked like half a dictator, but I really wouldn't know; my personal experience of dictators is slight, although not as slight as I'd like. To me he was a tallish, well-built character in his fifties, putting on a bit of a stomach, with a full but not too fleshy face, a hooked beak of a nose, neat greying hair and moustache, heavy eyebrows over slow dark eyes. He was wearing a snappy dark-blue uniform with five gold stars on the cuffs, gold wings and three rows of medal ribbons—which was restrained of him since he'd probably awarded most of them to himself.

He said in careful, almost perfect, English: 'I must congratulate you, Coronel. But—perhaps this would be better dealt with at the Hall of Justice?'

Ned jerked his head. 'It's his passengers. They're witnesses.'

Bosco swung his eyes slowly across us. He sized and priced me in a glance. The second glance got him Whitmore—and he knew him. Luiz took a moment longer, but he got the general idea. J.B. he ignored.

After a moment, he nodded and said thoughtfully: 'Ah-h-h. Yes. Perhaps you did the best thing, Coronel.' He took a long thin cigar from a breast pocket, and Miranda did a Billy-the-Kid draw with a silver lighter. Bosco breathed smoke, leaned his backside against the table, and said: 'Perhaps you would remind me of the full incident, Coronel.'

Ned said: 'It started with a radio call from Ramirez saying he'd spotted Carr's Dove and was going up closer to get a look at it. After that, nothing—until we got the word a few minutes later that a Vampire had crashed a couple of miles north of the field. I checked with Bartolomeo and found Carr had landed safely. I found him here. Him and Whitmore started a bit of a punch-up with the guards.'

Bosco looked at the gun in Ned's hand, then at Whitmore. Whitmore smiled his thin, confident smile. 'Two of your air cops tried to shove me around, General. I'm not complaining. They may be—when they get off the floor.'

The General smiled a little sadly. 'Nobody likes military policemen, Señor, not anywhere. But unfortunately they are necessary.' He looked back at Ned. 'And what were Ramirez' orders this morning?'

'Just a training flight. But we knew Carr's Dove was on its way, so he'd been asked to report it if he saw it.'

I asked: 'Any orders to bounce me?'

Ned took a deep breath. 'No. I'd told him to stay away from you.'

For all his eagerness to haul me into the scales of justice, Ned wasn't putting any gilding on the frame. In fact, it was hardly a frame at all.

So far.

The General turned to me. 'And you, Señor . . . ?'

I shrugged. 'Your boy made a pass at me. When he came in again I went into a spiral—to keep from under his guns. He stalled out of his turn and went in.'

I could feel Ned's eyes on me. The General asked Whitmore: 'And do you confirm this, Señor?'

'It all happened pretty quick,' Whitmore drawled, 'but that's how I recall it. I was up front with Carr.'

General Bosco sucked thoughtfully on his cigar, breathed smoke over our heads, and came to a decision. 'I think, Señores, we had all better have a drink.'

Still staring at me, Ned said slowly and clearly: 'You killed that boy, Carr. Deliberate.'

There were a few confused moments of a waiter asking What Drinks and J.B. asking What The Hell. When the smoke cleared the waiter had vanished and J.B. was smouldering silently with Luiz' hand clamped firmly on her

68

shoulder. The General was keeping Ned quiet with a steady dark stare.

Then he waved his cigar at the table. 'Perhaps, while we wait, Señor Whitmore would care to . . . ?'

Whitmore frowned, then shrugged, stepped up and took the dice from the croupier. 'We playing the house or just between ourselves?'

The cigar weaved a delicate *chandelle*. 'The house so kindly permits me to play just as among friends, so . . .' And he smiled sadly.

The house would so kindly permit him to rip off the roof, shoot down the chandeliers and borrow the manager's wife, too. The house couldn't stop him. He was General Bosco.

Whitmore tossed some money on the table. 'So fade me.'

The General nodded to Miranda, who said: 'General Bosco covers the bet.'

Bosco turned back to Ned. 'Now, Coronel, you were saying . . . ?'

Ned said flatly: 'Carr killed Ramirez. He started out to kill him, and he did.'

I said: 'I didn't start it, Ned.'

Whitmore spat on his hand and sent the dice across the table with an experienced flip.

The croupier chanted: '*Cinquo*. A point of five to make.'

The General smiled again. 'No win, no loss—yet. Please continue, Coronel.'

Ned was speaking to me now. 'I grant you didn't start it, Keith. But once *he* started it, you killed him. You dragged him down and stalled him. I don't know how—maybe with that old flaps trick. But I know you did it, and you know yourself.'

J.B. said icily: 'In an unarmed plane full of passengers? He killed your brave jet pilot?'

Whitmore rolled again. The croupier chanted: '*Ocho*. Eight. Still the point of five to make.'

Ned glanced quickly at the table, then shook his head. 'Guns ain't all of it, sweetheart. For some they ain't always enough when they got 'em, and some others don't always need 'em. What really matters is if you're a killer. Keith is.'

69

I said: 'He was still flying a fighter, Ned.' I stretched my hand. 'Give me your gun and I'll point it at you and you can guess if I'm going to shoot. Then tell me how it feels.'

'He wasn't going to shoot!'

I felt the cold anger rising inside. 'Wasn't he, Ned? Then I must have missed your postcard: Dear Keith, you're going to get beaten up by a boy in a Vamp but don't worry because he'll be disobeying orders and he probably won't disobey them as far as to shoot. So sorry I missed it, Ned, and put you to all this trouble. *So* sorry.'

The dice bounced. The croupier chanted: '*Seis*. Six. The point of five still to make.'

The General murmured: 'And still no win, no loss.'

Ned ignored both the dice and the general. His mouth twisted in disgust. 'Ah, don't bleed so easy, Keith.'

'*I'm* bleeding easy? I knock down one of your jets with an unarmed Dove and you start screaming murder?'

There was a long silence.

Then the dice galloped on the table. '*Siete*—seven. The shooter loses.'

The General said softly: 'So I win.'

J.B. was staring at me coldly: 'Are you admitting you deliberately made that jet crash?'

There was another silence, with just the rustle of Miranda picking up Whitmore's money.

I shrugged. 'Somehow, they never teach passive resistance in fighter squadrons. There's only one sure way to avoid getting shot down.'

Ned said: 'Shoot first.'

The General said, still softly: 'Or, of course, stay away.' He drew on his cigar. 'I believe Coronel Rafter met you in San Juan earlier this week and warned you that you were not any more welcome in the Republica. Perhaps you should have taken notice of that warning.'

'If you're closing Republica airspace you could announce it and get it in a Notam and make it official.'

'Ah, yes,' the cigar did another neat aerobatic. 'But we are not closing our airspace. We welcome airlines—even charter pilots—who bring genuine business to our island. Provided they are politically—shall we say?—neutral.'

'I'm not playing Republica politics.'

'Ah, but'—the cigar half-rolled off a loop—'we have heard other reports.'

'So I gathered. Part of the reason I came today was to talk that out and get it killed.'

The dark eyes studied me carefully. Then he said softly: 'You made a bad start to such talks, Señor Carr.'

Miranda said: 'General, do you wish to shoot?'

Bosco smiled quickly at the word, then shrugged and held out his hand for the dice. The croupier whipped them across.

Miranda chanted: 'The General bets whatever anybody else wishes to bet.'

Whitmore tossed some more notes on the table and went back to looking at J.B. and me. After a moment Luiz put down two ten-peso notes.

J.B. seemed to wake up and said: 'If your pilot had shot Walt Whitmore down, it would have made headlines all over the States. All over the world.'

'Most certainly.' The General shook the dice with a snap and threw them up the table. An 8. No win, no loss; 8 to make again. 'Most certainly—but what could my government have done then? We would have apologized, we would have tried and convicted the pilot himself. But what more could you have asked—as a democratic government yourself?'

I said: 'And reading between the headlines, the message would have got across: the Republica Air Force is a tough, shootin' air force.'

For once, his eyes moved quickly. I got a sharp dark glance. Then he took the dice from the croupier, shook them and threw them with exactly the same movement.

Three—a crap-out on the first throw, but now meaningless. Only an 8 or 7 counted now.

J.B. looked at me, then said carefully: 'General, if you were thinking of working up charges against Mr Carr, *that* could make a headline, too. The Boss Man is good copy even as a witness.'

Bosco lifted his shoulders fractionally and threw 10.

Whitmore's mind found the wavelength with a click. 'Unarmed passenger plane forces down jet fighter. I'd say that was news.'

'Film star bites dog,' Luiz murmured.

Whitmore smiled at Ned. 'That's a great squadron you're running there, Coronel.'

Ned's face shut as tight as a bank vault.

The General threw a 6.

J.B. said flatly: 'If you push charges, you'll get your air force laughed out of the air anywhere anybody can read a newspaper.'

Bosco sighed. 'It is possible that persons not familiar with aerial tactics might get the wrong impression.' He threw a 7, the croupier's face went stiff with horror. The General turned away. 'So—I lose. Coronel Rafter, I think we would be advised not to proceed against Señor Carr. You find sometimes that an act of mercy is better in the broad view than sticking to the letter of justice.'

It was gracefully done. It only missed out the other side of the coin: that the broad view in a dictatorship sometimes means chopping an innocent head as well.

Ned said tightly: 'You're the general, General.'

Bosco smiled his sad smile. 'I understand your feelings, Coronel. And I commend your zeal. But . . .' The cigar waved gracefully.

'A training crash,' Ned said.

Bosco nodded. 'A training crash. One has also to remember that Ramirez *was* disobeying orders.'

Ned's face closed up again. Then he looked at me and said slowly: 'That makes four. Three in Korea and one here. Another one and you'll be an ace. Don't try and make *that* one here, killer.'

'I'm a Dove pilot, Ned.'

'That,' the General said, 'is something we have still to discuss.'

In the silence there was just the faint rumble of dice on the table and then Luiz saying: 'Is this game over or does anybody want some of my money?'

He was rolling the dice hand-to-hand across the table, with the croupier giving him a worried look. But everybody else was looking at Bosco.

Ned said: 'You can't offer him a job in the squadron again—not after he's——'

'Of course.' The General held up his hand. 'That would hardly improve morale. Although—Señor Carr has more than lived up to the reputation you gave him, Coronel. So, it is a pity. But Señor'—he looked at me—'your Dove is rather old, I think?'

'About twelve years,' I said slowly. I couldn't see where this was going.

'Ah.' As if that explained something. 'The authorities at the airport inform me that it is in—a rather regrettable condition. But now I see it is not surprising.'

I knew what it explained now. I said grimly: 'Go on, General.'

The cigar fluttered. 'We have a duty—to others who use the airport, to those who live nearby. We should be failing this duty if we allowed an airplane to take off—to *try* to take off—which was not in proper condition.' He smiled—and not sadly. Not sadly at all. 'I am sure, Señor, that it will not take you long—or cost you much—to bring it up to the standards at which the airport authorities would permit you to take it off.'

'An eye for an eye,' I said grimly. 'A plane for a plane. So I lose the Dove.'

'But no. There is no question. Only it needs—what was the phrase?—ah, yes: a "check four", I think.'

'It isn't due a check four for another hundred hours.'

He smiled again. 'I fear one cannot stand too much on regulations and hours. One must use common sense in matters of air safety—as every newspaper would agree. The authorities believe a check four is needed, so . . .'

Whitmore said: 'I flew down in that plane, General. Now you're saying it ain't safe?'

'I am sure, Señor Whitmore, that you know much about aircraft engineering. But possibly not quite so much as our qualified engineers.'

73

J.B. said: 'You confiscate Carr's plane and your jet crash can *still* make a headline.'

The General said blandly: 'What crash?'

He looked at Ned, then at Miranda. 'Was there a crash, Capitan?'

Miranda spread his teeth in the big, homely smile of a hungry shark. 'I seem to recall a training crash; *mi* General —some time last week. A *teniente . . . teniente . . .*' he snapped his fingers, trying to remember '. . . Ramirez. I remember now.'

Luiz said suddenly: 'Film star bites dog. It *does* seem difficult to believe—especially if you cannot produce the dog.'

J.B. started to say something. I put a hand on her shoulder. 'They say the husband's usually the last to know, honey. Not this time. I've lost her.' Just like that. Maybe it's like losing a wife; I wouldn't know. I never had a wife. Only an airplane. Now, just the cold anger inside.

The General said to Whitmore: 'Naturally I must apologize for the inconvenience this causes you, Señor. But you understand it is also for your safety . . . Tickets for the Pan American flight to San Juan tonight will await you at the airport.'

'Tonight?' Whitmore said.

'Tonight,' the General said firmly. He looked around. 'I much regret, Señorita, Señores, but . . .' he turned to go.

Miranda waited just long enough to say, '*Rebelde!*'

I said to Ned: 'Only one thing I'm sorry about—that it wasn't Capitan Miranda in the Vamp. Except that he wouldn't have counted a whole kill, being only half a man.'

It wasn't the season's newest, snappiest insult. But for a man like Miranda it didn't have to be. He took a quick dancing step and led with his right.

I went in under the punch and hit him once just at the bottom of the ribs. Hard. Maybe not hard enough to pay for one confiscated airplane, but at least I was trying.

The two bodyguards moved quickly back, groping under their coats. The General snapped something, and they froze. He looked down at Miranda, sitting on the floor and trying to get his head up off his knees. The General said something else and the bodyguards moved warily to pick him up.

Whitmore drawled: 'I'll give you an eye-witness statement about that, too, General.'

'Tonight,' Bosco said quietly. 'For your own safety, Señor.' He led the way out.

★ 12 ★

I LOOKED around for my beer. Ned was still with us, watching me, completely expressionless. Luiz was still playing with the dice; Whitmore and J.B. were frowning at each other's feet as they chewed over the changed programme.

I found my glass, emptied it, and said: 'I seem to have bitched up the trip pretty thoroughly.'

Whitmore looked up, then shook his head. 'No sweat, fella. If they're going to pick on us, I'd rather it happened now than when we got the full unit in. And I still like the way you drop your shoulder in the punch.' He pulled out his cigarettes. 'So what's a check four gonna cost you, fella?'

'Three thousand pounds. Eight thousand dollars. No—more: they won't have engineers qualified on Doves down here, so I'd have to fly them in and put them up for a couple of weeks.' Then I shook my head. 'It doesn't make any odds. They're going to sit on the plane just as long as they want, no matter what I do or don't do.'

Ned gave one very small nod.

Whitmore grunted. 'Well, look's like you got trouble, fella. Maybe we can figure something out. I'm going to get some chow: we can still take a ride around the sights this afternoon, right? What time's that plane go?'

'About eleven,' Ned said.

Whitmore ignored him. 'Howsabout you, fella?'

'I,' I said firmly, 'am going to do a little drinking.'

He nodded appreciatively. 'Just stick around the hotel. We'll see you make the flight.' Finally he turned to Ned. 'Thanks for everything, Coronel.'

Ned just looked at him, stolid, expressionless. Whitmore and J.B. walked away.

75

Luiz came away from the table still idly shaking the dice in his hands; the croupier chased after him. Luiz said something fast and quiet in Spanish that stopped him like a slap in the face.

Then there were just Ned and me.

After a while he said: 'You want to get started on that drinking?'

'Yes; step aside. You're blocking the route to the bar.'

He stayed where he was. 'I ain't going to apologize to you, Keith. Frankly, I'd've liked to see you banged in jail a few months. But I didn't expect him to pinch your plane.'

'Don't cry too hard. You'll wet your pistol.'

'You don't have to believe me.'

'I don't even have to waste time deciding whether I believe you or not. Now stand aside.'

'I didn't expect him to ground you,' he said doggedly.

I just stared. But perhaps, in a way, I did believe him. Being in jail is one thing: you can get out of jail. Losing your plane is having the whole sky pulled from under your feet.

'All right,' I said. 'So I believe you. *Now* will you——'

'I'll buy you the first bottle. I owe you that for slugging Miranda. I been wanting to do that myself a long time.'

'So why didn't you?'

'I'm a colonel—remember? His superior officer. I ain't used to being a superior. You can't slug hardly anybody.'

We seemed to be walking out together. So—why not? Unless I was going to practise high dives into a whisky bottle in my own room, Ned was still better company than anybody I'd meet at the bar.

We got into a lift. On the way up, he said: 'You'll get the insurance on your plane, won't you?'

I looked at him. 'D'you want to bet? Confiscation'll come under "riots, strikes and civil disturbances" and on the standard policy you aren't insured against them. Anyway, I'd have to prove confiscation—and I can't see you helping me on that. I'm just grounded for safety reasons, and an insurance company isn't going to pay on *that*. Not after I swore to keep the plane up to standard.'

He frowned. 'Yeh. You really have got trouble.'

We got out at the top floor and walked down a normal hotel corridor and round a corner. I was just about to ask where the hell we were going, when he stopped outside an unnumbered door and started turning keys in a couple of locks that were a lot more serious than any an hotel normally uses.

It was a wide, cool room looking—surprisingly—inland. At first sight it seemed to be just another millionaire suite: lined with low expensive-looking Scandinavian cupboards and cabinets, thick green wall-to-wall carpeting, modern copper lampshades, ice-cold air-conditioning. Then you saw the touches that were Ned's: a heavy old green baize card table with a ring of tall leather chairs, the three telephones, the easel with a map board, the Braun T1000 VHF receiver on the window-sill.

That was why the room faced inland, of course: most of the air messages would be coming from inland.

Ned walked over to the receiver, switched it on and tuned it delicately. All he got was a faint crackle and hum. He picked up a red telephone, got an immediate answer, and said: 'Coronel Rafter at the Americana. I'll be here most the day.'

He put the phone down and waved at a cabinet. 'Start the round. I'll have a beer.'

The cabinet turned out to be a wood-covered refrigerator filled to withstand a long siege if you didn't happen to care about food. There were bottles of everything I could think of including several of Australian Swan beer. How Ned managed to get that hauled in across 9,000 miles . . . but perhaps being a superior officer has its compensations.

I poured his beer and gave myself a Scotch stiff enough to stand up without the glass. When I turned round Ned had dumped his gun and harness on the table and stripped off his flying suit, leaving him in just a pair of striped underpants. He took the beer, said 'Cheers,' and went out through the side door. I heard a shower start.

I took a long gulp of whisky just to set the tone for the afternoon, and wandered over to the receiver. It was a neat square job, a little smaller than a portable typewriter stood on end, well styled without being fussy: you could read the wavelength exactly. I read it.

Then I looked at the telephones: red, green, white. I wondered what the green one was for, then wondered about picking up the red one and telling the squadron to scramble and dive itself into the sea. In the end I just took another mouthful of whisky and walked over and picked up Ned's revolver.

It was a Smith & Wesson Magnum ·357. A squat, heavy gun as used by the Chicago police because it's supposed to drill clear through a car engine from end to end. Also as carried by most pilots in Korea in case we met the whole Chinese Army standing end to end. By putting both hands on the grip and holding very tight, you might actually have hit the Chinese Army. About hitting a car engine you'd better ask the Chicago police.

I put it back in the holster.

The receiver crackled and said faintly: '*Ensayo. Uno, dos, tres, cuatro.*' Another voice said: 'Okay. *Cinco, cinco.*'

Ned stuck his head out of the bathroom, dripping water 'What was that?'

'The squadron's gone on strike for a forty-whore week.

'What *was* it, sport?'

'Just testing.'

He ducked back and I walked over to the map on the easel. It was standard ICAO one-millionth-scale air map, but with a number of neat pen markings noting the airfields. There was the civil airport, the local base, and another military field up in a rather pointless position on the north coast. I knew about them. But I hadn't known about another base marked about sixty miles to the west, just before the real hills started. It was logical, though: most of the rebel troubles would come in those hills, and you could use a forward airstrip up there for both bringing in supplies and parking a flight of Vampires just a few minutes away from action.

Most of the rest of the markings I guessed were small-plane strips on the big plantations. Not long enough for

78

regular military use, but nice to know about in case you wanted to crash-land.

Ned came in wrapped in a crisp white towelling bath-robe that seemed oddly fancy with his great hairy hands and feet sticking out of it. He gave me a sharp look, but didn't tell me to get away from the map. I got away anyhow, sat down at the card table and began a count-down on my pipe.

'This is one of the best ops rooms I've ever seen,' I remarked.

'Just a week-end joint.' He nodded at the ceiling. 'The General's got the pent-house.'

That was logical, too, when you thought about it. It's easier to seal off the top of a big hotel against assassins than it would be a house. And it solves all the servant problems for you, too.

'What about General Castillo?'

He chuckled. 'He lives in a tent, poor bug-bitten bastard. Leading the noble army in the field.'

'And why isn't the noble Air Force in tents, too? Your forward base not secure enough? Or are you having supply problems?'

He smiled, but with his mouth firmly shut. He might be ready to talk about the Army; he wasn't going to spill any of the Air Force's secrets.

I took my pipe for a short walk to get it a bit of air it hadn't breathed three times already. At the end of it, I found myself by the refrigerator, so I filled up my glass again. Ned shook his head at a second beer. I walked back to the table and struck the third match.

'Feel like any food?' Ned asked.

'No, thanks.'

'I could get up some sandwiches.'

'If you want to eat them yourself.'

After a moment he asked: 'Like to suck a piece of ice?'

'No.'

'You're going to get loaded fast.'

'That's right. I got grounded today—remember?'

He nodded slowly. The red telephone buzzed.

He was there in a couple of strides. He listened for a

while, then said: 'Scramble the forward section. Tell 'em not to go above ten and tell the army to put down smoke *when* they see the planes—*not* before.' He put down the phone. 'Damn army's always putting down smoke markers the moment they run into anything. Rebels know what it means by now, so they scarper before we can get there.'

'How frightfully unsporting of them.'

He didn't answer. My crack just hung there with the pipe smoke and turned sour and dwindled and died. The room had gone very quiet. Only the radio breathed softly to itself.

After a time I got up to pour myself another drink, and found I was moving on tiptoe, shutting the refrigerator door as gently as I could. I opened my mouth to say something, then didn't. I just listened.

You don't have to like the man in the other cockpit. You can want to kill him—not angrily, but coldly and carefully enough to have trained yourself to wait until you're close enough to shoot at the cockpit, not just the plane. But you understand him; you can't help understanding him. Because the instruments he watches, the controls he handles, are the same as in your own cockpit. Because his problems of speed and height, range and fuel, sun and cloud, are your problems. You know him far better than you know a ground soldier on your own side, fighting for your own cause.

So you don't have to like him, or his cause either. But you do have to sit still and breathe quietly and listen when a man you know is going into action.

It took a long time. The air-conditioning built up a chill that made me shiver. Ned hunched on the far side of the table, just watching the radio.

Then suddenly it crackled fast Spanish. Ned grabbed the phone and yelled: 'Tell the stupid cows to speak English! Jiminez could be monitoring this channel!'

He slammed the phone down. 'Christ—nobody thinks a man who'll buy three-inch mortars might have the sense to buy a normal shortwave receiver as well.'

'And learn to speak English too, maybe.'

He shrugged. 'I'm trying to get 'em used to code, too. It takes time.'

The radio crackled faintly, but we weren't picking up the transmissions from the base: close as it was, there must have been a hill between it and the Americana.

Then, slowly and carefully, like a reciting schoolboy: 'Green leader calls "Goalpost". I have seen the smoke. It is a roadblock. With much *rebeldes*. I am going to shoot it.' Pause. 'Green two—I break left, break left, *now*!'

'Code,' I said softly. 'What does he say when he speaks in clear—tell you about his birthmarks?'

'He said "Goalpost", didn't he?'

'If you call that code for home base . . .' Neither of us were really listening—even to ourselves. We were both living the rolling turn, the long wriggling dive as you bring your guns to bear, and the last dangerous seconds as the ground rushes close and you're forcing the nose *down* because the range is shortening.

'Target hypnotism,' they call it—and, a couple of days later, a 'fighter pilot funeral' when they bury a box of sand with a few grain-sized pieces of you mixed in.

The radio gave a few distant crackles; now they were too low to reach over this range.

'They make two passes?' I asked.

'On a target like this, yeh.'

'Every man a hero.' The second pass is the worst. If there's anybody left alive on the ground (and if there isn't, why are you attacking again?) you've given him a dress rehearsal: he's got his eye in to your speed and angle.

But why should I care? If Jiminez' boys managed to knock down a Vampire—and damn little chance they stood with rifles, even light machine-guns, against a Vamp's four twenty-millimetre cannon—that suited me fine.

I still understood the man in the cockpit far better than the poor bastard with a rifle down at the roadblock.

Then, distant but getting louder quickly: '. . . have shoot our *munitio*. Roadblock is destroyed. Many *rebeldes* are dead——'

Ned growled: 'That means two men and a dog.'

81

'. . . Army advancing. I request instructions. Over.'

Ned looked at his watch and picked up the phone. 'Tell 'em to return Goalpost. And tell the army we're through for the day.'

He snapped off the radio. The room suddenly seemed much too cold, the whisky bitter on my tongue. Well, maybe the next one would taste better. I filled my glass, then opened a window to let in a little heat and the friendly, distant hum of traffic on the Avenida Independencia. I leant against the sill and sipped.

After a time, I said: 'And that concludes our Saturday afternoon programme of sport from the Free Republic.'

Ned looked at me, then shrugged and went to get himself another beer. 'You can't have all your battles big ones, Keith—not if you're a pro. It's the amateurs who feel brave just because it's D-Day; you know that.'

'I know pros aren't the answer in this place either, Ned.'

'Yeh? You think Jiminez'd sell off the Vamps if he got in?'

'I'll tell you one thing he'd sell off: you—in small pieces.'

He stared at me, then nodded slowly. Nobody builds up hate so much as a ground-attack pilot; a strafing fighter is partly a terror weapon, swooping omnipotent out of the sky, soaring away back. If you get hit by ground fire, you do your damnedest to land well away from the people you've been shooting up. Rules of war don't apply to a god who's fallen off his pedestal.

'Yeh, could happen,' he said finally. 'But—I wonder who'd get my job then. You? That what you pushing for?'

'I'm not pushing, Ned. I'm not a professional any more.'

He stared at me. Then he nodded and said slowly and perplexedly: 'Yeh, that's right, isn't it? If you were a pro, you'd have joined the firm when I offered the job. You worry me, Keith. I don't know if you're working for Jiminez or not—maybe not. But either way, the General made a mistake with you. You should've been in jail. Then we'd've known where you were and you'd have got your plane back at the end. Now—you're loose but you don't have a plane to fly. And that worries me. Because you're still a killer.'

The word had no sting; it was just a statement—a definition of a trade.

He ended up in front of me, stabbing a thick finger at my chest. 'I'll do what I can for you. Try to get your Dove back. I don't think I can do it, but I'll try. You need any money?'

'That could have been more tactfully put, Ned.'

He shook his head impatiently. 'You know I'm loaded right now—so d'you want any of it? Just to take yourself a quiet holiday somewhere for a couple of months?'

'What's all this to you, Ned?'

'If I can't have you in jail, maybe Miami Beach'll do. Just keeping out of the way. Otherwise—' he shrugged. '—I could end up having to kill you.'

'You could end up trying,' I snapped. 'And I mean end up.'

He grinned crookedly. 'You see?'

After a while I grinned back. 'This town ain't big enough for both of us—is that it?'

'It's a small town, all right—the whole damn Caribbean. Okay—' he rubbed the back of his neck thoughtfully '—we just have to wait and see. You want to go on talking politics, or just drink?'

I emptied my glass and handed it over. 'Let's just drink.'

Things got a little fuzzy after that. But somebody got me into a taxi around ten o'clock, and I came slightly awake at half-past eleven and found myself aviating towards San Juan aboard the World's Most Experienced Airline, eating a piece of the World's Most Experienced chicken and with a glass of beer in my other hand.

Luiz was sitting alongside me; J.B. and Whitmore just across the aisle, the two directors somewhere behind.

Luiz leant and dropped a pair of dice on my tray. 'A small souvenir of General Bosco.'

I blinked blearily at them, and the dots blinked blearily back. 'So?'

'My friend, they are loaded.'

I picked them up, dropped them into my glass of beer—

the old test for loaded dice. They tumbled slowly and showed a 6 and a 2. I drank them out, dropped them in again. I got a 4 and a 1.

'They don't seem to be winning anything for me. The General ought to fire his dice loaders.'

'My friend—do you think these belonged to the General?'

'You mean the Americana was giving him loaded dice?'

He smiled sunnily. 'So what could they lose?—he does not play against the house, only among his good friends. So the house gets his custom, they help him win a little, and his beautiful smile brightens their dark, drab lives. The stickman was highly annoyed when I first grabbed them before they could be changed and then walked off with them.'

I remembered that fuss with the croupier. 'But I still don't see which sides are weighted.'

He winced. 'My friend, one does not load the *side* of a dice these days—it is much too blatant. One loads a *corner*. Then, if all goes well, that corner must be on the table and one of only three faces will be at the top. I will show you.' He stretched his hand; I fished the dice out of my drink and passed them over. He turned them in his long brown fingers.

'Now these, although they are rather heavily loaded, so they almost always turn up "loaded" faces, are also rather subtle. Each is loaded at a different corner. One can show only a 1, 2 or 4; the other a 2, 4 or 6. Nice harmless numbers —but you can work out for yourself what they mean.'

The hell I could—in my state. I stared blearily. He sighed and explained: 'Two normal dice can throw thirty-six combinations: One 2, two 3s—and so on up to six 7s, then down again to one 12. But these can throw only nine combinations, including only one 7, one 3—but two 6s and two 8s. And no 2 or 11 or 12 and some others.

'So: in nine first throws the General will win once with a 7, lose once with a 3—enough to allay suspicion. But mostly he will throw something else and have to throw it again. Then he has a fifty-fifty chance, and if it is a 6 or an 8, he has a two-to-one chance. Overall it means . . .' he scribbled a quick formula on his menu card, 'it means he will win thirty-one times out of fifty-four. Say a three-to-two

84

advantage. Enough—but only enough that people will say the General is lucky. And it does a dictator no harm to be known as lucky.'

He handed the dice back. I turned them in my hand, looking for signs of the loading. A great hope; in my current condition I couldn't have seen signs of an elephant loaded into a telephone-box.

'How did you come to spot this?'

'I played with them on the table—and found I threw only those numbers. And also—I was born in this part of the world. One comes to expect dictators to play with loaded dice.'

'I know just what you mean.'

★ 13 ★

WE flew back to Kingston by a direct British West Indies flight the next afternoon. J.B. had rung ahead and there were a couple of film cars waiting at the airport to carry them back over to Ocho Rios. I dropped off at the Myrtle Bank hotel.

Whitmore lifted a big hand and said: 'Don't fret too hard, fella. You're still on the payroll. We'll call you.'

J.B. dug in her fat briefcase and came up with a wad of dollars. 'I make it we owe you for a three-hour ride. Two hundred and forty-four dollars, eighty cents—right?'

I shrugged.

Whitmore said: 'Call it $250. It ain't much of a bonus for knocking down a jet, but I don't know how we'd explain that in the budget.' He smiled. Joke.

I smiled back and said 'Thanks' and they drove away, leaving me standing on the hotel drive with my handful of money and the doorman looking at it curiously. After a while I walked through to the bar.

The next day I went through the proper motions without getting any further than I'd expected, which was exactly nowhere. The insurance company shook its head and regretted that confiscation wasn't covered. After them I tried various Jamaican authorities and the British High Commission to see if I could get a bit of diplomatic pressure on my side. Jamaican authority just didn't want to know; the Republica was some unknown quantity out of sight over the horizon . . . They were quite ready to believe they confiscated airplanes there; hell, they already believed they ate babies and danced naked in the streets at high noon there. So what could you do about it? It was another suburb.

The High Commission sympathized and said it would ask the Commonwealth Relations Office in London to ask the Foreign Office to ask the consul in Santo Bartolomeo . . . I clicked the loaded dice in my pocket and went away to ring Diego Ingles and tell him the flying lessons were off, indefinitely. I couldn't find him. I was back in the Myrtle Bank by five.

Tuesday was more of the same, only I was running short of people to complain to. So I tried the Flying Club, which sometimes chartered out small planes, to ask if they needed a pilot. But it was their slack season, too. I still couldn't reach Diego. I thought about the crop-spray boys—but that was a big decision, even if they really wanted me. A different type of flying, a different life. I decided to wait until I was off Whitmore's payroll. That day I was in the bar soon after four.

About an hour later the barman handed me the phone; it was J.B. 'The Boss Man wants to buy you a beer. Get yourself a taxi on over; we'll pay it. Okay?'

I thought of reminding her I had a jeep, then decided that if there was any serious drinking coming up, I didn't want *that* with me. 'All right—where to?'

'You know a house called Oranariz? He's rented it.'

I said I knew it and would be there in a couple of hours.

Jamaican taxis aren't surprised at the idea of a sixty-mile trip, so the doorman found one for me pretty easily. We went over the short, steep way, up into the hills to Castleton, down again to Port Maria and then along the north coast road.

Oranariz — which means 'golden nose' in Jamaican Spanish—is one of a collection of pricey modern houses around Oracabessa (golden mouth) near the Boscobel airstrip. They're mostly called Ora-something or just Golden Head, Goldeneye and so on. This one belonged to a writer who was rich enough to afford to live in London and rent off his Jamaican house most of the year. Visiting film stars often took it.

The house itself wasn't all that much—nothing like the 'Big Houses' the Victorian planters built in the hills so that they could take long walks without breathing the open air along with the workers—but what there was of it was good. A long, low bungalow built around three sides of a four-car courtyard, with a fashionable wood-tiled roof, windows with elegant white hurricane shutters, a wide marble-tiled patio around the outside walls. The big point was that it was private: it had its own walled-in three acres of jungle facing over a small cove and beach that couldn't be reached except from above—or by boat.

The road gate was open and J.B. met us in the courtyard, wearing a cool tube dress of white lace and carrying the usual wad of dollars. She paid off the driver and led the way through the house on to the patio facing the sea.

The first thing that hit me was a refrigerator of my own height, connected by a wire through an open window. On either side of it Whitmore and Luiz were stretched out in aluminium lounging chairs. The third person present was young Diego Ingles.

I was still wondering how he'd got into the charmed circle when Whitmore called: 'Hi, fella. Beer or whisky?'

'Beer, please.'

Luiz stretched an arm and yanked open the refrigerator door, Whitmore stuck in a hand and pulled out a bottle of Red Stripe, Luiz swung the door shut. It was a smooth piece of teamwork that didn't shift either of them an inch in their chairs.

Whitmore jammed the cap of the bottle against the arm of his metal chair, smacked it with a huge hand, and tossed the open bottle: it dropped neatly upright into my hands.

87

I took a swig, sat down in another chair, and told Diego: 'Been trying to find you since yesterday.'

He smiled his boyish smile. 'I have heard the sad news already, Señor. I am most sorry for you.'

Whitmore said: 'You remember you figured he could straighten out our Spanish for us?'

Diego waved a deprecating hand. 'I will do what I can, Señor Whitmore, but I am no writer . . .'

'Hell, it's your own language, isn't it? That's all we want. We damn sure don't need another lousy *writer*.' He looked back at me. 'We got some good news for you, too, fella. We got you another airplane. Show him the 'gram, J.B.'

She passed me a used cable form. It said: *Have found B-25 good condition Buenaventura stop price fifteen but can get for twelve stop delivery Barranquilla any time you want ends*. Signed with a Spanish name.

I handed it back thoughtfully. J.B. said: 'I've told him to close the deal—subject to our inspection—and get the plane to Barranquilla. We'll fly down as soon as we hear it's there —okay?'

'A twelve thousand dollar airplane that must be at least twenty years old,' I said slowly. 'She won't be in one-careful-little-old-lady-owner condition.'

'Will she fly?' Whitmore asked.

I shrugged. 'If she flies from Buenaventura to Barranquilla—and that's five hundred miles—she could do anything. You're quite sure she *is* at Buenaventura and not sitting at the back of a hangar in Barranquilla the whole time?'

There was a crossfire of startled looks. These people must have done plenty of wheeling and dealing in their time, but it seemed they hadn't tried buying an old airplane before.

Then Diego said carefully: 'I think, Señorita Penrose, you have not met this man—' he nodded at the cable in her hand '—but my family has done business with him many times. He is an honest agent.'

The suspicious tension faded. Whitmore stretched his legs again, scratched under his bush shirt, and said: 'So— okay. You can handle a B-25 okay, fella?'

88

Out behind him, on the edge of the patio, there was a humming-bird tree: a dead branch set in a block of concrete and carrying a dozen little narrow-necked jars of sugar-water. A few humming-birds were still around, whizzing in and hovering with flickering wings while they dipped their long beaks for the last snort of the evening. To them, flying was just flying, and no worry about what a new pair of wings might feel like . . . The hell with them; mere helicopter pilots.

I was trying to recall anything anybody had told me about the B-25, known also as the Mitchell. It wasn't much: except around South America nobody has flown them really seriously since the war, twenty years ago. All I could remember was that they were supposed to be good load-carriers, noisy as hell, and a little tricky until you knew them.

I said: 'I expect so.'

Whitmore said: 'Fine, fine. And we figured a new deal for you—after what happened Saturday. Give him the contract, J.B.'

She gave it me. It was the same as before, except for the pay. Instead of the $20-a-day retainer plus $10 a flying hour and costs, I was now getting a flat $100 a day. It was a nice gesture, seeing it was hardly his fault I'd lost the Dove, but it wasn't as generous as he probably thought; it would just about let me keep up the mortgage payments I had to go on making on the Dove, confiscated or not, and a bit towards the check four if that day ever came now. He still didn't really owe me anything anyway.

I put on a cheerful grin and said: 'Can I call you J.B.—on a $100 a day?'

'Sign the damn thing.'

I signed.

Luiz sighed. 'Always signing contracts. I tell you, my friend, you are going to end up with wet feet.'

Whitmore gave him a sharp glance, then came back to me. 'When we get the ship, you'll be working off the airstrip up the road—' he nodded towards Boscobel '—so we'll fix you a hotel room up here.'

I nodded. I had a feeling the Mitchell was going to be a

tightish squeeze on that 3,000-foot Boscobel runway: along with the other American wartime medium bombers, it had been designed specifically for the 6,000-foot strips that the Dakota had made a standard all over the world by 1940.

Diego said politely: 'Now there is another aircraft, Señor, may I perhaps continue my lessons?'

About that, I wasn't so sure. I didn't know how the Mitchell would handle yet, but I knew its age and I knew it was a military aeroplane built for the comfort of its bombs and not its pilots.

Whitmore chipped in: 'Hell, why not? Let the kid have a go—long as he pays his own fuel bills. Maybe you could use him as a co-pilot on the camera work.'

That wasn't a bad idea. If I was going to be flying around a load of cameramen and directors, all shouting for the impossible, it could be useful to have another pilot, however inexperienced, on board.

I shrugged, 'You're the Boss Man.'

'Okay. So the kid can fly.' The way he said it, the phrase went in capitals: The Kid. Diego had obviously joined the club—but I couldn't see quite why. He was a nice enough boy, but hardly a drink-from-the-bottle type, and certainly not a professional—at anything. And Whitmore obviously liked pros. That was why I was there: I'd once been a pro fighter pilot. It was why J.B. was allowed into what was a man's world—she was a pro lawyer. And Luiz, however much he bitched about getting his feet wet, stepped in and *got* them wet whenever the script said so.

But Diego? I couldn't see it.

I finished my beer and Whitmore and Luiz went through their routine and a fresh bottle arrived in my hands. The last light faded from the sky—Jamaican dawns and sunsets are fast, tropical affairs. A couple of lizards came out on the edge of the patio and took up what would be their regular sentry positions and froze there, waiting for a careless night insect.

'How's the film coming?' I asked conversationally. 'Re-written any good scripts recently?'

Luiz smiled; Whitmore bent an eyebrow at me. 'Fella, the

only script matters is the shooting script, the one you actually shoot from. And even that don't matter compared to the picture itself. You can't go handing out copies of the script and say, "We maybe made a lousy picture, but you'll like the script." '

J.B. said: 'We're three days behind schedule: that's nearly fifteen thousand dollars on the budget.'

Whitmore waved a bottle. 'So you're always behind on location shooting. You tell me a location picture that's been brought in on time. Hell—' he turned to Luiz—'remember down in Durango?'

Luiz chuckled and started to tell the story—about a film they'd made down in Mexico, five years before, where Whitmore hadn't been the producer. And the producer had sent in a popular singer to play the young cowboy part. After a couple of weeks, it turned out that the singer didn't know which side of a horse was up and which end of a gun was front.

Whitmore stopped the whole production dead for four days—with the producer and everybody back to the New York bankers having a coronary every hour on the hour—while he taught the boy to ride and how to pull a gun. At the end of it all, the singer had a broken guitar finger and the critics had hailed him as the man who'd acted rings around old One-Expression. And the film made a vast profit.

Diego laughed politely at the end, but I wasn't sure he saw the point. I wasn't sure I saw it myself, unless Whitmore was offering to him a short course in riding and twirling Colts in parallel with my flying lessons.

Soon after that, Diego remembered he had an eleven o'clock date in Kingston and did I want a ride back in his E-type? I didn't, of course, but it seemed the only way I'd stand even a chance of getting home that night, so I went with him.

As we blasted up into the hills out of Port Maria, he said: 'The new airplane, Señor—it is most exciting, no?'

'I hope not.'

He grinned. 'Ah, I forgot: you do not approve of risks.

But for me, an airplane that was once an airplane of war—it has, one should say, a *reality*.'

Not to me, it didn't. I didn't know much about Mitchells and even less about this particular one, but if it was like any warplane I'd met before it would be a lot more temperamental and liable to bust than any civilian aeroplane. A military plane is a racehorse: you spend most of your time working on it, getting it ready for Race Day. But if an airliner isn't plodding around like a carthorse it just isn't earning its keep.

'It'll be different from the Dove,' I said. 'And the experience won't be much use; you'll be flying planes that handle more like the Dove—unless your company goes crazy.'

'Perhaps. But to me, it is a challenge. To say—I flew *this* airplane.'

'It isn't likely to become all that famous. Just a few minutes in a film, that's all.'

'Truly, you are not romantic, Señor.' He grabbed the gear-lever and we went around a dark mountain corner on a prayer and very nearly a wing.

I said, when I had the breath: 'If that's romanticism, I'll take walking.'

He sounded suddenly contrite. 'You are right, of course. One must live to fly this airplane.' And he lifted his foot.

It was a nice thought, if a rather surprising one. I just hoped he wasn't storing up his 'romanticism' for when we got the Mitchell. But for the moment, just doing the rest of the journey less than twice as fast as I'd have liked was enough for me.

* 14 *

J.B. RANG me up at the Myrtle Bank two evenings later: the Mitchell had reached Barranquilla, so would I stay sober enough to catch a West Indian flight the next morning to connect with a Pan Am flight in San Juan to connect with

. . . Barranquilla isn't a main-line station. I told her to forget it, then rang a friend and bought two very unofficial seats on a Venezuelan cargo plane that was going out to Maracaibo in the morning. From there to Barranquilla is just 200 miles across the frontier.

We ended up hiring a small plane for the last leg, but we reached Barranquilla at four in the afternoon, about twelve hours ahead of her schedule. And there, waiting for us outside the end hangar, was the Mitchell.

Nowadays military airplanes have the same sleek good looks as civil aircraft; it wasn't always so, and the Mitchell came from that time. She was thin, box-sided, square-cut, with a long sneering transparent nose, high cranked wings, huge engines and propellers, fat over-sized main wheels like big boots. Just sitting there, she had the hunched, cluttered look of an old soldier loaded with all his equipment.

But this one was a very old soldier indeed.

J.B. was staring with an expression of sick disbelief. After a while she said quietly: 'Jesus Christ.'

'Right—now name me the co-pilot.' Then I shook my head. 'If she really flew in from Buenaventura, she must work better than she looks.'

I was trying to persuade myself. The transparent nose had gone smoky and crackled with tiny veins, like the nose of a hardened boozer; the bare aluminium parts, even the props, were covered with the gritty white lichens of oxidization; the painted parts—some idiot had painted the engines black to hide oil leaks, but also the one colour to over-heat them in this climate—were dulled and flaking. And the hydraulic system must have been leaking like an old shoe because the flaps were drooping half down, the bomb-bay doors half open.

I knew exactly what had happened. She hadn't been in the air for six months, and then somebody who knew a lot about airplanes but even more about money, had made her fit for just the 500-mile ride up from Buenaventura. In two ways, I had to take it from here.

I took a deep breath. 'All right. Now you find whoever's in charge. I want a Certificate of Airworthiness, the log-

93

books—there's three of them—and any pilot's notes and engineering manuals he's got. And *don't* pay him a peso until I've checked them and her.'

She looked at me rather doubtfully, then nodded and went off towards the offices built into the side of the hangar. I started a slow clockwise circuit of the Mitchell, kicking the tyres, squinting into the engines—rust on the cylinder head bolts, of course—banging the inspection panels.

Just below the cockpit there was a piece of over-fancy script, mostly washed and faded away by now. After a bit of twisting my head and puzzling, I made it out: *Beautiful Dreamer*, with a 1940's-style reclining nude to match. So she'd actually seen squadron service in the war, twenty years ago.

Well, whatever had happened, they'd brought her back —and walked away. And now they were Air Force generals or farmers or just your Friendly Home-Town Used-Car Dealer. And probably it would take them a lot of thinking even to remember the name they'd given her.

But think, boys, *try* and remember. Just what made her that little bit different from the thousands of other Mitchells they built? How did she fly better than the book says, and how worse? What systems never went wrong—and which never went right?

Just as man to man, boys—what's she like in bed? She's my girl now.

Then I shook my head and reached and slapped the metal below the cockpit—and nearly burned my hand off at the wrist. She'd been sitting in the sun all day. I took a pair of wash-leather flying gloves out of my hip pocket and pulled them on before I tried anything new.

J.B. came out of the hangar with a small, tubby man wearing sunglasses, a black moustache and a grease-stained white panama hat. She was carrying a handful of papers and not looking I-feel-like-singing about them.

'The certificate of airworthiness,' she recited tonelessly, 'was issued in Colombia two years ago and says it's *limitado*. Limited—what does that mean?'

'Mustn't ply for hire or reward. I'd expected that. If you own it, you can have it flown how you like. What about the logs?'

She handed them over, three unimpressive little mock-leather volumes like autograph books.

The aircraft one had a chit pinned in the front headed 'as removed from military records' which showed the Mitchell had done about six thousand hours before getting a us Air Force overhaul in 1951 which, it claimed, brought her back to the perfection of having done zero hours. But they'd sold her off to Colombia before they could prove themselves wrong.

In Colombia she'd flown another 1,500 hours as a bomber and been given another overhaul which—surprise, surprise —had once more restored her to zero hours condition. However, again she'd been sold off fast—for 900 hours as a freight transport, and then 300 as a private passenger plane. But apart from the delivery flight, carefully entered up as exactly two hours fifty minutes—she hadn't flown this year.

J.B. said sombrely: 'How does it look?'

I shrugged. 'About as I expected. These things might be honest, might not——'

'Could we sue on them?'

'If things go wrong, we and the plane'll be at the bottom of the Caribbean. Tell him you'll pay him when I've checked it over.'

She gave me a very steady look and said, deliberately tone-less: 'He doesn't speak English—he says. He also says he has another customer, and he wants his money right now.'

I grinned at the fat face under the greasy panama. I knew the 'another customer' line. 'Tell him,' I said, speaking slowly and carefully, 'that according to the log, this air-plane has, like his sister, been a virgin three times already. I will sleep with her tonight and give my decision tomorrow.'

Our Friendly Home-Town Used-Airplane Dealer had gone as rigid as a girder. I knew the don't-speak-English line, too. Everyone connected with airplanes *has* to speak English.

J.B. glanced sideways, saw interpretation was unnecessary, and asked me: 'Why tomorrow?'

'I won't do an air test until I've run up the engines properly, and I don't want to do that until this evening when the air's cooler. Tomorrow.'

She nodded, then handed me the last of the papers: a collection of stained, loose pages about the size of a science-fiction magazine. 'That's all he had.'

The top sheet was headed *Flight Handbook, B-25N; U.S.A.F.; revised to 15 August 1951.* Applied to this old lady, science-fiction was about what it would be. I sighed.

J.B. said quickly. 'If you want to say the hell with this and go back to Jamaica, I won't be part of any suit against you for breaking your contract.'

'Thanks. But . . .' I looked up at the Mitchell again. Ever since I'd learned to fly, I'd had one dream every few months: that I was sitting in a plane I didn't trust, and hadn't any proper instruction about—and I had to fly her. Now I was looking at my bad dream.

There's always a way to walk away: to walk away first.

'Thanks,' I said again. 'But I'm a pilot—and I don't have any other plane to fly. I'll tell you tomorrow.'

She looked at me hard for a moment, then turned to the man in the panama and started talking fast, fluent Spanish. I walked away, ducked under the belly of the Mitchell, and climbed up through the open hatch just forward of the bomb-bay.

I was in a narrow, hot dark cabin about as high as I could stand and not as wide as I could reach with both arms outspread. Ahead of me, up a high step, was a blaze of light coming in through the greenhouse roof on to the side-by-side pilots' seats. I stayed where I was, straddling the hatch, and looked slowly all around.

The dark green plastic sound-proofing on the metal skin was hanging loose by now, only kept in place by the criss-cross of pipes and cables and mess of switchboxes and boards of contact-breakers. Above me there was a filled-in circle in the roof where there had once been a gun-turret. Behind me, the metal box of the bomb-bay blocked off the aft end of the fuselage except for a small space at the top. And around my left knee, a small, square dark tunnel led forward under the pilots' seats to the bomb-aimer's position in the transparent nose.

Distant growls and hums off the airfield came up from the hatch at my feet. They annoyed me; I wanted to be alone with this bitch. I found a folding top hatch and slid it shut. The noise stopped.

I took a slow, deep breath. The Mitchell smelled. Of petrol and oil and hydraulic fluid and plastic and leather and sweat, but all adding up to some new, strange smell that would be the way all Mitchells smelled, because every type has its own smell. It was somehow interesting, but for some reason worrying, too.

I took a high step forward and, hunching myself up, eased into the left-hand pilot's seat, being very careful not to touch any lever or switch that might drop the whole plane on its backside. No switch should, of course, but who repairs safety locks after twenty years?

Under the transparent roof, the cockpit was like a furnace. The leather seat singed my bottom and I felt sweat start to trickle down my ribs. But I got myself as comfortable as I could, and started a careful look around.

It was as bad as I'd expected, or worse. How I'd ever make any sense of it or find any control in it . . . *that airspeed indicator reads up to 700 m.p.h.—must have come out of a crashed jet; no Mitchell ever did half that speed . . . and what instrument should be in that empty socket? . . .* Then I knew why the smell had worried me.

She was a woman I'd been warned off by everybody and my own common sense. And now I'd come close enough to get the smell of her in my nostrils.

Slowly, gently, I reached out my hands to touch her.

I was lying on my hotel bed reading a loose page of the Mitchell handbook that illustrated seven different types of smoke and flame that might be met coming out of its engines, and wondering which of them I'd meet coming out of the room's air-conditioner, when somebody knocked at the door.

I yelled 'Animo!' and J.B. walked in, wearing a skirt, a bra and an expression as if her best-rehearsed witness hadn't turned up in court.

'A spider the size of a horse came up the plug hole in my washbasin,' she announced coldly, 'and the telephone doesn't work.'

I smiled reassuringly. 'It's nice to know Barranquilla hasn't changed. The trick is to hit them both with your shoe.'

'Listen, chum: that spider wears the same size boots as I do only eight of them.'

'Use my washbasin, then.'

She looked at me, then it, suspiciously. But the first thing I'd done when I found there wasn't a spider in it at that particular moment was shove the plug in. When I'd found a plug, of course.

She discovered which tap worked and started splashing tepid water around herself. I put down my Smoke and Flame Identification Chart and watched. She had a slim, firm body and small sharp breasts more or less inside the thin bra. She caught my eye, but it didn't seem to bother her. She didn't flaunt her body, but maybe she used it a little defiantly, so as to sneer at people who thought it was the true J. B. Penrose.

When she'd finished drying herself on my towel, she just stood there and said: 'Well?'

'Sit down and talk it over.'

'I was just wondering,' she said heavily, 'if I had to spend the night with that damn tarantula or whatever. And what a brave fighter pilot might do about it.'

'That's what I'm prepared to talk about. Anyhow, what about the brave Hollywood lawyer? Why don't you slap a court order on him?'

'The hell with you, Carr.' But she grinned suddenly, vividly, and sat down on the end of the bed. I reached for the half-bottle of Scotch in my bag. 'Drink?'

She nodded, picked up the page of the *Handbook*, and started reading. 'Puffs of black smoke . . . thin wisps of bluish-grey smoke . . . variable grey smoke and bright flame . . . heavy black smoke—Christ, it sounds like the penalty clauses

I write in contracts. Do these things *happen* to that airplane?'

I winced; the flight handbooks have a certain realism you don't get from the manufacturer's brochures. 'Not all at once, I hope.' I passed her a fairly clean glass of neat Scotch.

'Thanks.' Then she turned suddenly serious. 'Look, Carr —you *don't* have to take on flying this old ship.'

'We'll manage.'

She eyed me carefully. 'You aren't trying to . . . to prove anything to the Boss Man, are you?'

'No. Flying airplanes is my trade.'

She nodded and we sipped silently for a while. Then I said: 'So—tell me about your early life and struggles.'

She smiled again. 'Early life spent in San Francisco. First struggle with a kid named Benny Zimmerman.'

'Who won?'

'Me. He's probably still walking around doubled up holding his . . . where I got him with my knee.'

'Mistake. It could become a habit.'

She looked at me. 'It has, chum. You don't win law-suits on your back.'

I gave her what was intended to be an encouraging and friendly smile. 'How did you get into the law-suit business?'

'Usual way: four years college—at Los Angeles. Couple of years law school.'

'Perhaps I meant "Why?" '

She considered, then said thoughtfully: 'I guess . . . I just like the law. I don't mean I'm a great crusader for justice, anything like that. I just like it as sort of machinery: a way of doing things exactly, of getting them just right.' She looked up and grinned. 'Maybe I just mean I like writing watertight contracts. Doesn't sound very noble, does it?'

'You're talking to a man whose first job was shooting down other pilots. Go on.'

'I don't mean squeezing anybody on the fine print, either —I just mean getting it *right*; so it's what everybody wanted and nobody wastes time breaking it or dodging it or fighting it. Maybe like a good airplane engine: so all the wheels really fit. Hollywood's built on contracts—well, so's any business, but pictures more than most. Nobody in pictures can remember what he promised five minutes back, even if he wants to. So—somebody's got to make the wheels fit. I try.'

I nodded slowly. 'Sounds worth doing . . . And I can vouch you're good at it.'

'Funny. I was expecting you to say something else.'

I raised my eyebrows. 'I like to think I'm a professional, too.'

'I don't mean that. I guess I was braced for you to ask "Wouldn't I be better off with a Man and a House and chasing a flock of kids around the backyard".' She frowned. 'Or maybe why wasn't I lying on my back shouting "Come and get it"? A girl doesn't get much room for manoeuvre between those two ideas.'

'Or, "If she won't hop into *my* bed, she *must* be Lesbian." Right?'

'Yes, I've heard the bastards say that, too.'

I spun the Scotch bottle along the bed to her. 'Well, it was you who chose to live in that stronghold of Victorian morality called Hollywood.'

'I did that,' she said grimly. 'Thank God for smog and Communism. They broaden the conversation there, anyway.'

I eyed her nearly bare upper half thoughtfully. 'Actually, I wasn't trying to broaden the conversation.'

She looked up quickly. 'You don't have to make a pass at me just because we're stuck in the same hotel.'

'That wasn't why. I've just got a feeling about you . . . And me. It scares me, a bit.'

For a long time, we looked at each other down the length of the bed. And the room was very still—except for the air-conditioner wheezing like an old lecher peering through the key-hole.

Then she said, in a small, shivery voice: 'I know, Keith.' Then shook her head. 'I told you I wasn't settling for just a brand on the backside. Nor a one-night stand in some fly-blown hotel——'

'Spider-blown, please.'

She grinned exasperatedly. 'Okay. But I still mean it: get tangled up with me and you'll have one hell of a job getting clear again. I'm not one of your North-Coast tourists looking for a quick tumble under the mango trees with the hired help, no strings attached, back to mummy in two weeks.'

'You're pretty clear about what you think I think, aren't you?'

After a moment she said quietly: 'I'm sorry. I guess being a lawyer *and* Hollywood—it makes you too suspicious. I like you, Keith. You're an independent sort of character . . .'

'Come up this end.'

She hesitated, stood up, walked three paces and sat down beside me. A deliberate, but perhaps wary, movement.

I reached and put my hands on her bare shoulders. 'You're a pretty independent character yourself. I'm not trying to spoil that, nor take advantage of it. And I'm not kidding myself I could own it—or want to. I just like it.'

She ran a finger down my forehead, my nose, across my chin, splitting my face neatly in two. 'You know,' she said thoughtfully, 'if you cut your hair more often and shave a bit closer, you'd be quite a handsome guy.'

I pulled her down—or she leant—and kissed her.

Then she pulled back and there was a flicker of worry in her eyes. 'It scares me, too, Keith. *And* you've got a plane to fly tomorrow.'

'I always have.' But she held back against my pull.

'You don't *have* to fly this one. I'll back you right up if you want to go back and say it just won't do.'

'If she won't fly with me she *must* be a Lesbian.'

She grinned quickly. 'And you don't even know my name —what the J.B. stands for. I thought Englishmen never seduced girls without being properly introduced.'

'You're thinking of two Englishmen in a railway carriage.'

'Fact? I didn't realize your railways were so exciting.'

After a while, I said: 'You could always tell me your name.'

She smiled again—but then stood up. 'Keith—if it's

what I want, it'll wait. A bit, anyway.' And again, the flicker of worry that I couldn't quite understand.

But gradually the mood dwindled and died like smoke on a light wind. I said: 'There'll come a day.'

'I hope so, Keith.' She stooped quickly, kissed me, and was gone.

A couple of seconds later she was back. '*What* about that spider?'

I sighed and handed over the remains of the Scotch. 'Sprinkle that on him. He'll curl up like Benny Zimmerman.'

She grinned, touched my nose with one finger, and was gone again.

One of these days I'll remember to bring a cheaper spider-killer than Scotch to South America.

★ 15 ★

At seven-thirty the next morning we—the Mitchell and I— lined up on the runway. It was the still clear time between the land breeze and the sea breeze, between the morning mist and the heat haze. As good as I'd ever get.

The cockpit windows were open and the engines were giving off a terrific dry clatter a few feet from either ear, sounding as if they were trying to eat their own insides. But it was the same noise they'd made at the run-up the night before, so perhaps it was the sound Wright Cyclones always made.

I looked carefully around the cluttered cockpit. The flight instruments were still dead; I wouldn't know about them until we were in the air. But the engine instruments all seemed to be registering. *Supercharger to low gear; booster pumps to 'emergency'; mixture* . . . I had the page of the flight manual which gave the landing and take-off checklists, but nothing to show at what speed she left the ground—or ought to. Well, I could guess: it was going to be over 100 m.p.h., probably nearer—— No. Stop guessing, Carr. You're going to get the fastest flying lesson of your life on this runway. Don't cloud your tiny mind with preconceptions.

A Spanish accent in my headphones said: 'Mitchell on runway, you're clear to take off.'

I pressed the transmit button on the wheel. 'Thank you, tower.'

A last slow look around. Engine and oil temperatures going up . . . throttle and pitch locks *off* . . . flaps full up —I'll use them when I've learnt to trust them . . . harness and hatches all secure . . . No parachute. But nobody jumps from a first flight; nobody writes a divorce clause into a marriage; nobody has a taxi waiting at the door when he gets into bed with the girl for the first time.

Nobody jumps from a first flight. Not in time, anyway.

The tower said languidly: 'Mitchell, you are still clear to take off.'

D'you think I'm sitting here waiting for a sun-tan, you stupid fat slob? 'Thank you, tower.'

But the engines were collecting a tan: the temperatures were on the edge of the red line. Still, one last, slow look around . . . ah, the hell with it. She's an airplane and I'm a pilot. And neither of us virgins. *Something'll* happen. I pushed the throttles to thirty inches of boost and flipped off the brakes.

Suddenly we were running.

No control, none at all. The wheel limp and loose, the rudder pedals flopping meaninglessly . . . and beginning to swing left. *Left?* Why the hell *left?* Wake up, Carr: these are American engines, turning the opposite way to British ones, so we swing left, not right . . . Dab of brakes . . . more. Jerk. Straight again . . . But a bad start.

Still no control . . . 50 m.p.h. . . . and *still* no—yes, now. The pedals hardening, the wheel growing stiff in my hands . . . now, control . . . touch of right rudder, nicely done, you're no beginner, Carr—did she notice that? . . . 60 . . . more rudder . . . 70 . . . 75 . . . nosewheel should come unstuck now, back on the wheel, back more—*God, but she's heavy. Wake up, you over-fed bitch* . . . The nose suddenly pivoting at the sky. *Hold it down, careful, don't try and rush things.*

Eighty . . . 85 . . . How much runway have we used? And what happened to that extra 4,000 feet they've talked about building all these years? . . . 90 . . . coming up to 95 . . . getting time to fly. Slight back pressure on the wheel—and nothing. Nothing.

One hundred . . . I *felt* back on the wheel, gentle fingertip movements searching ever-so-delicately for a response, a waking, a willingness . . . ahead the end of the runway, the scrubland beyond, and then the roofs of the town . . .

One hundred and five . . . I got firmer on the wheel . . .

One hundred and ten . . . *Damn it, I'm the boss around here. Now* FLY, *you bitch!*

And suddenly but smoothly, to show that *now* was exactly her moment, she flew.

The scrubland flicked beneath, then the town itself. At 175 m.p.h. I let her lift into a shallow climb—and we were running gay and young up the morning sky, twisting, solid but fast on the controls, into a wide climbing turn.

Finally I levelled off, throttled back, and stared, rather surprised, round the cockpit. It was still a junkshop window of non-matching instruments, sweat-corroded levers wrapped in sticky black tape, cheerful little notices saying *limiting speed 349 m.p.h.* with the 349 scratched out and 275 scratched in. She was an old over-painted hag, but she'd once been young and powerful, and she hadn't forgotten the great days.

There had to be a reason why she'd lasted twenty years, longer than I'd been flying myself.

So perhaps, after all, there was more than money in it. 'I'm sorry,' I said softly, 'that I called you a bitch.'

I had her refuelled while J.B. settled our account and we flew out, all three of us this time, for Kingston at nine-thirty. I was anxious to get airborne before the midday heat.

A full set of airline radio equipment would have cost three times as much as we were paying for the entire aeroplane, so we weren't over-equipped in that direction. The Mitchell had a ten-channel VHF set without crystals in half the channels, an elderly radio-compass, and that was all. So a

500-mile ride over the sea left an awkward gap in the middle where I couldn't raise a single station. Not that I was worried about navigation—Jamaica's too big to miss entirely—but I'd have liked to have someone to say good-bye to if the occasion arose.

But it didn't. We landed at Palisadoes soon after noon.

I planned to keep the Mitchell there a few days, learning about her while I had a long runway for errors, and getting her hydraulics patched up. We parked off behind the pier of cargo sheds and went to phone Whitmore.

He wasn't available, but J.B. got Luiz at Oranariz. After a bit of a chat she put me on for a technical report.

'Tell Whitmore,' I reported, 'that she's a tired old lady, but still a lady. There's a bit of a bombsight mounting left in the nose, so you can probably fix a camera on that. And you could work another sideways out of the old gun windows down behind the bomb-bay, if you want to. We've got about three hundred dollars-worth of work to do on the hydraulics and re-wiring the intercom system. But that should cover it.'

'Fine. Get J.B. to sign you an okay, and you can get somebody started on it.'

'And tell him I'll fly her up to Ocho Rios as soon as it's done. Two to three days.'

'I will tell him. Have you seen Diego Ingles yet?'

'No. Was he supposed to be here?'

'I expected him to be. He and I drove down last night to meet you when we thought you were coming then. I had to be back at work today, but he was most anxious to see the new airplane so he stayed.'

'Well, it's a bit early for him to be up and about yet. You want to speak to J.B. again?'

'No—only tell her to hurry back. One of the extras has broken his ankle and talks of suing us for a million bucks. We want her to break his spirit also.'

I rang off and passed on the message. J.B.'s eyes glittered ferociously. 'Goddamned extras who try and make a name by doing something crazy in camera and break their necks and *then* sue *us*. I'll see that bastard never works in pictures again.'

Suddenly she wanted to be off and into the fight. I watched her go. She was quite a lawyer. Perhaps even quite a woman —if her lawyer let her be.

I went upstairs and had my usual lunch of beer and hot dogs before starting work on the Mitchell. Word of her had got around already—an airport's a small village when it comes to gossip—and the refuelling supervisor was almost polite to me. I knew why, too: the Mitchell's fuel consumption seemed to work out around 145 gallons an hour—five times as much as the Dove's.

After that I waved Whitmore's name and income around the hangars until I had a couple of mechanics tracing down the hydraulic lines. I could see from their faces that they didn't believe what they were finding and couldn't find anything they might have believed.

But she was like that all the way through. As a plane built towards the end of the war, she had started life full of hasty modifications: extra gun hatches chopped out all over, chunks of armour plate slapped on here and there, auxiliary fuel tanks stuffed into every corner. And since then, most of the gun hatches had been roughly sealed up, yet another tank had been built into the bomb bay, somebody had added three swivelling armchairs and piece of carpet in the narrow cabin behind the bomb-bay, carved out four portholes and installed a hot-air system that looked like two metal pythons in position 69.

I had a short sentimental moment of wanting to strip her down and bring her back to being *Beautiful Dreamer* again. But the idea passed: she had more 'improvements' to come, yet another job to do. And at her age, that was glory enough. I went back to work with an uneasy feeling that the same thought might apply to pilots.

By five o'clock, when my mechanics started showing symptoms of raging thirst, we had a rough idea of how the system worked, even if not why, and had found two leaking joints, a sticky valve and a shaky pump. After an hour of overtime rates we had the pump stripped and knew what parts we needed. I sent an Aircraft-On-Ground cable to North

106

American in California asking them to air-freight spares if they had any left, then called it a day.

Diego still hadn't shown up, which was odd if he really wanted to meet the Mitchell—but not so odd if he'd found something else twenty years old and rather less modified. Airplanes ran a bad fourth to sex in his life.

By the time I'd cured my own thirst and went over to collect the jeep from the cargo pier, we were into the short tropical twilight. The tall lights around the loading bay came on as I walked across, turning the concrete blue and cold in contradiction to the soft warm air. Everybody else had gone—cargo planes, without passengers to worry about, work union hours—and all the sheds were locked except the last, which never held anything but my jeep and a few cargo trolleys.

I drove round the end of the terminal pier heading for the back gate, slowing up for a last look at the Mitchell. She stood there, dark, lonely, but with that watchful look all nose-wheel airplanes have, unable to sit back and rest on their tails. A cluttered old lady on sentry duty . . .

Hell, I was getting sentimental about that box of junk. Still, I didn't have any other airplane to get sentimental about now. Or maybe it was because she'd once fought a war.

I was about to pull away when I remembered the heap of plastic covers that I'd used to stretch over the Dove's engines and cockpit when she was standing in the sun. Without the Dove, they'd sat in the back seat of the jeep all week, and I was lucky nobody had pinched them. There are enough Jamaicans for whom a few square feet of plastic are halfway to a house. Now, maybe, the Mitchell could use them. I got out and yanked them off the seat.

Then I knew what had made Diego late.

He'd been there some time, so he just stuck out over the side of the jeep, stiff as the plank from the side of a pirate galleon. Then the drag of the covers, as I dropped them, toppled him over and he fell with a sound I can hear again whenever I close my eyes. I closed my eyes then, too.

When I had them open and focused again, he was lying

beside the back wheel, in the curled, crunched shape set by the space behind the jeep's front seats. Not because I wanted to, but because I had to know, I rolled him so he balanced on his back, and in the dim back-glow of the neon lights on the far side of the cargo pier I could see the splatter of black blood on his white shirt front. When I looked closer, there wasn't just one hole, but dozens of small ones.

Then I started the long walk back across the bright cold concrete to the warm lights of the terminal. Except that I ran a lot of it.

★ 16 ★

'A SHOTGUN,' said the inspector. 'When you think about it, that tells us quite a lot.'

There were two of them: an English inspector and a Jamaican sergeant. The inspector was a man with pale cold eyes, a neat little moustache, clipped hair and the general finicky-tough look you get from Englishmen who come out to be cops in somebody else's country. He was wearing a summer suit, but made it look a lot smarter than the sergeant's uniform. The sergeant was a long, loose man with a thin bony face and big solemn eyes.

It was nearly ten o'clock and we were still up in an office near the top of the control tower. A dusty-white room lined with the usual maps covered with the usual coloured strings and wax-pencil scribbles. There was an old travel-agent's model of a DC-7C on the desk and the inspector couldn't keep his hands off it; twizzling it on its stand, flicking the propellers.

The sergeant said gravely: 'Not many shotguns in Jamaica, sir.'

'Exactly. It's not a *native* weapon. That's one thing. Second, it means premeditation; you don't just happen to have a shotgun with you. And finally, it means he wasn't killed here.'

He looked at me, with the hint of a triumphant smile behind the toughness, waiting for me to ask why.

I said: 'You mean the noise?'

He frowned and spun a couple of propellers quickly. 'Yes, exactly. I know the airport's a noisy place, but they'd still have heard a shotgun up here. If he was killed here some time last night.' And he nodded out of the window towards the end cargo shed, 200 yards away.

In the cold neon light there was a little huddle of vehicles: ambulance, police jeep, motorcycles, and dark figures moving slowly around them, measuring, searching, conferring—probably telling each other that a shotgun would have been heard up in the control tower.

I said: 'You've got a perfect place for a murder just outside: the road to Port Royal. There isn't a house on it for five miles. So why don't you throw him in the bushes or chuck him in the sea there? Why go to the risk of bringing him into the airport and dumping him in my jeep?'

He flicked another propeller and gave me a crafty look. 'Perhaps he wanted to throw suspicion on you—had you thought of that?'

I shook my head. 'I don't see that, either. If he knew my jeep was a safe place to hide the body, he'd have to know I was away for the night—in Colombia. So I'd have an alibi anyway.'

'Ah yes.' He flipped back through his notebook. 'An alibi which will be backed up by an American girl lawyer, who will be here shortly. An American—girl—lawyer.'

He made it sound like an insult.

It had been a long, full day. I felt like yawning, thought about not, then went ahead and yawned in his face.

'You don't seem very interested!' he barked. 'I thought this man was a friend of yours.'

I shrugged. 'I was teaching him to fly twins. I was making money out of him.'

The sergeant said: 'You had your airplane confiscated in Santo Bartolomeo the other day.'

The inspector jerked around. 'Where d'you hear this?'

The sergeant waved a long thin hand in a helpless gesture. 'I just heard it around, sir.'

The inspector glared, then turned back to me. 'So you didn't have an airplane any more at the time?'

'True. But at the time I was still in Barranquilla.'

'Ha.' He twizzled the model into a flat spin. 'Well, what d'you suggest?'

'That he was waiting for me last night. He'd wait by my jeep because that's the one place he couldn't miss me. Somebody shot him and stuffed him under the covers as the nearest hiding place.'

He smiled thinly. 'You're forgetting the noise, aren't you? Have you ever heard a shotgun?'

The sergeant said: 'He must have, sir. Fighter pilots train with shotguns and clay pigeons. Something about learning deflection shooting.'

The inspector jerked around again. 'I suppose you just heard *that* around, too?'

The sergeant smiled apologetically.

I said: 'Maybe it wasn't a shotgun.'

'You really think so? I know doctors are wrong most of the time, but not even a doctor could get a shotgun wound wrong.'

I just shrugged again. I could perhaps have added something to his store of knowledge on the subject, but his sneer at J.B. had got me niggled. And *he* was supposed to be the detective around here; let him detect something. Or ask his sergeant.

I just said: 'It's still the simplest solution.'

'Possibly,' he conceded. 'But let's consider the motive. What can you offer?'

'From some hints he dropped, he'd got a sex life like a tomcat with reheat. Maybe he picked on somebody whose husband owned a . . . a shotgun.'

'Yes—' He nodded. '—Yes, that's possible. A planter, somebody who lives out of Kingston. Somebody who'd need a shotgun for the mongoose.'

Oddly, the mongoose is a pest in Jamaica. Somebody brought them in some time back—probably from India—to get rid of the snakes. They did that, then started on the chickens as a dessert.

'But,' the inspector added, 'why come out to the airport to kill him?'

Because you couldn't have found him to kill him anywhere else in the last few days: he'd been up in Ocho Rios with Whitmore. And probably when Luiz drove him down last night, they stopped for a drink in Kingston—and at one of Diego's boozing-places, because Luiz wouldn't know Kingston. And if you were an angry husband, you could have been haunting Diego's favourite joints the last few days, waiting for him. Then all you had to do was trail him to the airport, wait until Luiz went back, come quietly up in the dark cargo shed, and—bang.

Still assuming it was a shotgun, of course.

I was getting tired, and he was still supposed to be the detective. 'I don't know.'

He smiled. Above us, in the control room, a loudspeaker echoed, and far off I heard the whistle of a Viscount on the approach. The ten-thirty from Miami.

The phone rang. The inspector snatched it up, grunted several times, put it down.

Then he stood up. 'Your witness is here, Mr Carr. Miss— ah—Penrose. And Mr Luiz Monterrey. I'll lead the way.'

We wound down the concrete stairs. J.B. and Luiz were waiting on the edge of the loading area, escorted by a small posse of uniformed police.

J.B. saw me and said immediately: 'If they're trying to involve you, Carr, you don't have to say a damn thing without a lawyer present. If you haven't got your own man, I probably know enough Jamaican law to help out.'

The inspector was staring at her as if she'd sprouted a forked tail and spat on *Moriarty's Police Law* into the bargain.

Before he could explode, I said: 'Skip that. Just tell the man where I was last night.'

'In Barranquilla,' she said crisply. 'If you don't like my word, you can check the hotel, the airport authorities, the guy we bought a plane off and the charter pilot who flew us in. You want their names?'

'Later, perhaps later.' He cleared his throat, then turned

to Luiz. 'And if you're Mr Monterrey, I believe you drove the dead man down last night?'

Luiz opened his mouth, but was drowned by the sound of the Viscount rolling up to the ramp behind him. When its engines died, he said: 'We came in by the back gate, past the flying club, at about seven. We had a drink in the terminal, then I left about half-past nine. I'd parked my car over there—' he nodded at the cargo pier '—and he walked over with me, and said he'd wait a while. He still thought Señor Carr might come in that night.'

'I see.' The inspector turned to me. 'Were you planning to come back last night?'

'If the plane had been in better shape, I might have. As it was . . .'

He nodded, then announced: 'I understand you all knew the dead man. So I will now ask you to make a formal identification. You may be called on to repeat this at the coroner's inquest.'

Luiz and I started simultaneously to protest on J.B.'s behalf. But she cut us off: 'I've had dead clients before.'

The inspector marched us off across the bright cold concrete towards the group at the cargo shed.

When we were lined up outside the ambulance, the sergeant gave a couple of orders in the broad Jamaican he saved for talking to constables, and somebody opened the doors and put on the lights.

In turn, we stepped up inside, looked, stepped down. It was warm inside the ambulance and it smelt of something. When I got down, I could feel the cold sick sweat on my forehead.

The inspector said softly: 'I'd have thought you'd seen dead men before, Mr Carr—in Korea.'

'No. Pilots only kill them. You don't see them.'

He grunted, then raised his voice. 'Do you identify this man?'

J.B. said: 'That's the man I met as Diego Ingles.'

He frowned at her careful legal phrasing, then turned to me. I nodded. 'That's Ingles.'

Luiz said: 'Yes.'

A constable in a white motorcycle crash helmet handed over a bunch of papers. The inspector thumbed through them, picked out a small booklet. After a moment he said: 'I have a passport here, found on the dead man. The full name appears to be Diego Jiminez Ingles.'

I said: 'Say that again.'

He looked at me, surprised. 'Does this contradict anything you understood?'

Not now; not any longer. I should have remembered, of course; Spanish custom uses both father's and mother's family names—but it puts father first. The son of Juan Smith Jones is Roberto Smith Brown—it's the middle name that matters. I should have remembered.

'Jiminez,' I said slowly. 'Perhaps that changes your case for you a little, Inspector.'

'I *beg* your pardon?' He looked annoyed.

This was carrying Jamaican disinterest in the rest of the Caribbean a bit far.

'Jiminez, for Christ's sake. The rebel leader in the Republica Libra. Diego must have been his son.'

He glanced at the sergeant. 'You didn't hear *this*—?'

'I've heard of the man Jiminez, sir,' the sergeant said—a little reluctantly. 'But I hadn't seen the passport, of course, sir.'

The inspector glared down at the passport as if it should have *Son of well-known rebel leader* stamped on it. 'This is a *Venezuelan* passport.'

I said: 'So his mother's family was Venezuelan. And probably loaded. That's maybe where Jiminez is getting his backing. And you let him in here, without noticing a thing.'

'I wasn't teaching him to fly,' he said stiffly.

Then I knew where all my troubles had come from. The FBI knew who Diego was, the Republica knew. It just hadn't occurred to them I could be stupid enough not to know. So I'd been written down as a rebel.

So I'd lost the Dove.

Then I remembered something else and swung round on

J.B. 'You must have had his name on a contract. He was working for—'

'No. He wasn't on contract—Eady plan, you remember? He was strictly off the budget, just helping out for drinks and expenses.'

I frowned at her, at the ambulance, finally back at the inspector.

He said: 'How did you mean—this changes the case?'

'My God—I was teaching him to fly twins. He must have been planning to fly arms or something into the Republica—and they guessed it.'

He made a noise in his throat. 'So you think he was—assassinated?' he asked distastefully.

'Well, at least it's a thought.'

He did some deep detecting on the thought, then smiled. 'But that would mean sending in a . . . a murderer, probably by airline. And *that* would mean trying to carry a shotgun through the Customs. They couldn't—'

'*Forget* about shotguns. Haven't you ever heard of a snake pistol?'

He hadn't; not on an island where the mongoose is the problem.

I sighed. 'Just take an ordinary revolver—a thirty-eight or bigger—bore out the rifling, pull the bullets out of the cartridges. Put in a wad, fill them up with birdshot, seal them with wax or soap—and you've got a shotgun pistol. Spreads enough to kill a snake at twenty paces with a snap shot. And it'll kill men at short range—if you're the sort who couldn't hit a battalion of barn doors at ten feet.

'*And* it'll fit in your pocket *and* it doesn't make any more noise than an ordinary thirty-eight. And the Republica's snake country.'

There was a long hush while everybody looked at me.

Then the inspector said. 'How do you happen to know this, Mr Carr?'

J.B. said quickly: 'You don't have to answer—'

'The hell with that. I converted my own revolver in Korea. *I'm* a lousy pistol shot; with a snake gun at least I could kill snakes.'

The inspector turned to the sergeant. 'You didn't happen to know about snake pistols, did you?'

The sergeant gave me a reproachful stare, then shook his head. 'No, sir,' he said sadly.

The inspector came back to me. 'Some people might think you withheld this significant information for a remarkable time.'

'Some people might think *I* was supposed to be the detective around here.'

His eyes glittered. 'You wouldn't happen to carry a snake pistol these days?'

Steam started to come out of J.B.'s ears. I just smiled sweetly.

Luiz said quickly: 'Inspector, my friend—let me make a small suggestion. Possibly you should not worry so much about Señor Carr, but go and ring one of your ministers and tell him that you have a murder which will, tomorrow, bring the Venezuelan consul, a rich family in Caracas, quite possibly the Republica and most certainly some American newsmen from Miami—all asking awkward questions.'

The inspector stared. He hadn't thought about the international aspect of Diego's death—no local would. But no island is an island.

Luiz smiled with infinite Spanish sadness. 'Politics, you know, my friend.'

The inspector suddenly knew. He held the word *politics* on his tongue a moment, despising the taste of it. Then, reluctantly, he swallowed.

'None of you will be leaving Jamaica, of course,' he said officially.

'We got a picture to finish,' J.B. pointed out.

'Ha. Very well—you can go.' He swung around and marched off towards the terminal. The sergeant gave me a final sad look, and ambled after.

Luiz watched them go, then said: 'We've got a company car outside. Can we drop you?'

The jeep was back in the cargo shed, being crawled over by experts. I nodded, and we walked slowly back across the bright loading bay.

J.B. said suddenly: 'We got a public relations angle of our own to figure out. I don't want anybody trying to tie the Boss Man in with a revolution.'

'Just don't let him write Diego's murder into the script, then,' I suggested.

Luiz made a wincing noise.

Halfway round the sandspit road into Kingston, J.B. said: 'Tell the driver where you want to be dropped.'

But away from the police, I'd had time to catch up on my thinking. About time, too.

I said: 'I think I'll come all the way with you. I'd like a word with Whitmore.'

'He'll be asleep by the time we get in.'

'No—I don't think so. And if he is—well, you'll just have to wake him.'

She said, shocked: 'We can't do *that*.'

'Just tell him I've finally woken up myself.'

After a time, she leant forward and told the driver to go straight through for the north coast.

* 17 *

It was one in the morning by the time we got to Oranariz, but there was a glow of light from the back of the bungalow. J.B. led the way round and up on to the patio.

Whitmore was sitting, stretched in his usual chair beside the refrigerator, and wrapped in a weird mixture of beach clothes and Bolivar Smith clothes, topped with an oily old beaded-and-fringed Red Indian jacket. He had a bottle of rye whisky at one side, a heap of account books, scripts and western novels at the other.

He saw me, squinted in surprise, then said evenly: 'Hi, fella. Beer or whisky?'

'Both.'

'Bad as that, huh?'

I just shrugged. Luiz walked across and opened the

116

refrigerator door, Whitmore did his bottle-opening act, and tossed over a Red Stripe. Luiz found glasses and poured shots of rye for J.B. and my other hand.

She had flopped into a chair, suddenly white and drained. She took a gulp at the whisky, then said rapidly: 'Well, it's true, all right. He must've got killed soon after Luiz left him last night. Seems he got shot with a "snake pistol"—Carr figured that out. Apparently it's some sort of—'

'I know snake guns,' Whitmore said. He glanced at me, then back at J.B. 'So what did the cops say?'

'They took statements. They tried to walk over Carr a bit, but all they got was sore feet. That's about all. Except one piece of news: it seems Diego was really—'

'Hold on,' I said. '*I'll* tell this part.'

Everybody looked at me: Whitmore and Luiz with calm professional faces, J.B. with a series of expressions that were probably just her exercising her face. Then she nodded and took another gulp of whisky.

I said: 'Diego was Jiminez's son. And you knew it all along.'

I hadn't expected a vast reaction, not from these three. What I got was exactly nothing. The two actors went on looking like studio pictures of themselves, J.B. went on nuzzling her glass.

Then Whitmore said calmly: 'Why d'you think that, fella?'

Suddenly what I was going to say seemed ridiculous out here on a quiet patio overlooking the dark sea, with no sound but the gurgling of the refrigerator, the hums and bumps of insects beating themselves on the lights along the patio roof.

I drank quickly from both hands and said: 'That trip we did to Santo Bartolomeo—'

'You suggested that yourself,' Luiz said.

'Oh, I remember. You know, I was rather disappointed, that first day on location; I thought I hadn't seen any real acting. I was wrong; I saw some great acting. That question was a pure frame. You asked me for the nearest Spanish-style locations: you knew I *had* to say the Republica. And you asked me for somebody who spoke perfect Spanish. Another frame: you already knew I knew Diego; that was just a way of getting him up here without surprising me.'

'Why the hell should we care about you?' J.B. asked politely.

'I'll come to that. My point is Diego got *me* into your job, not the other way around. You already knew him—and who he was.'

'You're guessing pretty wild, fella.'

'You forget I've seen her at work.' I nodded at J.B. 'The day she hired me, she had a complete breakdown on my costs, she knew all my flying history, she probably has a set of my grandmother's fingerprints. Don't tell me she'd let Diego get mixed up with you without even knowing his *name*. I just don't believe she'd fall down on the job that far.'

There was another silence. Then Whitmore said, still calm: 'Okay—so we knew. So what? He was a good kid. And he still spoke Spanish.'

'You asked me another question that day,' I said. 'You asked me about a camera plane: something with twin engines where you could put a camera in the nose. That was a frame, too: the answer *had* to be a bomber, like the Mitchell. And then *Diego's* agent found one for you—and you gave *Diego* the okay to fly in it with me. *Just what the hell were you and him planning with that bomber?*'

After a while, Luiz sighed and said: 'We've been called, Walt. Time to turn up our cards.'

Whitmore frowned, grunted, and lifted his huge shoulders in a slow shrug. 'Okay, so you guessed it. Well, I guess after we'd finished with the plane and the kid knew how to fly it, we were going to let him use it.'

'For what?'

He shrugged again. 'He had an idea he could get hold of some bombs, then if all the jets were lined up, the way we saw them, he could have—' he snapped his fingers '—like that. Knock 'em all out in one pass. Change the whole balance in the Republica.'

'You were going to back a *bombing* raid?' I asked incredulously.

'Hell—you saw what bastards were running the place, when we were down there.'

I stared around: at J.B., who was hunched in her chair, staring resolutely into her whisky; at Luiz, leaning on the refrigerator, thoughtfully opening and closing the door.

'You all knew this?' I asked.

J.B. took a fast jolt of rye. 'I knew. Hell, I advised it, in a way.'

I said: 'This isn't just a cow-town with a crook sheriff and a drunken mayor; this is somebody's country. Somebody *else's* country.'

Luiz flipped the door shut with a thud. 'It was my country —once. Long ago, and under a different name, of course. But I went to school with Jiminez. He is a good man. So —perhaps you could say it is all my fault.' He frowned suddenly and very sadly. 'Perhaps, anyway.'

Whitmore said: 'Hell, no. I'd've backed the kid anyhow.'

'I see.' I nodded. 'I see. Well, at least that means it doesn't matter so much that he got killed, does it?'

Luiz stared sharply; Whitmore frowned. 'How d'you figure out *that*?'

'Because the poor bastard would've killed himself anyway, trying to handle that Mitchell. And if he didn't he'd certainly have got himself killed in the attack. He only had to miss one jet—one—and he'd've had Ned Rafter sitting on his tail inside three minutes.'

'He was a good kid,' Whitmore said.

'He was a sports-car driver. That Mitchell's a professional airplane—and an air war's a professional business, too. It isn't as easy as it looks in the movies. Why the hell d'you think the Republica's paying Ned a thousand dollars a week or whatever?'

He'd looked a little pained at the crack about the movies. But then he sighed heavily. 'Well—yeah, maybe you're right. But we had a sort of other idea, too. We kind of thought you might take it over. How d'you feel?'

119

What I felt was that the world was coming loose at the hinges if I was really sitting here with a drink in either hand being asked if I just happened to feel like going on a mission to bomb the bejazus out of somebody's air force.

And what's so odd about that? Less than two weeks back you were offered a job at $750 a week to fly jets against somebody else's rebels in somebody else's hills. You didn't think that was so odd. All right, now the other side's made you an offer.

Well, maybe so—but these people aren't rebels; they're two Hollywood stars and a top American lawyer. The thing's crazy. It's like a Walt Whitmore film.

So? Maybe that's exactly what he wants. He's spent the last thirty years playing this part in the movies—maybe he wants to have a crack at it in real life. Maybe he thinks it's just that simple. Haven't you ever heard an actor talking politics before, Carr?

'You're a pro,' Whitmore said.

'No. That was a long time ago.'

Luiz said: 'Such as last Saturday, over Santo Bartolomeo?'

I gave him a look, then said carefully: 'Look—Diego's been murdered already. That means——'

'Yeah.' He nodded decisively. 'I'd kind of hate to drop it now the kid got dead.'

'The Diego Jiminez Ingles Memorial Bombing Mission,' I said grimly. 'But that means they know something's up. They've already got me on the list—probably they know about the Mitchell, by now.'

Luiz moved his shoulders delicately. 'It will, indeed, be more difficult. For myself, I do not think one old bomber, one pilot—and a *fighter* pilot, too—could do this thing.'

'Hell, I could *do* it,' I said. 'I've practised ground-attack work, and if they're lined up like we saw them——' Then I looked at him and said slowly: 'You bastard. You tricky bastard.'

He smiled softly.

Whitmore said impatiently: 'You fly this mission and you'll get your plane back.'

After a moment, I said: 'How the hell can you promise that?'

'We can get you a written guarantee from Jiminez: when he takes over, first thing he'll do is let you take your plane out. Okay?'

J.B. suddenly shook her head. 'Let's level with him, Boss. We've *got* a written guarantee from Jiminez. Got it that afternoon in Santo Bartolomeo. That was the real point of the trip: we'd arranged to meet Jiminez just out of town. By then you'd lost your plane, so we asked him for the guarantee. Just in case.'

'Just in case,' I said thoughtfully.

'You're a free man, Carr,' she snapped. But she didn't look at me. 'You haven't signed any contract for this. And the film job holds, whatever you do.'

But how free was I—without that Dove? I still owed money on her, and as soon as the film work was finished, I'd start missing payments on her. And London would start firing off sixteen-inch lawyers at me. I'd live through it—but I'd never own a plane again. It still wasn't a very good reason for getting mixed up in someone else's war.

I said: 'That guarantee may not be worth anything, of course . . .'

'I personally will back Jiminez's word,' Luiz said sharply.

'Yes? But you can't guarantee he'll win his revolution, whatever I do. He may never get near the Dove.'

Luiz glanced at Whitmore. After a while, Whitmore said: 'So put it this way: you fly the mission and you get *some* plane. If Jiminez don't get in or don't pay out, you keep the B-25. Fly it, sell it, do what you like. It must be worth something. Maybe even the twelve grand I paid for it. All yours, fella.'

I smiled. 'And if I get pinched in the process, the airplane'll turn out to be mine, not yours—right?'

He shrugged; a huge slow movement. 'You get yourself caught, fella, and I guess the generals won't worry too much about whose plane it was.'

He had a point there, of course.

'He hasn't said he'll do it, yet,' J.B. said.

'Haven't I?' I said. 'Oh, I'll do it, all right.'

This time she looked at me, quietly, carefully. And maybe even a little disappointed. Then she took a deep breath. 'Okay—so the next problem: we're going to have newspaper men down from Miami by noon. If they see that bomber, they might start getting some right ideas. Where can we hide it?'

'*Hide* it?' My mouth stayed open. But I saw her point. Now I knew why we'd got that Mitchell, it seemed horribly obvious. *A tommy-gun under the pillow, Inspector? Oh, yes—that's in case a spider comes up the plughole.*

'Would it help if we brought it up here, to the Ocho Rios strip?' she asked.

'Christ, the hydraulic pump's off one engine——' Then I thought about it. 'I can fly it like that, probably. But not to here. Your newsmen'll want to interview Whitmore: they might take the local flight into Ocho Rios. No—I'll run it up to the Port Antonio strip. No reason why they should go there.'

'Get it there before lunch.'

I nodded meekly.

'And when they get on to you, don't try and dodge them: that'll just make them suspicious. Just tell 'em the story. But maybe play down the ride into Santo Bartolomeo a bit.'

I nodded again, looked at the drinks in my hands, then remembered I was going to be flying before lunch and put them down. J.B. saw the move and stood up. 'You can get a room at the Shaw Park, Carr. I'll come down with you.'

Whitmore stood up slowly and stretched himself, an enormous movement that made the broad patio seem like a bathing hut. 'See you in a coupla days, fella. We'll figure the details then.'

Luiz nodded politely as we went out.

Out in the dim quiet parking bay, with the chauffeur asleep behind the wheel, J.B. paused before opening the car door and said quietly: 'Well, seems you've got a new job, Carr.'

I nodded slowly. 'It does seem that way, doesn't it?'

'Just as a matter of interest—why did you take it?'

'You talked me into it.'

'You're still a free man, Carr,' she snapped.

'Am I? Well—I'm getting the Dove back. And maybe something to do with Diego getting killed.'

She was quiet for a while, then asked gently: 'Do you miss the war flying much?'

'The RAF didn't exactly fire me, you know: not after Korea. I'd have a squadron by now, maybe a wing.'

'So why'd you quit?'

I shrugged. 'No matter how many rings you've got on your sleeve, there's always somebody with more. Now, at least I can tell anybody to take a running bite at his own backside.'

'Like you did the Boss Man.'

I looked at her curiously. 'I thought you were helping plan this attack?'

'I was. When it was just young Diego's stunt, it seemed . . . ah, hell.' She sounded angry, but uncertain about what. 'Just the way when the Boss Man calls for a posse to trail the bad men, everybody jumps on a horse.'

'He's buying the horses. Now wake up the driver and tell him he's picked to lead a battalion of tanks into Santo Bartolomeo on Tuesday.'

She gave one fast, hard look and jerked the car door viciously.

★ 18 ★

I GOT the Mitchell off the ground just before the first airliner from Miami got in, and had an interesting flight to Port Antonio—nearly fifty miles east along the coast from Ocho Rios—with the loose hydraulic pipes sealed off with corks and the wheels hanging down all the way.

But at least J.B. had been right about the newspapermen: they were filling the Myrtle Bank like thirsty locusts when I got back in the afternoon, queueing up on the bar stools to borrow the phone and ring home to say it was a great story and send more money.

They were right, too, although the best of it was in the diplomatic rumpus, which mostly by-passed Jamaica. Venezuela kicked off by sounding worried about the safety of its citizens, but a little embarrassed about them turning out to be Republica revolutionaries. The Ingles/Jiminez family was less inhibited, and came in calling the Republica régime several things—all of which were probably true, but hardly rare in that part of the world. And dead on cue, the Republica boosted its own tough image by carefully muddling who'd insulted them and inviting Venezuela to step outside and say that again—remembering, of course, that 'outside' was a safe 500 miles of sea.

That took the first two days, after which the Ministry of Foreign Insults in each country handed the file down to the clerks to keep the row going for the usual fortnight with the usual notes and leaks.

With all this going on, nobody even tried to tie Whitmore in with the political side of Diego's death. After all, you don't suspect Hollywood of revolutionary politics any more than you do the Catholic Church. Sure, some film stars have friends on the shady side of the street, but how about the Church in its time? In Hollywood, a rebel is still a man who drives a Porsche instead of a Jaguar and comes to cocktail parties in a dirty tee shirt.

Even I got off lightly. The newspapermen came in with a fixed idea about me: with my Korean experience, I was obviously a restless-war-hero-looking-for-trouble. But that itself made me conventional and dull—they'd spent years writing the same story about pilots who'd flown for or against Castro. With the diplomatic fuss, the family angle and Whitmore there wasn't much room for me anyway.

Nobody went near Port Antonio.

Come Sunday lunchtime most of the journalists had got all the local colour, heat and smell they could stand from Kingston and had either flown home or evacuated to the north coast to pester Whitmore. So I was quietly water-logging my sorrows in the Myrtle Bank when J.B. came on the phone telling me to turn out and help a company car meet the five o'clock plane.

Apparently somebody from the Jiminez/Ingles family was flying in from Caracas to collect Diego's body, and since the film company was shooting that day, it was thought that I'd add tone to the proceedings by forming a guard of honour. Myself, I wasn't so sure, but she'd rung off before I could think up an excuse. So by five I was waiting outside Customs in my Sunday suit, at least seven-eighths shaven and three parts sober.

I missed her the first time. Rather, I didn't exactly miss her—I'd have to be blind to do that—but I didn't immedi-ately think of her as somebody who'd come to collect a corpse. Although she *was* dressed in black: a silk sheath dress high at the neck and nearly as high at the knees, a black silk headscarf and a vast black crocodile handbag.

I was looking at her in the general way you look at *Caneton a l'orange* even when you know you're going to have the hamburger, when she caught my eye, came straight over and asked: "Capitan Carr?"

'Uh . . . just Keith Carr. You're Miss . . . ah . . .' I tried to remember just what Diego's name *had* been, after all.

But she stuck out a slim brown hand and said: 'Juanita Jiminez.'

I just waved my head up and down. At a distance she'd been attractive; close up, she had the punch of a thirty-millimetre cannon. I was trying to work out how this girl could be Diego's sister. Well, maybe they had the same dark hair and big dark eyes, and if you had hauled Diego's stomach up eighteen inches and split it into two . . . Her centre of gravity was definitely forward. It's a good thing on airplanes and women both.

I came awake abruptly and said: 'There's a company car outside. If you'll point out your luggage, I'll put it aboard and the driver'll take you wherever you're staying.'

'But you're taking me there, aren't you?' The dark eyes looked infinitely sad.

'Am I? Where?'

'The Shaw Park.' Spanish-style, she rolled several imaginary R's at the end of Shaw. 'It's beyond Kingston, I think.'

J.B. might at least have told me. 'It's sixty miles beyond——' Then I started thinking what else I'd rather do that evening than ride sixty miles over the hills pointing out the sights to Miss Jiminez.

I nodded. 'Of course.' I went to collect her luggage. Perhaps she had owned it already, but it looked very much as if she'd bought it especially for the trip. It was black, brand new—and crocodile skin. The two cases, with their stainless-steel fittings, must have cost a good £500.

When I got it back to base, the party had grown: the inspector and the sergeant. I still couldn't remember their names, so I just said hopefully: 'You've met, have you?'

The inspector coughed and said heavily: 'You're looking after Miss . . . ah . . . Jiminez, I gather.'

'That's right.'

'I was just asking what she could tell us about her brother's . . . ah . . . activities. It might give us a lead.'

'I understand, Coronel,' she said sadly, 'that he was murdered by gangsters from the Republica. Have you caught them yet?'

He coughed awkwardly. 'Well . . . no, not yet, quite. Trouble is, Mr. Carr didn't find your brother's . . . ah . . . your brother until twenty-four hours later.' He gave me a look which made the whole thing my fault.

She looked at me soulfully. 'And you were teaching him to fly, Capitan?'

'That's right.' I looked back at the inspector. 'Although I didn't know what it was for.'

She said: 'He was very devoted to his father's cause.'

Well, maybe—after women and his Jaguar E-type. But I stayed shut up. After a time, the inspector said gallantly: 'Well, a man should be——' then caught the sergeant's eye, and added: 'Depends on what cause, of course.'

Nobody said anything and we had a bit of rich dark Spanish gloom. Then the inspector said: 'So you can't think of anybody your brother knew particularly in Kingston?'

'Only Capitan Carr, Coronel.'

He grunted. I noticed he wasn't objecting to the 'Coronel' title. After a little more gloom, he said: 'If you want to make arrangements for your ... ah ... brother, I see no objections. I've already spoken to the coroner and since there's obviously no possible dispute over the ... ah ... cause of death, he's been released for—well, you can make any arrangements you like. The inquest may be delayed.'

And I could guess why. After three days of international politics and American journalists over a murder he'd probably decided was unsolvable, the last thing he'd want would be to remind everybody about it by staging an inquest in a hurry. This one was an inquest that would take up five minutes of a wet Monday morning in the middle of the next banana-loading strike.

'Please call on me at any time,' he finished—a little hopefully, I thought. She gave him a vast sad smile and he rocked, lifted his hand to salute, remembered he was in plain clothes, and tottered away with the sergeant loping after him.

She said contemptuously: '*They* will never catch them.'

I didn't think so myself, but all I did was make soothing noises and start humping her cases towards the exit.

Around the Palisadoes road and through Kingston itself I kept talking and pointing out the sights—mostly to give my hands something to do apart from grab. The back seat there, with her tight skirt riding up a little beyond loud-hailing distance of her knees, was definitely a one-thought situation.

She listened, nodded and smiled politely until Tom Pringle's Cotton Tree on the Spanish Town road finally exhausted my local knowledge. Then she said calmly: 'Now you will fly the bomber instead of Diego?'

I jumped and looked quickly at the driver. But I'd forgotten that it was one of those old-fashioned long Cadillacs some Jamaican car-hire firms use—with a glass partition behind the driver. Closed.

Still, our security didn't sound too good if the news had already spread as far as Caracas.

I asked cautiously: 'Why d'you think that?'

Her eyes got wide, and maybe a little disappointed. 'But of course, Capitan—I assumed it. You will want to revenge Diego.'

Well—that or get my Dove back or something. I nodded.

She smiled, then said thoughtfully: 'It is very good. It is the classic use of air power, as your Lord Trenchard said. To destroy the enemy air force on the ground.'

I said: 'Huh?'

'Indeed, it is the most pure of all tactics. Captain Liddell Hart wrote it: "fixing combined with the decisive manoeuvre". You are fixing the enemy's attention with your frontal attack, my father is manoeuvring on the flanks, one might say, to bring about Clausewitz's "decisive battle".'

This time I didn't say anything. I just let my jaw dangle against my chest. After a time she noticed my expression had changed from the hungry leer which I'd been wearing ever since we met, and asked: 'You know Clausewitz, of course, Capitan?'

'He was the German general who . . . well, it was in Napoleon's time, wasn't it?'

'He wrote *On War*,' she said, a little austerely.

'Yes, I expect he did.' Not quite my brightest and best remark, but I was still going through the disorientated feeling you might get if the airplane had suddenly decided to fly backwards.

'But you must have read his books in your Air Force. He has been much misunderstood, but he is still the basis of all strategy.'

I nodded helpfully. 'I'm sure they read him at the *top* of the RAF but I was pretty close to the bottom. They didn't consult me much on strategy.'

She frowned. 'Was that why you left your Air Force?'

I waved a helpless hand. 'Look—I was just a pilot. A bullet. The air marshals pulled the trigger and I went where I was pointed. That's all.'

But that wasn't quite the impression I'd planned to give. I'd been thinking more along the lines of The Dashing

Debonair Aviator Flying Fearless Into The Eye Of The Hurricane.

The hell with you, Clausewitz. I hope your tent leaked on campaigns and your publishers cheated you on royalties.

'Now that,' I said, pointing, 'is the original church of Spanish Town. You should see some of the inscriptions on the gravestones from the plague days——'

'Your Lord Nelson was here before he became a Lord, I think,' she said.

'Yes, that's down at Port Royal——'

'He was not a strategist, of course, but a very good tactician.'

I thought of asking whether she meant Trafalgar or Lady Hamilton, but decided not to. I said: 'At one time, Spanish Town was the capital of——'

She said: 'Only the Nile and Copenhagen were his important battles of course. In each he used the factor of surprise in the most interesting way . . .'

In the next hour I learnt a lot about Nelson. I also picked up some good stuff about Marlborough, the Schlieffen Plan, the two Moltkes, Foch and Hannibal.

Somehow, it still wasn't the car drive I'd planned.

★ 19 ★

It was twilight when we pulled into Shaw Park. J.B.'s Avanti and Whitmore's white station wagon were parked there, so I leant on the bell of Apartment C.

Luiz opened the door. He started to smile at me, then caught the view over my shoulder and went into shock. It was nice to see it happen to a professional.

He recovered quickly and made an elegant gesture that just happened to shove me out of the line of sight. 'Señorita Jiminez? I am called Luiz Monterrey. I knew your father. May I express my sorrow at the death of your brother? I should wear mourning'—he was still in film clothes; he plucked distastefully at the torn, smudged frilly shirt—'but an actor must wear mourning in his heart. That, I do. But you must be tired, please——' I was suddenly alone on the doorstep.

He was a pro, all right.

I hauled the luggage out of the car to release the driver for other company business, and walked into Apartment C myself. And straight into the muzzle of a gun.

I recognized it as one of the lever-action rifles they'd used in the river-crossing scene; the face behind it seemed vaguely familiar from the film-set, too.

'Blanks, I trust?' I said.

'You could find out—the hard way.' The face was grim and steady. 'Now say somep'n about who you are and why.'

J.B. came around the corner of the passage. 'All right, Doug—he's one of ours.'

The rifle drooped towards the floor—a little disappointed, I thought.

'After Diego,' J.B. explained, 'the Boss Man started taking a few precautions. He's licensed to have real ammunition for that thing in case he wants to go hunting alligators down on the Black River. Come on through.'

I dumped the luggage just inside the door, and said to the man Doug: 'You're in a bad position there: coming in with the light behind me I could have been Santa Claus or Fidel Castro. Either way, you could have made a bad mistake.'

'Only if you was Santy Claus,' he said calmly.

In the living-room facing over the patio and beach, Whitmore was offering Miss Jiminez a drink and she was saying she'd rather have a wash and brush up first. J.B. led her off through the bedroom.

Whitmore waved at me, then sprawled himself down on the sofa. 'Buy yourself a drink, fella.' The room was littered with bottles, glasses, dirty plates—they'd obviously just finished dinner—and yellow pages of shooting scripts. I started searching.

'Hell,' he said thoughtfully, 'that's quite a piece of tail you brought in.'

Luiz over-acted an anguished wince.

Whitmore grinned at him. 'If you wanna go riding without a horse, fella, I ain't competing.'

'You gringo peasant.'

Whitmore grinned even wider. Then he turned back to me. 'How's this airplane look?'

Luiz shook his head. 'A girl like that comes in—and the man wants to talk about airplanes.'

'I already said my piece about her and you didn't seem to like it.'

J.B. came back. 'Didn't know what I was letting you in for, Carr. That's quite a piece of——'

'My God,' Luiz said, 'Americans.'

J.B. looked at him, surprised, then smiled wickedly. 'You really getting hot pants about her, Luiz? I'll get you a pass key for her room.'

'What about this airplane?' Whitmore roared.

By then I'd found myself an unopened bottle of Red Stripe and half a plate of not-quite-cold prawns and rice. I swallowed and said: 'I've had a couple of men working on it at Port Antonio—I paid their fares from Kingston each day, if that's all right—and North American sent in some parts yesterday, so . . .' I gave him a fairly full progress report. It added up to the hope that the Mitchell would be ready for an air-test the next afternoon.

'After that,' I said, 'you can start filming as soon as you can fit cameras. But she'll need some more work before she does a bombing raid—if you still want to go on with that.'

He stared. 'Hell, yes. What's the matter?'

'Nothing,' I shook my head. 'Just—just every time I think of it, the crazier it sounds.'

'It'll work, won't it?'

'Yes, I think it'll work.'

'Okay, then. So what needs doing to her?'

I listed the items. I wanted to rip out all the excess weight —those seats and central heating in the rear, the bomb-bay tank. I'd learnt, from gossip around the airport, that some Mitchells had been fitted with such tanks in the war, so I hoped that it had been normal to leave the bomb rails and shackles in above them. If so, all I'd need to do was make sure they worked and then rewire the release mechanism.

Luiz said thoughtfully: 'You will have to work carefully, my friend. If the generals hear we are re-converting the airplane to a bomber . . .' he shrugged.

'She's in the script now,' Whitmore said. 'We can cover a lot of the work as dolling her up for the picture.'

Luiz looked doubtful.

I said: 'Frankly, I don't think there's much we can do on the security side except not make it too obvious. They must know we've got the Mitchell and if they believe I may be going to use it against them, we can't stop 'em believing, whatever we do. Still, once we've got the big changes made on her, I'll take over rigging her for bombing myself. That's as secure as we can get.'

They might have wanted to argue the point, but just then Miss Jiminez came back into the room. Maybe looking a little fresher, although I hadn't noticed anything wrong in that department before.

Whitmore stayed sprawled where he was. I bent myself into that half-on-the-feet position the British use for showing they're being polite. Luiz went across the room like a pouncing tiger and started easing her into a chair like a foot into a shoe.

'A drink, Señorita?' he suggested. 'Or may I show you to your room? And I will arrange dinner.'

She hit him with a ten-kilowatt smile and said she'd settle for a gin and tonic.

The conversation lapsed. Beyond the open french windows the sky darkened and the sea breathed politely on the empty beach. A fat lizard came out to stand sentry duty in the light spilling on to the patio.

Finally I said: 'Any idea of when this raid's supposed to come off?'

Luiz spun round and snapped: 'We are not discussing that any more.'

I smiled crookedly: I had a pretty good idea of what was going to happen now.

It did. Miss Jiminez looked up brightly. 'You are talking about the bombing of the generals' airplanes?'

Luiz said soothingly: 'Señorita, you need not concern yourself——'

'But that is what I am here for.'

He looked baffled. Whitmore said slowly: 'I thought you came to take home your brother.'

'I came to avenge him. I will have him sent home tomorrow. I will stay here.'

Luiz chewed his lip. Whitmore put on a puzzled frown. J.B. gave me a sharp glance, but didn't say anything.

I said: 'Well—when?'

'When the airplane is ready,' Miss Jiminez said, 'I will inform my father. After that, he will give one day's warning.'

I nodded. 'When are the bombs coming? And what bombs?'

'Diego was fixing that,' Whitmore said. 'We ain't heard anything since—I'm trying to get in touch again.'

Luiz stopped eating his lip and said: 'Four 500-pounders.'

'High-explosive?'

'Yes.'

I nodded again. The Mitchell would carry 2,000 pounds, all right. In fact, given a long enough runway, I was pretty sure the Mitchell would carry everything you could cram into her and your Uncle Harry's bathtub besides. She was a hell of a load-carrier—given a long enough runway. But that was the problem: I couldn't see the authorities at Palisadoes or Montego Bay, which had the long runways, giving flight clearance to this particular jaunt.

I looked at Miss Jiminez. 'I want your father to understand that I can't do this attack at just any time of day. It's got to be——'

She gave me a smile that raised flash burns. 'But of course. As your Kitchener of Khartoum once said, "We have to make war as we must, and not as we would like to." It must be dawn or dusk.'

Everybody was staring at her. I shook my head and muttered: 'You ain't heard nothing yet.' Then louder: 'That's right. They seem to send at least a section up to

133

forward base near the mountains during the day——'

'At Cordillera,' she said.

'That's the place, is it? But they don't seem to leave aircraft on it overnight. I'd guess Ned's scared of guerrilla raids and doesn't trust the army to——'

'The generals do not trust each other,' she said. 'General Bosco has been recruiting ground troops for his Air Force—like your RAF Regiment—to become an airfield defence unit. He now has about three thousand men. Some are seconded from his other branches; many of the non-commissioned officers were once policemen.'

Now Luiz was really staring. Then he shook his head to see if he was still awake, and asked: 'Señorita, how do you know these things?'

She seemed surprised. 'Señor, you forget who is my father.'

Whitmore said: 'Your father's 500 miles from Caracas.'

'Señor Whitmore, the Republica is not closed like a door. Letters come. Airplanes land there.'

Luiz persisted. 'But your brother did not know all these things.'

'My brother was my mother's son,' she said—quite sharply. 'I am my father's daughter. Diego knew what I told him.'

I'd begun to suspect something like that. I'd never seen Diego as the hard-working spider in the middle of an intelligence web. And the link between the Republica and Caracas —because of the common language and something of a common history—would be much stronger than between the Republica and Jamaica.

But mostly, I was interested in the news of the trouble between the Air Force and the Army. I saw why Ned had worked the cumbersome old system of controlling ground-attack fighters from right back at home base instead of letting the Army direct them on target from up on the front line—the way Ned himself had learnt it in Korea.

But that wasn't the point right now. I said: 'Right—I attack at first light or last light. All things considered, it had better be——'

'Dusk would be best,' Miss Jiminez said briskly. 'You

would be more certain to catch all of them on the ground, then.'

'It had better be dawn,' I said firmly.

I got a sharp, rather startled, look.

'Purely military problem,' I said soothingly. 'With bombs and full fuel that plane's going to be pretty heavy for a short strip like Boscobel or Port Antonio. So I want the air as cool as I can get it for take-off; more power for the engines, more lift for the wings. If I go in at last light, I take off in the afternoon: If I attack at first light, I take off around two in the morning. It's as simple as that.'

She frowned. 'Capitan, even Clausewitz believed that a "purely military judgment is a distinction which cannot be allowed".'

'He should've tried flying an overloaded Mitchell off a 3,000-foot runway in hot weather before he started making wild statements like that.'

'One cannot avoid all risks, Capitan. As Clausewitz said——'

'Clausewitz never said one horse made a cavalry charge. If I miss a couple of Vampires, the attack's still eighty per cent successful. But if I pile into the trees on take-off, you've got a hundred per cent flop. There won't be *any* attack.'

There'd be a few per cent of Keith Carr missing, too, if I went tree-pruning with a load of 500-pounders. But probably Clausewitz had said something reassuring about that as well, so I kept quiet.

Whitmore said firmly: 'Okay, so you hit 'em at sun-up. If they do get any jets up, you're going to have to come a-running. Be daylight.'

I just nodded. Speed wouldn't be much help against a Vampire that could go twice my speed and more. And no clouds to hide in, not around dawn. 'But at least I won't be making a night landing on a strip that doesn't have any lighting.'

Nobody had thought of that, of course. Whitmore crooked his eyebrows and said: 'But you'll have to take off in the dark—how about that?'

'A sight easier than landing. I can do it with just a hurricane lamp planted at the end of the strip.'

There was a silence while everybody thought up the next problem.

J.B. said suddenly: 'What about radar? Won't they see you coming?'

I had my mouth open when Miss Jiminez said: 'There is no radar in the Caribbean except at Puerto Rico and Cuba. You should know these things if you wish to help.'

J.B.'s face shut with a snap like a rat-trap.

Luiz said: 'Señorita Penrose only does our legal work; she does not pretend to be a general.'

'She makes contracts for my father to sign,' Miss Jiminez said scornfully.

Whitmore came to the rescue again. 'All right, kids. This is just a planning session. The real fighting comes later—and Carr does that.' He looked at me. 'Anything more, fella?'

There was one thing that had better be said, but I was uneasy about saying it in front of Miss Jiminez. I dug out my pipe and started to fill it while I gave myself time to think. Whitmore sighed, grunted, and threw me a cigarette.

I lit it, decided I'd better say my piece anyway, and said: 'Just one thing: we're dealing with an old airplane. It could go unserviceable—seriously—at any time. So the attack could be called off at the last minute.' I turned to Miss Jiminez. 'If your father's depending on the raid, you'd better tell him not to move until he *knows* it's coming off.'

There was no warmth in her look now. It was a hard searchlight stare. 'Capitan—the attack *must* happen. You must take *any* risk.'

There wasn't much warmth in my look, either. 'I'll give you a quotation you don't know: Keith Carr is not, repeat *not* expendable. Source, Keith Carr.'

'Capitan, you have joined a noble cause,' she blazed. 'It is too late to remember you are a coward, now.'

'I haven't joined a damn thing. I'm just a hired hand. I'll fly the raid if——'

'For money!' She bounced up, feet spread, hands on hips,

136

her dark eyes glaring furiously. 'Teach me to fly it, then. *I* will make the attack!'

I just stared at her: a magnificent, angry huntress, dominating the room, turning Whitmore into a small boy flopped in a corner.

Then I shook my head and said: 'That isn't the point anyway. A starter motor could go, a tyre could burst. Then we wouldn't even get her off the ground—nobody could. Just tell your father we *can't* give a guarantee.'

She went on standing there. Luiz said judiciously: 'Perhaps we could give the most careful overhaul, then . . .' he waved a hopeful hand.

'Overhauls wouldn't do it,' I said wearily. 'She's just too old—all of her. If we started that we'd find we needed new wings, fuselage, tail, engines . . . a new airplane. I'll check her out on the film flying and fix anything that busts, but she'll still be held together by rust and habit—and even the rust's a bit past it by now. Well, maybe the habit'll keep up long enough. If it does, I'll fly the attack.'

Whitmore nodded. 'Okay, that sounds good enough.' He looked at Miss Jiminez. 'Better tell your old man the position. He can move when he knows Carr's on his way.'

She went on looking at me. 'Perhaps,' she said coldly, 'if the Capitan keeps his courage in his wallet, he wants us to pay him a little more courage.'

Whitmore said firmly: 'Planning session's over. We got a movie to make tomorrow.'

She gave me one last glare, announced: 'I am eating,' and marched out.

In the silence there was just the click of her heels down the passage to the front door.

Luiz said softly: 'She should have been her brother.'

J.B. stared at him incredulously, 'Jesus, Luiz's gone queer.'

There was a sudden moment of pain on his face, then he smiled and shrugged. 'In political terms only, of course.' Then he hurried out after her.

When he heard the apartment door shut, Whitmore shook his head and said: 'She's really got him jumping, huh?'

137

'He's probably rehearsing to play the lead in *The Clause-witz Story*,' J.B. said sourly.

'Yeah? And I play the small fat guy Napoleon?'

'You could still do most of the scenes on a horse,' I pointed out.

He just looked at me. 'Thanks, fella.' Then he finished his drink, lit a cigarette, and reached for one of the yellow scripts.

'So,' he said after a while, 'if you get the ship ready in a coupla days, we'll schedule the flying shots so you'll be clear whenever Jiminez rings the bell.'

'We've got Roddie's church, too,' J.B. said. 'Should be ready in a day or two.'

'You're actually building a Spanish church?' I asked.

Whitmore looked up. 'Sure. You want us to haul the whole unit to Mexico just for a three-minute sequence?'

J.B. said: 'In films, it's always cheaper to bring the mountain to Mahomet—with Mahomet on union rates.'

I shook my head; it would obviously be stupid to ask if it wouldn't be cheaper still to write the church out of the script. Anyway, it was nice to know a business where the costs were higher than in aviation.

Whitmore made a note on his script, then stood up and stretched. 'So if you're working on her up this end of the island, you better move in here.' He looked at J.B. 'We got a room booked?'

She nodded.

I said: 'If it'll save you money, I don't mind moving in with J.B. She's got space.' I waved a hand around the big suite.

'Pull your throat in, Carr,' she snapped.

Whitmore grinned. 'Suddenly everybody's sex-crazy.' He nodded at me. 'I don't mind, fella. But if she talks contract law in her sleep don't blame me and don't try to stop her. That's what she's hired for.'

'Get out, you broken-down old cow-catcher.' The anger wasn't entirely faked either.

He just grinned again, waved in one of his big, slow gestures, and strolled whistling down the passage.

J.B. looked at me. 'Your room number's 17, Carr——'

'Fine.'

'——at the Plantation Inn.'

I winced. It was only a few hundred yards up the road, but damn it all . . .

'You don't trust yourself in the same hotel as me?' I asked. She just went on looking.

'One last drink,' I suggested. 'Before the intrepid aviator wings off on the dawn patrol.'

'If you're going to work for us we'd better put a real writer on your dialogue. All right—a Scotch. A thin one.'

I mixed it, found myself a bottle of Red Stripe, and sat down again. The evening wound down gently; the surf hissed politely on the beach beyond the patio; the lizard sentries drowsed at their posts.

After a while, she said quietly: 'Carr—why *are* you flying this raid?'

'I'm making a profit at it—I'm getting an airplane out of it, one way or another.'

She shook her head impatiently. 'You're not a damn fool, Carr. I know your record; I saw you figure out everything we'd been up to with Diego and getting that bomber. *You* know you could've tried other ways of getting your plane back. Diplomatic pressure, spilling the story to the papers, bringing law-suits—I'd've been forced to help you, morally, anyway. But this way you may not get your plane but you damn sure will get run out of the Caribbean.'

The grey list. I shrugged, then asked: 'That's my legal position, is it?'

'Ah, *legally* you probably aren't too badly off. It doesn't seem to be an offence in Jamaica to start a war as long as you don't start it here. They might get you under the Foreign Recruitment Law, but they need an order in council to bring that into force. And they'll get you for having bombs —unless you swear you picked them up *en route*. But all that isn't the real trouble.'

'I know.'

'A pilot's always vulnerable. If they want to get you, they

139

can trip you up on a dozen licensing troubles, safety standards . . . They'll run you out.'

'I know.'

She eyed me carefully. 'You're *not* a damn fool, not that way.' Then she tossed her empty glass on to the crowded table; two other glasses toppled, rolled, smashed on the floor. She watched them, expressionless. Then said quietly: 'When you first walked in here, I thought you were a pretty tough independent character. I thought maybe you'd be able to tell the Boss Man to go climb a tree. But then he calls for a posse and everybody grabs a deputy's badge and jumps on a horse—and then they can say "I rode with Whitmore." I've seen it happen before.'

'You think that's why I'm going?'

'Isn't it?' she flared. 'It isn't for your plane—and you don't give a damn about Jiminez, *that's* for sure. Well, you've joined the posse; the Boss Man thinks you're really one of the boys. That's wonderful.'

I stood up. The evening was dead. Among other things. 'Room 17, I think you said? And the desk knows I'm coming?'

She nodded. I found my own way out. And I didn't feel a thing. And that was pain enough.

★ 20 ★

THE next morning I got the boys down at Port Antonio to work stripping out the seats and bomb-bay tank from the Mitchell, then wangled a company car over to Kingston to pick up my jeep (the cops had finally got tired of finding each other's fingerprints on it) and a suitcase of dirty shirts I'd been saving until my laundry could go on the company's bill.

By the time I'd got back to Port Antonio via dumping the jeep at Boscobel, they'd nearly finished. The seats, the central heating and the bomb-bay tank were all out, and they were just sealing off the ends of the fuel feed, which seemed to have been designed by a kitten and a ball of wool.

140

Then I fired them, handed over a wad of Whitmore's dollars and let them find their own way back to Palisadoes. When they were out of sight, I took out my torch and ducked down for a private look around the bay itself.

Standing on the ground, I was inside it from about my hips up: a hot, dark metal box full of old oily grime and petrol fumes. About eight feet lengthways, nearly four wide, and six high. And the first quick flash of the torch convinced me the attack was off: the roof of the bay was quite bare.

I ducked out for a breath of air and a reconsideration. To be quite honest, as an ex-fighter pilot I couldn't remember ever having seen a bomb rail or shackle before; they were just words I'd picked up. But I was quite certain the roof of that bay didn't have any, and just as certain that anything that'll hold a 500-pound bomb can't be knocked up in a dull evening with a cigar box and a couple of rusty hairpins.

And it isn't something you put a 'wanted' ad in the *Daily Gleaner* for, either.

I took a deep breath and ducked in again just to make sure.

The roof of the bay was still empty. But when I turned the torch on the sides, they were lined with heavy metal stringers that seemed far too strong just to support the thin metal of the box—it wasn't even the outside skin of the aeroplane itself. And spaced along them, two to each side, were four thin, irregular-shaped steel boxes. I stared at them in the torchlight. They were just over a foot long, with two flat hooks sticking down at either end.

I dipped a finger in a pool of petrol on the tarmac beneath and rubbed it over one of the boxes. And I knew the attack was on again.

Surprisingly clear and non-rusty under the grime, the lettering came up: *Bomb Shackle Mk. 5*.

'You know, they must've hung the bombs on the *sides* of the bay, one above the other, and let 'em roll out and down,' I said. 'I suppose I should have guessed: you wouldn't need a bay six foot high if you were just going to hang 'em from the roof, and I suppose it must've worked—as long as you pressed the buttons in the right order—but still——'

'Will it work now?' Whitmore asked.

He and Luiz had been waiting for me on the Boscobel strip when I flew the Mitchell in soon after five. Apparently J.B. was off visiting a sick contract and Miss Jiminez had decided, after all, that she'd better go and watch Diego's coffin being shoved aboard a Venezuelan freight plane.

'With a lot of work,' I said slowly. I held up the shackle I'd managed to get off the rail. 'The shackles are in pretty good condition—I suppose because the thing was being used as a bomber in Colombia up to a couple of years back. You get the shackles off the rails, hook on the bombs—two hooks, you wouldn't want a bomb waggling around on just one— winch the whole lot up, fit the shackle back on to the rail. Then these'—I tapped a couple of little levers sticking out of the top of the shackle—'fitted into some sort of release gear.

'The trouble is,' I went on, 'that all that gear's gone. It must've worked on electro-magnets, with a coil in the circuit to step up the power, and probably the whole thing dupli- cated to avoid hang-ups. And on top of *that*, a fusing circuit —you wouldn't take off with the bombs fused and there's no way of getting at them from inside the plane.'

Whitmore nodded, reached out, and pushed the hooks closed. Then slapped the trip levers with a huge finger. The hooks came open with a vicious little *clack*.

It was a cold shivery sound in the hot sun. Whitmore looked at Luiz and grinned slowly. 'Sounds simple enough.'

'Simple?' I stared at him.

'Hell, fella—one thing a film unit's got is electricians. We got 'em like that guy in The book had pimples.'

'Job,' Luiz said. 'And boils.'

Whitmore jerked his head. 'He played a Bible picture once. Anyhow, I'll get the boys down to work on her tomorrow. Hell, she's in the script—so why can't she drop a few bombs? Rig some dummies outa beer cans or something. Have 'em going off along the river, bang-bang-bang; use dummy charges. We got a scene there.'

He walked off to look at my jeep.

Luiz sighed. 'Another scene where I get my feet wet.'

I grinned, then asked: 'Can they really do it?'

142

'My friend—you recall we are already building a fifty-foot church for this picture? A little matter like arranging a bomb-release circuit . . . They will do it.'

Whitmore walked back. 'That your jeep, fella?'

I'd said 'Yes' before I realized my mistake. They needed an old, battered jeep for the scene outside the church. Of course.

The next morning, the boys moved in. They were either good electricians or good actors; either way, they knew more about what they were doing than I did. So I just suggested where they could mount the release buttons—over some of the empty sockets at the top of the instrument panel—and left them to get on with it.

The art director had also arrived, without his crocodile jacket, but with a couple of scene-painters to help give the Mitchell a little movie makeup. This consisted of spraying her silver, shoving a couple of painted broomsticks in the nose and tail positions to look like machine guns, and inventing Amazonian Air Force insignia for her wings and sides. I tried to help on this last one by pointing out that every combination of shapes and colours they dreamed up had already been used by a real South American country.

Finally the art director told me they'd use a mixture of Malayan and Congolese symbols—a completely *darling* yellow star on a totally *ravishing* square of ultramarine (he was going to redecorate his bathroom in *exactly* the same colours just as *soon* as he got home)—and meantime would I *please* GO AWAY?

So I checked up on the weather—a maximum of 15 knots from 70 degrees, with a slightly suspicious circular disturbance north of Barbados—then went away to the Golden Head Tavern, just up the road.

At that time of day, the little bar was quiet, almost empty. The only other customer was sitting up at the bar, his back to me.

I went up and ordered a Red Stripe. The customer said quietly: 'Can I buy you that one?'

A knobbly, tanned face, cropped greying hair, milky-

143

coffee-coloured suit. It took a moment to place him, he was so far out of place.

Then I had it. 'Agent Ellis, I believe? Aren't you on CIA territory?'

He smiled easily. 'I'm on holiday. But you know—the Bureau once had a sort of responsibility out this way. The Caribbean, South America. Counter-espionage, in the war. Before they invented the CIA.'

FBI small talk again.

My beer arrived and I said: 'Here's to your *holiday*. Hope you don't get troubled by work.'

'No trouble.' He drank. 'Heard I might find you here, these days. Remembered I'd promised you something.' He felt in a side pocket and handed over a small rectangle of brass.

On it, engraved in neat capitals, was IT'D SCREW ME UP ALL OVER THE CARIBBEAN. Then I remembered the phrase, back in the bar of the Sheraton at San Juan.

I grinned, turning the plate in my hands. A small hole at each corner, ready to be pinned to an instrument panel. And a lot neater than any of the notices I'd met pinned to panels in any airplane before. It was a professional job and it must have cost him money.

'Why the hell did you do this?' I asked.

He looked down at his glass and frowned thoughtfully. 'You're a trained fighting man, Carr. You did a good job in Korea and I happen to think that's important. But it isn't a very saleable talent. Well, we taught it you—so maybe we owe you something.' He nodded at the plate. 'That, anyway.'

'You're wrong, of course,' I said softly. 'A good fighter pilot's never working for anybody but himself.'

'Maybe. You still did a good job. And I think that about covers it. Unless it's too late, of course.'

I twisted my eyebrows at him. 'What d'you mean?'

'I hear you lost your plane in the Republica a couple of weeks back.'

'That's right.'

'And now you have an old bombing plane.'

'Walt Whitmore has it.'

'And you fly it.'

I nodded. But if news of the Mitchell was spreading so far and so wide, perhaps it was time to put my cards on the table. I mean pretend to. I said: 'So? You think Whitmore wants to get mixed up in Republica politics?'

He sipped his beer, frowned, and sipped again. 'No-o,' he said finally. 'That's what I can't figure. Nothing in his file suggests he'd do anything so altruistic. Hell, nothing in his file suggests he knows any words that long. And I can't see why else he'd get involved. But——'

'You've got a file on *Whitmore*?'

'Sure. We've got a file on everybody with that much money—if we know they've got it. There's two things make a crook: one's wanting a million, the other's having it.'

'I'd settle for less.'

'And your plane back, perhaps? You wouldn't have done a deal with Jiminez, would you?'

'I wouldn't know Jiminez from the cat's grandmother.'

'You knew his son.'

'I didn't *know* I knew his son—not until after he got shot. By the people you seem so fond of back in the Republica.'

He eyed me thoughtfully. 'Now there's a funny thing. Because political assassination's mostly an amateur business. Tends to make a man a martyr. You know people have been writing *Diego* on the walls in Santo Bartolomeo this last week? Me, I wouldn't have thought he rated it, from what I'd heard.'

I just shrugged.

He ploughed on regardless. 'Particularly dictators don't like assassination. Not since Trujillo got his, anyway. Could plant an idea, you know.' He stood up from his bar stool. 'I better get on with my holiday.'

The little brass plaque was lying on the counter. I pushed it towards him. 'You forgot something.'

He looked down at it and sighed. 'I thought it might be too late.'

'No—just that I already have a souvenir.' I tossed the pair of dice on the bar-top. 'These were pinched off General

Bosco. I'll roll you for the next beer—if I do the rolling.'

The barman materialized at my elbow. 'No dicing allowed, sir—now *you* know that,' he said reproachfully.

'We're not playing. These are joke dice; my friend's buying into the company that makes them.'

That got me looks from both Ellis and the barman. But after a moment, the barman faded suspiciously away again.

Ellis juggled the dice in his hand. 'Dictator's dice, huh? Well, I'm not surprised; anybody who shoots dice with a dictator deserves it. Don't get me wrong, Carr: I don't think Castillo and Bosco are saints. But loaded dice don't kill anybody; revolutions do. And never dictators. They've always got a bag of gold bars packed, a fast car to catch the last plane out. It's the poor hungry bastards out on the street to buy a can of beans who get killed by revolutions.' He leant a hand on the bar. 'I *told* you, Carr: 150 revolutions in the last 150 years—and a lot more that didn't work. And how many real democracies and stable economies have you got south of Mexico? But almost all of them killed somebody.'

'A little softer on the violins,' I said sourly, 'and you'll have it in the top ten next week.'

His face got cold and tight. 'All right, Carr; all right. I'm just a sort of cop. They give me a gun so I guess I'm allowed to kill people. But basically I'm supposed to bring them back alive. Now you tell me about fighter pilots.'

'You missed out something about your job: it's pensionable—if you keep your record nice and clean. You think you're *stopping* a revolution in the Republica by running around Jamaica and Puerto Rico waving your little grey list? You're just keeping your record clean.'

For a moment, I thought he was going to hit me. But he'd been in the FBI too long for that. After a moment he said quietly: 'It's the professionals who do the real killing, Carr. Give the guy in the street a gun and he wouldn't know if he was going to hit a barn door or next Tuesday.' He reached and picked up the metal plaque. 'I guess it was too late all along. Maybe it'll be in time for someone else.' He slipped it in his pocket.

Just to needle him, I said: 'You could be wrong, of

146

course. If Jiminez ever took over, your State Department might suddenly decide he was a good thing and everybody who helped him was a hero.'

'Sure. Or they might just be smart enough to guess that most of the people who helped were the people who turn up helping any revolution. And a Government Department never throws away a list, Carr. They get paid on the number of filing cabinets they can fill up.'

There wasn't anything to say to that, so I didn't say it. He just looked at me a few moments longer and then walked quietly away, out into the high midday sun.

By the time I got back to Boscobel, the scene-painters had finished and gone and the Mitchell stood glowing silver in the afternoon sun and looking, oddly, more shabby than ever. Maybe that the paint didn't so much hide the wrinkles and dents as suggest somebody wanted them hidden. On film, she'd probably look clean and new; close up, on the ground, she was an honourable old lady with paint forced on her face by some young creep in a pink mesh shirt.

The electricians were still working, so I just handed out a few 'Jolly good show—you chaps really *do* know your business, what?' remarks such as pilots use for ground crews who are doing something totally incomprehensible. And went away again.

I hoped they did know their business, though. After sixteen years' flying, the most important thing I'd learned about electricity in airplanes is that it's the first thing to go wrong.

I checked the weather again with a phone call to Palisadoes met office—tomorrow's wind was forecast the same as today's, but the circular disturbance was getting a little more circular and disturbing. Still, it hadn't grown up enough to earn a name yet.

But that night, it did: Hurricane Clara.

21

SHE was the third ugly sister of the season—Annette and
Belinda having come and gone in the usual way: a couple
of days snarling around outside Barbados and Martinique,
then crawling off north-east to die in some uninhabited
corner of the Atlantic.

Clara had started the same way. But that night she came
to a near-stop a couple of hundred miles north of Antigua,
wound herself up into fury and headed westwards. By nine
o'clock in the morning, when I first heard of her from the
Palisadoes met office, she was already north of Puerto Rico
and still coming.

I had another cup of coffee while I thought about it, then
got the desk to call me a taxi—the art director had confiscated my jeep the day before—and went up to the church
location, where they were supposed to be starting filming.
They were—or at least, everybody was there and well into
the day's snoozing and poker playing. It was as quiet as I'd
learnt to expect it: the only sound was a monotonous drone
that was half the generator truck, half the sound man swearing at his equipment.

Roddie's church was a pretty impressive affair: fifty feet
tall, twin-towered, built of four-hundred-year-old stone with
moss in the cracks. You had to get within a few feet to see
the stone was rough-plastered boards, the moss plastic, and
the whole thing just a façade pinned on scaffolding.

J.B., Luiz, Whitmore and Miss Jiminez were sitting around
my jeep under the shade of a palm at the edge of the plaza
and drinking coffee out of paper cups. Whitmore seemed
pleased to see me; Miss Jiminez looked as if she could have
managed without.

'She all ready to go?' Whitmore asked.

'Getting on that way.'

J.B. handed me a cup of coffee.

'Thanks.' I thought of telling them about Agent Ellis
popping up over here, but decided not. If I thought he
represented an extra risk, it was up to me to say so—and

cancel the raid. I was still a free man—as J.B. would have pointed out.

I said: 'I need to see the bombs before I do the final work. Heard any more about them?'

Whitmore grunted. 'Supposed to be sailing yesterday. We should get 'em maybe tomorrow.'

'All good modern stuff, non-corroded, guaranteed to explode in the right time and place and not before. Am I right?'

He shrugged. 'Fella, we just got to wait and see.'

I nodded, looked up at the church. 'How long were you planning on shooting here?'

'Today, maybe a coupla scenes tomorrow.'

'I should try and get it finished today; there may be a hurricane heading this way.'

The director called: 'Walt: we're ready to go.'

He said to me: 'Stick around,' then climbed into the jeep. Several people shouted 'Quiet,' the camera crew laid down their cards, and Whitmore drove the jeep up in front of the church, stopped, got out, looked around, lit a cigarette.

The director shouted: 'Cut!' Then they did it three more times.

Luiz passed me a script so that I could see what was going on. Bolivar Smith comes into the plaza with his load of guns (the back of the jeep was stacked with empty rifle boxes) to meet the rebel chief but can't find anybody but a lovable old priest. However, the lovable old priest goes into a bit of useful dialogue which tells the audience that (a) Amazonia is a poor but lovable country run by a cruel dictator, and (b) Whitmore is a hard-hearted gun-runner who's ready to sell his goods to the dictator if the rebels can't find the pesos to pay for them.

This, of course, is before the love of a peasant girl (the girl whose scenes Whitmore had shot in a hurry a month before because he couldn't stand her) converts him not only to handing over the guns for free but leading the rebellion for them as well.

And they live happily ever after in a real democracy with a stable economy.

149

He walked back, leaving the jeep in front of the church while the camera crew produced a burst of energy and shifted the camera a few yards forward.

'So what's about this hurricane?'

'The eye can't get here in less than two days even if it's coming and it probably isn't. But it sounds pretty wide, and you can get some rough stuff at the edges. You remember Hurricane Flora, a couple of years ago? It hit Cuba, two-three hundred miles north—but we got sixty-knot winds and several inches of rain down here. It washed out half the mountain roads, knocked out telephone lines and fouled the water supplies.' I nodded at the church. 'And I don't think *that'll* take sixty knots.'

'You're damn right, fella.' He frowned thoughtfully.

'And I may want to get the Mitchell off the island. *She* won't take sixty-knot winds, either.'

'Yeah. Well—let us know if you're going. Now—anything more you want for the plane? Howsabout armament?'

I shrugged. 'If you can find a couple of Browning ·50s and a few hundred rounds, I'll take them along.'

'Pretty big order.' He frowned. 'I can get a coupla tommy-guns or automatic rifles, but . . .'

'Skip it, then. They'd be just a dead weight. I wasn't counting on anything, anyhow.'

J.B. said: 'You're going to do it unarmed?'

'A Vampire carries four twenty-millimetre cannon. If they get one of them up, a tommy-gun won't make any odds. You don't shoot down airplanes with tommy-guns.' Then I remembered Whitmore planned to do just that—in the film 'Begging Mr Whitmore's pardon, of course.'

Luiz smiled and said: 'In the air you need firepower. An aerial machine gun fires at about twice the normal rate of a ground gun.' Then, seeing my expression, he explained: 'I was a gunner in the Air Corps during the war.'

Miss Jiminez jerked around to stare at him: this was something he hadn't told her, either. She'd been thinking of him as an actor and—*abracadabra*—he was suddenly a warrior. A toad turned into a prince.

I asked: 'What'd you fly in?'

'Some B-20s—once or twice even the Mitchell.'

'Where'd you get to?'

He gave Miss Jiminez the sad apologetic smile of a prince about to turn back into a toad and said, to me: 'Texas. They made me an instructor. Possibly they decided actors were too valuable to risk in combat. Or just possibly they were keeping back the best men to defend Texas. After all—Texas never *did* get invaded. Can I be sure that was not my doing?'

I grinned sympathetically. Like most fighter pilots, I had a low opinion of air gunners' usefulness—and a high regard for their problems. A fighter pilot just has to point his aeroplane and press the trigger—and damn few are even much good at that. An air gunner is shooting sideways, upwards and downwards from a moving platform at a moving target —and with usually only a quarter of the firepower of the fighter he's shooting at.

But Miss Jiminez had missed one point: Luiz must have been good. They might have kept him off operations because he was Hollywood, but that wasn't why they'd made him an instructor: they didn't want the gunners who *were* going operational trained half-heartedly.

Under his Beverly Hills-Spanish manners, I was beginning to see Luiz as a tough, competent character.

The director called: 'Walt—we're ready.'

An elderly actor whom I hadn't met but recognized from several other Whitmore films was standing by the church doorway, dressed in a dusty set of priest's robes. Whitmore walked over and stood near him; somebody put a part-smoked cigarette in his hand; the director moved him a couple of inches and then scurried back behind the camera and started the scene going.

The priest said politely: 'You are looking for someone, Señor?'

Whitmore: 'Just a guy, Father.'

'On business, Señor?'

'He ordered some . . . merchandise. I just hauled it in over the hills.'

The priest nodded. 'That is your hoss in the—goddamn it, I mean *jeep*.'

The director howled: 'Cut!'

The priest shook his head and spat sadly. 'Hell, Boss, I *knew* I'd forget this one ain't a Western.'

Behind me, J.B. said softly: 'Don't we all?'

I got to Boscobel soon after eleven, and for once the joint was jumping. Mechanics and pilots were shoving the crop-spraying planes into the single hangar; other pilots and a couple of local farmers who owned light planes were crowding the counter of the terminal hut, studying a weather chart, listening to a transistor radio, yelling at the clerk to ring Palisadoes met office yet again.

I asked the latest news and five people told me. Clara was still moving along roughly in our direction—slightly south of westwards, and had last been seen about two hundred and fifty miles north-east of the Republica.

'She's big,' a spray pilot added. 'Fifty-knot gusts reported 300 miles ahead of the eye.'

'But what d'you bet we learn from the Republica and Haiti and Cuba?' the man at the radio asked sourly.

That was a snag—three snags. Clara would be affecting the Republica now, probably Haiti and Cuba by midnight. But all three were notoriously bad at broadcasting useful weather reports. Cuba and the Republica because they were just naturally secretive, Haiti because it's just Haiti.

And while American weather flights would track the eye of the hurricane well enough they wouldn't necessarily check all its edges—and it was the edges, particularly the leading edge, that interested me.

The spray pilot said cheerfully: 'Sorry there's no room in the hangar, Keith.'

'I'll send you a postcard from Caracas,' I said. 'Sun shining, light sea breeze, wish you were here.'

The man with the radio chuckled. 'Just after he'd got the girl from Caracas installed at Shaw Park. Man, have you *seen* her?' He took his hands off the radio long enough to make Miss Jiminez-shaped gestures in the air.

'I've seen her,' the spray pilot said. 'You know, Keith— I'd say God was watching you. You bring in a girl and He

152

sends a hurricane to test you: if it's really love you wouldn't let a little wind stop you.'

'As the actress said to the bishop,' the radio man added.

I stepped to the door and looked up at the sky. So, super-stitiously, did every other pilot in the group. But it was still clear and blue except for the fluffy white cumulus building up on the Blue Mountains; the wind was the normal gentle easterly. Nothing to see—yet.

But the eye of a hurricane isn't big; the hard core, the 150-m.p.h. winds spinning around the calm centre, isn't usually more than forty miles across. And that's the part that does the real damage: guts houses, throws steamers halfway up Main Street, flips heavy aircraft on their backs. But it's still only the yolk of a broken egg; the white spreads far and wide. Clara could be changing clouds 1,000 miles from her eye, dragging winds into an anti-clockwise spiral 500 miles ahead.

And there was our trouble: coming as she was, the first hint we'd get of Clara would be a shift of wind so it came from the north. And with only an east-west runway—like every runway in Jamaica—a north wind would be a cross-wind. It might be too much crosswind to risk a take-off. So I could find myself pinned down with the eye still nearly five hundred miles off—and even if it didn't arrive for another twenty-four hours, me and the Mitchell would still be here when it did.

The spray pilot asked: 'Going this afternoon?'

It would make sense. Yet the first wind-shift could hardly come before three o'clock in the morning. And it might not come at all. Sooner or later Clara would *have* to recurve—turn north and east. And Caracas, or any other safe airport south of here, was a lot of petrol away . . .

'I'll wait,' I decided.

'It must be love,' the radio man said.

The spray pilot snorted. 'If he's got any sense he'll be sleeping with the plane tonight.'

I nodded. It would be nice to trust the met office to ring me at the hotel if the wind shifted northerly and reached more than, say, fifteen knots, but . . . I'd be sleeping with the plane. I was the aircraft captain.

I walked up the runway to see how the electricians were getting on and warn them not to leave any loose ends this evening. But they were just about finished. A new set of clean, bright plastic-covered wires threaded along the dowdy soundproofing behind the cockpit; a neat little panel of one master switch and four press-buttons on the instrument panel.

'Works okay,' the chief assured me. 'And when they've finished the scene, we'll strip it out. Can use them coils and magnets again. Unless you was thinking of setting up professionally as a bomber?'

Big joke. Everybody laughed brightly.

I had a quick drink at the Golden Head, then back to the hotel to stockpile a little sleep, stopping on the way to buy an oil lamp.

At seven I woke up and rang the Palisadoes met office— and Clara was still coming. Reports were also in about what she'd done to Puerto Rico during the early morning: trees and telephone lines down, flooding, landslips in the interior —the usual catalogue. But all at a range of three hundred miles at least. The Republica must have got the same treatment during the day. Well, I just hoped General Bosco got caught out of doors without a raincoat.

But not me. I wanted no part at all of sister Clara. She sounded a very big girl by now.

I washed, had a solitary drink at the bar, a leisurely dinner, and finally forced myself to head for Boscobel at half-past nine.

★ 22 ★

At this time, I had the strip to myself. The terminal hut was dark and locked, the hangar of small planes quiet. At this end of the island, Hurricane Clara was strictly my problem from now on.

154

I walked down to the east end of the runway with the hurricane lamp, lit it, and hung it up on a tree just right of the runway. At 3,000 feet it would be just a spark of light, but that's all you really need for a night takeoff: an aiming point. As long as I remembered to aim left of it.

I walked back up to the Mitchell. There, I took off the rudder control locks so that the first north wind would bang the rudders and wake me—in the unlikely event of my being asleep. Then, because you don't officially start a sleepless night until you start trying to sleep, I sat down against the nosewheel, lit my pipe, and breathed smoke at the sky.

It drifted away slowly. The night was very still, very clear and very dark, with that gigantic echoing distant darkness you only get in the tropics. Not quiet, though: the trees and bushes—not quite a jungle—on either side of the runway buzzed and clicked and purred busily, with an occasional squawk or squeal to break the monotony. But a tropical night never gets spooky the way a northern night can. At least, not on an island where the worst things that can bite you are scorpions and hotels.

I smoked and looked at several thousand stars and wondered if, somewhere out there among the bug-eyed green monsters, there wasn't some poor bug-eyed green bastard sitting under an old bomber waiting for an ammonia storm and looking out at the stars and wondering if, somewhere out there . . .

On an engineering-type guess at the stars and odds involved, I decided there probably was. And maybe he was even thinking about how he'd come to get mixed up in somebody else's war and trying to work out how he felt about it. And perhaps remembering that he'd have no bomb-aimer, so he'd have to go in low, like a fighter-bomber, and wondering how low he dared go with 500-pounders. Even assuming the delayed-action fuses worked on bombs that had probably been stockpiled for years in the steam heat of some Central American hideout . . .

I banged my pipe out on the brake drum and went to bed.

I didn't know what woke me, except that I wasn't much

asleep anyway and tuned to catch the first sound at the start of the north wind. I just found myself sitting up among the engine and cockpit covers in the rear fuselage and listening.

Nothing.

So I went through the usual charade of pretending I was going to get back to sleep without getting up to make sure there was nothing. After a bit of that, I crawled over to one of the old gun windows.

Two men, walking up the runway in the starlight towards me.

A couple of old crop-spraying friends come to tell me Clara had recurved north and I could cease my lonely vigil? Like Hell. I woke up with a jolt. As the two rounded the end of the wing, they both pulled out knives.

For a moment I thought about sealing myself up tight in the Mitchell. I could probably have done it: an airplane is a fairly solid affair. All I needed to do was jam the floor hatch tight . . . Then I knew I'd got to go down there.

Oh yes? And with what?—against two knives.

No use looking around; it was as dark as the inside of a coffin in here. I wondered if I'd left any tools lying around —but I knew I hadn't. And somebody would have pinched them anyway.

Then I remembered the tail 'gun', the piece of painted broomstick stuck through the rear-gunner's window. I crawled quickly and, I hoped, quietly back there.

It jammed for a second, then slid free; it was only held in by insulation tape. About three feet long and smooth in my hands, which suddenly seemed damp.

I poked a cautious eyebrow up into the transparent aiming blister above. They were standing a few yards off, staring at the side of the airplane. I froze, thinking they'd heard me. But they seemed to be discussing something. Finally one of them got out a piece of paper, looked carefully around, and struck a match to read it by. The other leant in over his shoulder.

Two sharp Spanish faces, one with a small black moustache. Open-necked white shirts. I couldn't see any more. The match died. They looked back at the airplane, discussed a little more—then moved forward, under the wing.

I crawled for the hatch. It was open, for ventilation and wind noise. I eased down, hoping that the little collapsible step wouldn't creak. But it was too rusty and jammed-up for that. Me and my broomstick arrived on the tarmac a few feet behind the wing without being spotted.

One of them was bending down beside the starboard wheel, the other out by the nose. I took three long careful steps and, as I reached the wing, ran.

The man by the nose saw me and yelled. The other jerked up and around, his hands and knife coming up in front of his chest. I swung the stick like a baseball bat.

It crashed through his hands and thumped on his chest; he bounced back against the engine. But he still had the knife.

I lunged with the stick, like a bayonet. He said the Spanish for 'Oof' and folded forwards—and the knife clinked on the tarmac.

But now the second man was coming around the propeller. I stooped, grabbed the knife, and waggled it fiercely, to show him I was in the same business by now. He stopped.

'*Avanze, amigo,*' I suggested. I wanted him under the wing with me. If he knew about knife-fighting, he knew about it in the open and the light. I didn't know any more than you pick up from American films about teenage life in the rich suburbs. But under the wing was my world. I'd worked here, had an instinctive feel of heights, distances, obstructions.

Slowly, he hunched into the knife-fighting crouch, the blade weaving hypnotically in front of him. He knew, all right.

I shortened my left-hand grip on the stick for a quicker swing and copied his crouch.

'You may have plane tickets,' I said conversationally, 'but they won't be any use tomorrow. All flights'll be cancelled. There's a hurricane coming—*un huracán*—so you'll be stuck here. Just waiting in the final departure lounge, for the police. It'll be like picking money out of the gutter. *Apúrese, amigo.*'

He *apúresed*, all right—a fast sliding step and a wriggling

157

thrust with the knife. I caught it on the stick and tried to twitch the knife out of his hand; no luck. I lunged myself and he stepped back and banged into a propeller blade and swore, but when I lunged again he'd slipped away.

He circled towards the wingtip, rotating me so that my back was to the first friend, still gasping and grunting down by the wheel—but due to wake up and join the party at any moment.

All right: if his pal had decided he should play a part, let him play a part. I stepped aside and back, dropped the stick and grabbed the man up by shoving a forearm under his chin and lifting. Then I banged the haft of the knife against his ribs. I thought I heard both of them gasp.

'You understand,' I said to the one with the knife, 'that if this fight is to go on I must first kill your friend. *Es justo*, no?'

'*Como usted quiera.*' As you like. But perhaps not quite nonchalant enough to be convincing. The man on my arm squirmed nervously.

I said: '*Como usted quiera*,' and swung the knife wide so it glinted in the starlight.

The other man said: 'No!'

I waited. Car headlights swept across the airstrip. Two cars.

I yipped: '*Policia!*' although I didn't think it was.

The man with the knife looked—at the cars, at me, at the trees on the edge of the runway. Suddenly he chose the trees.

I let the man on my arm drop and he dropped, saying something both unmistakable and unforgivable about his partner's mother as he went down.

I warned him not to hurry off, then stepped out to meet the cars. As they pulled up, I recognized them: Whitmore's station-wagon, J.B.'s Avanti. The gang was all here—right down to Miss Jiminez.

Whitmore stepped out, saw the knife in my hand, and said: 'We're friends. You don't need that, fella.'

'Not mine. Belongs to a couple of gents who came calling.' And nodded at the man under the wing. 'The other's heading for the hills.'

That stiffened them. Then Miss Jiminez plunged a hand

158

into her vast crocodile bag and came up with a silver-plated automatic. 'Where are they? They killed my brother.' The pistol swung in a rather too comprehensive sweep.

'Not with knives, they didn't,' I said mildly.

Whitmore and Luiz walked up under the wing and came out half-carrying the man over to the cars' headlights.

'What are you all doing here?' I asked. I'd finally had time to look at my watch, and it was just past one in the morning.

J.B. said: 'We got some news. It can wait, though.'

In the pool of light from the headlights Miss Jiminez was pointing the gun at the trio of Whitmore, Luiz and the man.

Whitmore said testily: 'Put that damn thing away.'

Reluctantly, she decided it wasn't really necessary and tucked it back in her bag. 'But he must talk. We must *make* him to talk.'

In the light, the man looked about fortyish, medium high, medium fat and much more than medium frightened.

Whitmore said: 'You heard the lady, Start talking.'

The man shrugged and muttered: 'No unnerstan'.'

Whitmore clamped a vast hand on his shoulder and shook him like a jammed door. Miss Jiminez said: 'We must make him to talk now. Some torture.' She looked around for inspiration.

I said: 'Why don't I start up an engine and you feed his arm into the propeller? By the time you reach his elbow he'll probably be talking a blue streak.'

J.B. said: 'Are you *serious*?'

I shrugged. 'As much as anybody here. What do we want him to talk about? Where he comes from?—we know where he comes from. Who sent him?—we know who sent him. What for?—we know. Ask him about the weather in Santo Bartolomeo and throw him away.'

Whitmore let go and stood back. 'You could have a point there, fella.'

Miss Jiminez stared: 'You mean—to let him go free?'

I said: 'Unless you want him as a souvenir.'

She frowned, trying to adjust to the idea. Then she said slowly: 'But a principle of good counter-espionage is never

159

to give the enemy even a negative report—unless it is deceptive, of course. Do we wish him to report failure?'

'But his pal got away anyhow; we can't stop *him* reporting. Just hope he knows dictators well enough to be scared of saying he fell down on the job.' I walked over to the man and, standing clear of his breath, ran my hands through his pockets. As I expected, I came up with a passport.

I looked up in time to catch a stare of sullen hatred. 'Now look,' I said quietly, 'I just saved your life. Not your job, perhaps, but at least your life. Don't come looking for this passport: I'll burn it. And don't come looking for me; you aren't good enough. *Vamos, amigo.*'

He went, reluctantly and unbelieving at first, then accelerating. By the time he reached the trees he was in top gear.

I tapped the passport against the knife, still in my hand. 'It'll delay him, even if he dares go back there. And taking a man's passport is a pretty childish punishment: he'll hate to admit to it.'

J.B. said: 'What I don't see is why they didn't use guns. I mean, if they used one at a busy airport like Kingston at around nine o'clock, why not on a deserted airstrip at one in the morning?'

The legal mind.

I said: 'They weren't after me—just the Mitchell. Going to slash her tyres. They didn't know I was here at all. Spent an age standing out there arguing if it was the right plane. I suppose the markings threw them off.' I nodded at that 'Amazonian' insignia on her flank.

Whitmore said: 'That'd have fixed her, huh? Slashed tyres?'

'No spares. They must've guessed that. But I could get some in a few days. They should have guessed that, too.'

'A few days is all they need.'

'What d'you mean?'

He jerked his head. 'Juanita—she got a radio message from her old man. He wants the attack for—' he looked at his watch '—thirty hours' time.'

After a while, I said slowly: 'Well, if the bombs are here by then—and I can rig a fusing circuit——'

Whitmore said flatly: 'No bombs.' Then to J.B.: 'Tell him.'

She unfolded a copy of the *Miami Herald* and read tonelessly: ' "Four airplane bombs were found hidden under the nets of a fishing boat boarded by a Guatemalan Navy patrol boat in the Gulf of Honduras last night. The destination of the bombs is not known for certain, but it was surmised that they were headed for anti-Castro rebels in Cuba or possibly even Florida . . ." Well, they're wrong.'

'They aren't likely to be wrong for ever. What happens when the boat crew talks?'

Whitmore said: 'They didn't know. We were dealing with a guy in Kingston and he was sending out a boat to meet 'em halfway.'

Then I remembered Agent Ellis and his 'holiday'. If the FBI had once had contacts here, Ellis was old enough to have known them—and bright enough to have remembered them.

He should be able to claim expenses on this holiday.

But I just nodded and said: 'Well—that seems to do it. So Jiminez can't move. Anyway, we could have a hurricane here tomorrow.'

Luiz said quietly: 'That is exactly the point, my friend: the hurricane. The Republica has had bad winds and rain all day. Telephones are out, roads are blocked by landslips, communications are mostly gone. The army is stranded in the hills, the jets have been grounded all day. That is what Jiminez wants: he can take over Santo Bartolomeo before anybody knows.' He sighed. 'It makes sense . . . so he moves at midnight. In twenty-three hours' time.'

'It makes sense if the Vampires were blown around, or if Ned flew them off the island——'

'The message,' Miss Jiminez said, 'says they are still there and they were not harmed.'

'Then tell him not to move! Christ, with the Vamps loose——'

'Capitan,' she said calmly, 'we have solved the problem. You will drop mortar shells instead.'

Whitmore said quickly: 'Seems there's a shipment of 3-inch mortar shells on the way to Jiminez. We can get 'em diverted here before tomorrow night.'

Miss Jiminez said: 'For the same weight, you can carry nearly two hundred shells. In fact, it might be better than bombs anyway.'

I looked carefully around them. 'Mortar shells?' I said. 'Two hundred of them? How do I attach them to just four shackles? And fused, I suppose—*live*, before I took off. It just needs one to shake loose among two hundred . . . I want a fast take-off, but not without the plane.'

Miss Jiminez gave me a look that made it clear Clausewitz wouldn't have condescended to fight in the same war as me. Even on the other side.

J.B. said: 'Well, no posse, no horse—better turn in your badge, Carr.'

Whitmore heaved his shoulders, growled: 'I suppose we could always throw rocks at them.'

'We'd bloody well better, if he's really going to make his move,' I growled. Then an idea struck. 'Although bricks would be better.'

They stared at me. Whitmore said: 'Bricks? D'you mean that?'

'Yes, I mean it.'

'*Bricks?* What'd they do to jets?'

'Ever seen a jet fighter that's hit a brick wall at 150 miles an hour?'

After a while he said: 'Yeah—I mean no, but I get the idea.'

'It works the other way round, too. We throw the brick wall at the jets—at 150 miles an hour.'

J.B. said: 'D'you think a brick would knock out a jet?'

'Hell, you run into a bird at that speed and it'll knock a hole in a metal skin. And Vampire fuselages aren't even metal: they're plywood. With a lot of delicate stuff inside: radio, hydraulics, ancillary drives. We won't turn them into scrap, like a bomb would, but I'm damned if I'd fly a fighter with several brick-sized holes in it. We'll wreck some and

162

knock out the rest for several days—and that's all you need, isn't it?'

Luiz said: 'One day is probably all we need.'

Whitmore asked quietly: 'How about loading bricks on just four shackles?'

'Yes.' That was a point I hadn't thought out. There was another silence while they let me get down to it.

Suddenly I remembered I was giving up smoking. 'Anybody got a cigarette?'

Without a word, Whitmore handed one over: Luiz flicked a Zippo under my nose.

'Thanks.' I went back to deep thought. It was very quiet in the cold, still glare of light from the headlamps. The things in the trees had given up squawking and squealing and either got down to business quietly or knocked off for the night. The stars were still there, but somehow flatter and dimmer, as if already touched by the dust of the coming day. I didn't know anybody up there.

Whitmore said gently: 'Well, fella?'

'Nets,' I decided. 'Fisherman's nets.'

'Huh?'

'When I first came out here, I knew a pilot who was using an old bomber to fly nitro-glycerine up to a mining company in the Andes. You know how nitro behaves? Well, he slung it in a fisherman's net in the bomb bay. So it was a sort of hammock, cushioned against rough air bumps. But if he got stuck in really bad weather, he could open the bay doors, press the shackle release—and no nitro to worry about.'

'And it worked?' Luiz asked.

'Fine. Until one day some fool pressed the release when they were still refuelling on the ground. That was five years back and on a clear day you can still hear the echoes. But he wasn't a particular friend of mine anyhow.'

A short silence. Then Luiz said quietly: 'My friend, are you cheering yourself up with these little stories?'

I grinned. 'Sorry. But I think we can do the same thing. Except use several nets, stretched along the bomb-bay in layers. With bricks on each. Then I can release them in sequence, one-to-three-four, right down the line.'

Whitmore frowned. 'Would that give you enough spread to hit eleven jets?'

'I think so. The bricks'll be pouring out of just one end of the net, so that'll give them a spread. And they aren't streamlined, so some'll topple and slow up a bit, some'll fall end-on, and that'll spread them a bit more. And I'll be going in low—hundred feet or so—so they'll still have most of their forward speed. So those that miss will probably bounce or slide, and that could rip off a wheel—at 150.'

Whitmore looked around at each of us in turn. 'Well,' he said finally, 'that seems the best we can do—right?'

Miss Jiminez said: 'You are really going to drop just bricks on these airplanes?'

'We ain't got anything else, honey. You heard what Carr said; it adds up. Anyhow—if he just knocks out half of them, we're fifty per cent ahead of the game. Your old man's going to move anyway, right?'

She frowned. 'He seems to be taking the "calculated risk": that he will gain more from the hurricane than he will lose from Capitan Carr.'

I said: 'Thanks.'

'All right, then,' Whitmore said soothingly. 'Tell J.B. what you need and she can track it down in the morning.'

'I need four nets—strong, but not too big. You'll get them in Kingston or MoBay, probably. Then I'd like the remains of that drum of control cable your boys were using to rig the bomb release. And the bricks. Say two thousand pounds of bricks. Don't know where you'd get them.'

Luiz said: 'Roddie used some bricks for the foundation of his church.'

Whitmore snapped his fingers. 'That's right. We're tearing the thing down tomorrow anyway. We just send the bricks along here.'

Luiz smiled, a little wanly. 'There is a philosophy there somewhere, Walt. An illusion of a church is used for a real bombing raid.'

'Hell, are you getting religion?'

'No.' Luiz shook his head. 'Come to think of it, it is not a new philosophy.'

164

THE glow of the station-wagon's lights faded up the coast road. J.B. watched it out of sight, her hand on the Avanti's door.

Then she said: 'So you talked yourself right back into the war. Nobody else would've thought of bricks and nets; the whole deal would've been off.'

'A good deputy's supposed to put up ideas to the sheriff, isn't he?'

She may have winced. 'I might have been wrong about you, Carr. You've really worked on this thing, you really want to go . . . Why?'

I took a deep breath. 'I suppose, because Ned Rafter's there.'

'You mean it's just a private war between you two?' She looked at me curiously, her face very still in the soft underglow from the car's headlights.

I shrugged. 'I suppose, in a way.'

'Just because he beat you? Took your plane off you? So now you've got to beat him?'

'No.'

'He called you a killer.'

'Ah, he's been seeing too many movies. There shouldn't be anybody but killers in fighters.'

'The boy in that jet over Santo Bartolomeo.' And her voice was as cold and distant as the tall night.

I nodded. 'That's right. You'd thought I got into combat in Korea by accident? That I'd shot down three Migs by mistake? Of course I'm a killer; it was my job. And it's the only way I can fight a war—if I'm fighting one.'

'A private war.'

I blew up. 'Christ, so what about your tall friend? I know why Luiz is in it—but Whitmore isn't exactly a great liberal leader.'

She stared. 'At least you're right there. Whenever he talks politics he ends up about three goose-steps to the right of the Nazi Party.'

'That's what I guessed. Well, that shouldn't put him behind Jiminez, but there he is, all right. If *that* isn't a private war . . .'

'You didn't *know*?'

'Know what?'

'I heard him *tell* you. He's got $250,000 in profits frozen in the Republica. And he's also got a piece of paper saying the first thing Jiminez does when he takes over will be unfreeze them. Along with your airplane.'

I just nodded stupidly. But he *had* told me about that money, back in the bar at Santo Bartolomeo. I said slowly: 'And I thought he just wanted to play Bolivar Smith in real life for once.'

'Well, maybe . . . but not at less than his normal rates.'

I found myself laughing softly. 'Well, it sort of restores your faith in human nature. What's good for Walt Whitmore is good for the Republica.'

She looked up sharply. 'You aren't exactly a great Jiminez-for-Presidente man yourself, are you?'

'I don't give a damn about Jiminez; never have. It's not my business. Not my country.'

'So you're just going because you want to get that man Rafter.'

'Well, somebody's got to, haven't they?'

There was a long silence. Then she said curiously: 'Just what d'you mean?'

'*Somebody's* got to stop Ned and those Vamps getting off the ground when Jiminez moves. I'd just as soon stop Jiminez moving—but I can't. So somebody'll get killed. Somebody'll poop off guns in the streets, stick somebody else against a wall. All right, so that's normal. But the Vamps aren't.'

She frowned. 'I still don't get it . . .'

'You wouldn't. Not you, not Whitmore, not Jiminez, not even the generals. None of you's ever seen a real pro like Ned leading a squadron on ground-attack. But I've seen it. I saw Ned and just five planes behind him take out a village in Korea. Napalm and cannon fire. It took them forty-five

166

seconds and then there just wasn't any village. Imagine him and ten planes loose over a nice crowded target like Santo Bartolomeo. No anti-aircraft fire, and maybe six or seven missions a day. Their base is only a few miles out. After that, the town'll just be a dirty word in the history books. And win, lose or draw won't matter. There won't be the pieces to pick up. Nor the people.'

After a time she asked: 'Would the generals really do that?'

'I told you, *they* don't know. Only Ned and I know . . .' Then, quieter: 'Yes, they'll do it. They'll have to: with the Army stuck in the hills, Ned and the Vamps are the only weapon they've got. They'll use him.'

'Only you're going to stop him.'

'Hurricane permitting.'

She nodded, then walked slowly and thoughtfully out across the headlights to the Mitchell and stood looking up at the shining wrinkled side. And said softly: 'And that's the only reason?'

'Call it good commercial sense, if you like,' I growled. 'There won't be much trade for a charter pilot to pick up in SB after Ned and the boys have worked the town over.'

'I like your noble reasons better, Keith.' Then her voice got serious again. 'It's not something personal against Rafter?'

'I left that business eight years back—remember?'

'Was . . . this sort of thing why?'

'Perhaps. Or perhaps because you get to like it. You like seeing a man go down burning.' I shrugged. 'Why not? Most people who're good at their jobs like the job—and I was good, all right. But—I didn't have to like liking it. And I couldn't change: go on shooting down fighters but change the reasons. I couldn't think "That's a blow for freedom and democracy" or "That's probably saved a pal's life." I'd always be doing it because I was Keith Carr, the Great Unbeatable—because I liked it.'

'But—tomorrow?'

I smiled. 'You don't count the ones you knock out on the ground anyway. Old fighter pilot tradition.'

167

She looked up at me. 'Keith—I'm sorry; I was wrong about you . . .' She shivered, as if from a sudden wind or an old memory. But there wasn't any wind. 'Give me a cigarette, will you?'

'Sorry.'

'Of course: you aren't an owner-smoker. Some in the car.'

I found a pack on the crash-pad above the dashboard. I also found the headlight switch and turned it off. Then I walked back to her in the quiet, dusty starlight.

We lit the cigarettes. For a long time nobody said anything. Far down the strip a small light twinkled like a fallen star; my oil lamp, waiting patiently to become a flarepath. Waiting for the north wind.

I reached and ran a hand through her long, tangled silky hair. She stiffened. 'Wait—Keith . . . You know I fixed this whole thing. I got Jiminez's signature on his promise to the Boss Man, that afternoon.'

'I'd guessed that. A nice watertight contract?'

'Look—I'm Whitmore's *lawyer*.' There was a small, desperate edge to her voice. 'I *had* to say it was a good deal. He spends twelve thousand on the airplane and a few hundred on you—and most of it deductible—for a chance, a good chance, at a quarter of a million. I *had* to say that's a good deal. But not for you. You don't have to be any part of it.'

'I know. I'm a free man.'

'Keith, you could get killed.'

'Not me. I told you: I was good. The type that waits until he's got the height and he's up-sun and can get the other fighter in the back. We don't take risks. We don't gamble. We cheat.'

'Korea was a long time ago,' she said doubtfully. 'You could have forgotten——'

I stretched my hands and laid them on her shoulders. 'Like I had over Santo Bartolomeo that day?'

And suddenly she was holding me, her strong body straining against me, her hair flooding my eyes. And whispering: 'Keith—don't get yourself killed, just *don't* . . .'

Then the dusty starlight and the lamp glittering at the

end of the strip and the north wind itself, if it were there, were something in another country, beyond another hill.

Much later, and much sleepier, she said: 'You *are* slipping, you know ... you forgot to ask me what the J.B. is for.'

'Yes. You must tell me sometime, when we've got nothing better to talk about.'

'I will. I absolutely insist on you knowing. Besides, you might lose your British citizenship if they found out you didn't even know my name.' Then her voice changed. 'What about that man—Colonel Rafter?'

'What about him?'

'If you raid him tomorrow—won't he have to come after you?'

'I don't think so. Ned's a commercial pilot. He flies ground-attack, but just the way Pan Am flies passengers. He won't like it—but he won't come chasing me unless he's got a nice watertight contract saying he'll make a profit out of it.'

She was quiet for a while. I gave up groping around the engine covers for the cigarettes and just lay, watching the dim square of light that was a gun window.

Her voice was sleepy again when she said: 'You know, I've never been seduced in an airplane before. I wonder, if it was flying ...'

'Greedy.'

She chuckled softly. 'Maybe sometime then. Keith—do I get to go with you?'

'Where?'

'Wherever you go—when you get run out of the Caribbean on a rail.'

'Hmm. It may not be exactly a Man and a Home and a Back Yard and ... I don't know what it'll be.'

'I think I'd like that.'

I frowned. 'What about Whitmore?'

'You're going to need a hot lawyer a lot more than he will, after tomorrow. And I don't think you could afford my fees.'

'Why d'you think I seduced you?'

She laughed sleepily and put her arms around me again.

I was woken by a banging on the fuselage side. The morning sun was streaming dustily through the gun windows; the fuselage was stuffy—and empty, apart from the rumpled engine covers.

One of the spray pilots shoved his head up through the aft hatch. 'God, but you charter pilots really believe in your sleep. It's nine o'clock.'

I stared at him blearily. 'What's the weather?'

He grinned. 'No hurricane. She recurved; turned northwest four-five hours ago. So no trip to Caracas.' He looked around the fuselage. 'Well, at least you had a quiet night.'

I nodded. 'Yes. A quiet night.'

★ 24 ★

I STAGGERED down to the Golden Head for a wash and several cups of coffee. I'd finally found J.B.'s pack of cigarettes; I lit one and just sat, brooding.

A quiet night. And suddenly, something in your life that you may never say goodbye to. Something fixed; a commitment. Funny how it changes a man. And funny how it doesn't. I was still Keith Carr, still unbeatable, still going on a visit to Ned Rafter in . . . about seventeen hours' time.

I was back with the Mitchell by ten.

Until the nets and bricks arrived, I couldn't do much practical work, so I sat down in the shade of a wing to work out the theory. I'd said a fighter pilot could do any low-level attack—but perhaps mostly because, like most fighter pilots, I'd never had a high opinion of bomber pilots. In fact, like most fighter pilots, I'd never had a very high opinion of any other pilot.

Now, it began to look a little complicated.

Say I was going in at 150 m.p.h. at 100 feet. In falling a mere 100 feet, a brick would hardly lose any of its forward speed—it would hit the ground when I was still dead overhead. I suddenly became glad I wasn't using bombs.

Working backwards from that, I had to drop the first

170

bricks as many seconds before I passed over the first Vampire as it took a brick to fall 100 feet. Let that be known as Carr's First Law. On to Number Two.

A brick accelerates downwards at 32 feet per second per second—ignoring air resistance. So it falls 16 feet in the first second, 48 in the second, 80 in the third—say two-and-a-half seconds for 100 feet. Bung in air resistance and call it three: I dropped three seconds early. Carr's Second Law.

Number Three was easy: at 150 m.p.h. I was doing just over 200 feet a second, so I dropped a bit more than 600 feet early . . . It seemed a hell of a long way. But it was right.

That left me with just the problems of holding precise speed, height and course and judging exactly 600 and a few feet. Possibly bomber pilots did need a trace of intelligence. The few that ever hit anything, that is.

Whitmore's white station-wagon swung in through the gates and trundled slowly up the runway. I watched it quietly, almost apprehensively. It stopped; Luiz got out. Only Luiz.

I went over to help him unload. He took the bundle of nets, I picked up the small drum of cable.

'From Montego Bay,' he said, carrying the bundle. 'Officially, we are supposed to be having a fishing scene but —such scenes often get cut.'

'All deductible, anyway.'

He dumped the bundle and gave me a look. I avoided it, put down the drum, and started unpicking the nets. 'Whitmore or J.B. coming down?' I asked casually.

'Perhaps when they have the church sequence finished. I spoke to J.B. on the phone. She seemed . . . tired.' Again he tried to catch my eye, but I went on sorting the nets.

They turned out to be about a three-quarter-inch mesh, roughly circular, perhaps ten feet in diameter. I didn't know anything about fishing, but I guessed these had been the type used for casting into the surf—before the snorkel-fisher tourists had chased every fish outside the reef.

Luiz was fingering the end of the cable. 'Why do you need this, my friend?'

'Thread it around the edge of the nets to take the weight.'

I held up the net itself: the edging was thick, rough string, stiff with creosote or something. 'Each net's to hold about five hundred pounds, remember.'

He looked at the cable doubtfully. 'Five hundred pounds . . .'

'Not so much. Just imagine four girls hanging on one end.'

'What a remarkable imagination you have, my friend. But I shall try.' He closed his eyes and smiled dreamily.

I said: 'Oh God.'

He opened his eyes. 'What is it?'

I'd just realized it might be more than 500 pounds—and also why bombers flew so sedately to the target, as if they were afraid of waking the air gunners. You've got a hook that'll take a 500-pounder—but then you do just a one-g turn and the pull on that hook doubles. In fighters, I'd done more than six-g turns. If I'd been carrying a 500-pounder then, the pull on the hook would have topped 3,000 pounds . . .

'I think it'll work,' I said. 'But it'll be a damn gentle ride.'

'I am happy to hear it,' he said. 'Because I am coming also.'

I glared. 'Like hell you are.'

'You recall I was once a gunner?' He beckoned me over to the station-wagon and pointed in through the back window. On the floor lay a fat, heavy-looking rifle. After a moment, I remembered it as something the Americans had used in Korea: the BAR, Browning Automatic Rifle.

After a few more moments I said: 'So you were an air gunner—and you want to bring *that* on an air attack?'

He shrugged, nodded.

I said: 'What is it—·30 calibre? And a cyclic rate of about five hundred rounds a minute?'

He nodded again.

'I see. In Korea we were using Sabres armed with six ·50 calibre guns firing 1,200 rounds a minute each. Thirty or forty times the punch of just that thing. And even then we'd have done better with twenty-millimetre cannons. Christ, *you* know all this, Luiz.'

He smiled deprecatingly. 'My friend—I was good. And I might be lucky.'

'You aren't asking because you're either good or lucky.'

He just said: 'You are worried about the extra weight?'

'Not so much . . .' Him and the gun would only add 200 pounds or less, and that could be balanced by using him as co-pilot, to yank up the undercart the instant we broke ground. I'd prefer an extra 200 pounds than the extra seconds of drag from leaving the wheels down if I couldn't spare a hand at the moment of take-off.

I shrugged. 'All right: you've re-enlisted.'

He nodded graciously—but still didn't tell me why he was coming. It might be because he didn't want just to stand by with Miss Jiminez looking on. Or perhaps as a political commissar, to make sure my resolution didn't get a little weary in the wee small hours.

He picked up one of the nets. 'Perhaps you will show me how I am to do this threading.'

It was a long, hard grind in the sun, and we had to invent the details by trial and error; there's no manual of how to load a bomber with nets full of bricks.

In the end we doubled over the nets—I didn't like cutting and weakening them—into palliasses the dimensions of the bay: about eight by three-and-a-bit. Then I started screwing big ringbolts in four layers, along the bomb rails and at each end of the bay. The cables would be threaded through them as well as the mesh, each end of each cable ending in a loop hooked into a shackle; it had suddenly become useful having two hooks on each shackle.

When I pressed the button, the cables would jump off the hooks, the weight of bricks would force down the net and pull the free cables back through the mesh and ringbolts, letting more and more of the net loose until the load spilled out. That was the theory, anyway.

I knew the cables would jam after a few feet—but all I needed was one end to stay free long enough to open enough net. And I'd have 500 pounds of bricks pulling on it for me.

It was crude and it wasn't going to empty each net in one

173

sudden jerk—but I didn't want it to. I wanted to spill a steady stream of bricks over a whole line of Vampires, not four loads on just four of them.

'But how do you know, my friend,' Luiz asked, 'that they will be neatly lined up for you?'

'We know they are normally, and if Ned doesn't know we're coming . . . Anyway, did you ever see a military air-field where the planes weren't lined up?'

'No-o. But I only saw training fields. There, they lined up even the potatoes at lunchtime.'

'Well, there's a good reason for lining up planes. You can run the refuelling bowsers and rearming trucks and servicing gang right down them, one-two-three-four. Commanders are always getting caught with their planes lined up because they like fast servicing better than dispersing the damn things all over the field.'

'Let us hope so,' he said solemnly, sucking a finger that had got stabbed on an end of cable.

We had a wash, several dabs of iodine, a couple of beers and a light lunch at the Golden Head and were back with the Mitchell by two.

By then I had half the ringbolts in place and Luiz had got two cables cut to the right length and the ends spliced and bound into loops. But still no bricks. And no J.B.

We soldiered on. We had the airstrip to ourselves and the afternoon sun. With its British traditions, Jamaica doesn't have an official siesta—just that everybody goes to sleep in the afternoons.

The inside of the bomb-bay was like a Turkish bath gone critical. I ducked out, lay down under the shadow of the wing, and said: 'Give me a cigarette, will you?'

He threw the pack across.

'Thanks.' I lit one, puffed smoke at the wing above, and asked: 'How much chance does Jiminez stand—if we get the Vamps, I mean?'

He considered. Then: 'Good, I would think. Of course, he is taking a risk at this time of year, with the university on vacation.'

'He's what?'

'The university students, my friend, are always a strong force in any liberal revolution. To make the move when they are on holiday, scattered all over the country, is to forgo valuable support. But the hurricane gives him a great chance to take Santo Bartolomeo. If he can do that, then . . .' He shrugged.

'Then what? He won't have the whole country. And the Army'll roll home sometime—with tanks and artillery and——'

'A revolution is not a war, my friend. It is not even truly a military affair. After all—who is the enemy? Just a few leaders, that is all. Do army officers wish to be at war with the civil servants? The soldiers with the peasants? Does the whole Army wish to fight a colonial war in its own country, among its own homes and wives and children?

'A revolution is an affair of *belief*. You have won when enough people believe you have won. So if you hold the capital, if you name a new government, broadcast on the radio, re-open shops and businesses—and perhaps a foreign government recognizes you—then people say "It is all over; it has happened." Then, truly it *has* happened. If Jiminez can do all these things before the Army can get home—then it will not come home shooting. To do so would be to start a civil war.'

I nodded thoughtfully—and painfully, since I'd forgotten my head was resting on the tarmac. 'But if Jiminez can't hold Santo Bartolomeo that long?'

There was a silence. Then he said quietly: 'Then he has lost. Finished. That is the other side of the coin. People will never believe a man has won if he has once lost before. Until now, Jiminez has been fighting a guerrilla war: never trying to hold on to a position, dodging away into the hills—just keeping his cause alive. But now, he must hold Bartolomeo. Tonight he commits himself—forever.'

'You really have been listening to Miss Jiminez.'

He looked at me, and his dark eyes suddenly seemed very old. Then he smiled sadly. 'My friend, I had no need. In the Republica every child learns reading, writing—and revolution.'

The load arrived soon after four. Two small lorries, each stacked with dirty yellowish bricks. The driver of the first asked me who I was, consulted a paper, then nodded to his two mates to start unloading.

To keep from helping, he offered me a cigarette and asked: 'What you building, man?'

I thought of saying something clever and cryptic like 'a new country', but settled for: 'Shed where I can lock up tools without them getting pinched.'

He believed that. 'Anything getting stolen in Jamaica, man.' He told me about the number of times people had swiped his lorries, and spun it out until every brick was stacked beside the runway.

Luiz had faded quietly away into the Mitchell while this was going on. I suppose the sight of a film star getting his hands dirty might have been suspicious. When the lorries had gone, he came out.

I picked up a brick. 'I'm going to sneak this on to the luggage scales in the terminal hut to find out what they weigh. You can start threading up the first net.

He just nodded, picked up a brick for himself, and bounced it thoughtfully in his hand. I left him to it.

A brick turned out to weigh five and a half pounds as near as dammit, which made 360 to a 2,000-pounds load, or ninety to a net. We got the first net strung—it had to be in place before loading—and started filling it up. It wasn't particularly hard work, just long. We alternated between the one who hauled the bricks and the one who stood bent in the bomb-bay slipping them in over the edge of the net.

We had forty or fifty in when a long black Cadillac—a film company car—whooshed up the runway. Miss Jiminez climbed out; alone.

She smiled at Luiz, then handed me an envelope. I ripped it open.

Dear Keith,

Sorry, but I've got to go down to Kingston on business with Walt. Anyhow, it wouldn't look so good if we were all of us up there today. Suspicious.

Here's your final shooting script:

There are just ten, not eleven, jets now. According to a message from Miss J's old man, they crashed another last week.

Sunrise in SB is at 5.22 tomorrow.

The weather there is supposed to be pretty cloudy. This is a good thing, isn't it? Means you have somewhere to hide. Anyway, for God's sake don't take any risks. You hear me?

And when you get back, if I'm not around DON'T TALK to anyone. Stay under cover until I can tell you what to say.

Look after yourself, Keith;

J.B.

I grinned. It was somehow a very J.B. letter.

Then I shrugged, stuffed it in my pocket, and looked around. Luiz and Miss Jiminez were talking quietly by the bomb-bay.

'They aren't coming down,' I said.

Luiz nodded, as if he wasn't surprised, then said: 'Juanita would very much like to see if the nets work.'

'I'd like to see myself. Climb in and pull the plug.'

'Oh no, my friend. *I* want to watch.'

We glared at each other.

He turned to Miss Jiminez. 'Juanita—perhaps you would care to press the very button which will, tomorrow, strike out such a blow for your father's cause?'

Her eyes glittered. She'd just *love* to.

'You speak like snake, with forked tongue,' I whispered, remembering a line from several Whitmore Westerns.

'My own hands,' he said grimly, 'they loaded that net. I want to *see*.' He shunted her up through the forward hatch.

I shooed the company car away; this was a strictly private demonstration. Luiz dropped out of the hatch again. 'I think she understands the idea. I told her to——'

She understood it.

The net suddenly sagged below the bay, then poured bricks on to the tarmac in a clattering roar. Yellow dust exploded up around the plane.

I said: 'About a half-second delay. That means I'd better drop at . . .' I tried to think where.

Luiz said: 'My God. It works.'

But we were working by the station-wagon's headlights before we had all four nets strung and loaded, brick by filthy, heavy, sharp-edged brick. Any time the Bricklayers' Union wants to bar me from ever handling a brick again, I'll come out and picket myself.

Miss Jiminez didn't last the course: the dirty, slogging little details of war didn't seem to be anything Clausewitz had said much about. She pushed off at dusk.

It was eight o'clock by the time Luiz and I were cleaned up and sitting down at the long Spanish bar of the Plantation Inn.

He said thoughtfully: 'You may have a drag problem, from those nets hanging down after the bricks are gone.'

I'd realized that already, but without seeing any way around it. 'It may not be too bad. If it is, you can try hacking open the bomb-bay with the fire axe and cutting them loose.'

He seemed a little dubious about that, but just grunted and looked at his watch. 'At what time do we take off?'

I pulled J.B.'s letter from my pocket and uncrumpled it. 'Sunrise is at five twenty-two—so it'll be light enough for an attack about fifteen minutes before. Say five minutes after five. It's about four hundred and fifty miles; two and a half hours at normal cruise. Let's aim at a two o'clock take-off and give ourselves half an hour in hand for bad weather or getting lost or a wing falling off.'

He nodded. 'So I'll pick you up at—quarter-past one?'

'Fine.' I finished my drink, stood up, turned away. Then turned back. 'Just why are you really coming on this trip?'

He shrugged. 'Perhaps—I rehearsed being a gunner for three years, in the war. I want to play it, just once, for the camera.'

'Luiz, you're a damned liar.'

But he just smiled. After a moment, I went away.

I had my room door half open before I realized the light was on inside. And not only the light. Miss Jiminez.

This time, she was out of mourning. She was out of practically everything, everything being a tight white silk Chinese dress with a slit skirt reaching almost to journey's end and a high collar with a big cutaway just below to give a fine close-up of her strategic high ground.

I leant limply back on the door, shoving it closed. The last thing I wanted right now was a briefing on what Clausewitz said about how to drop bricks on a line of jet fighters.

I didn't get it. She stood up, slowly, gracefully, and said gently: 'This is an early celebration of tomorrow, Capitan. Would you like a drink?'

There, on the bedside table, was a half-bottle of champagne in a silver ice-bucket. Two glasses.

I nodded blankly and she poured the stuff out—expertly, too. She handed me one and smiled softly. 'To tomorrow, then. I think in England you say "confusion to the enemy"?'

'Er—yes.' Well, that or 'Request take-off', anyway.

'Confusion to the enemy.' She drank, watching me across the glass. I took a quick swallow.

There was a short pause. Then I said: 'Well—it's nice of you to drop in and wish me luck.'

She straightened herself, put her head slightly back and slightly to one side and said simply: 'Capitan, I just wanted to be sure you had—everything you needed.'

My mouth may have been open; I know my eyes were. She might have made it more obvious by having herself brought in naked on a plate with water-cress round the edges, but only might.

But I just couldn't see why. I've got a fairly high opinion of myself—anyway, nobody has a higher one—but I didn't see how I'd suddenly jumped into the class, and bed, of a rich Venezuelan society girl who was well known to despise my strategic reading.

179

She said: 'Tomorrow you must be most brave, most noble, Capitan.'

Then it clicked. She was ready to lay down her . . . well, just lay down, for her father's cause. To ensure my devotion to duty.

Suddenly she was just a big, busty girl in a tarty dress. And I remembered a strong, small body against me in the silence of the Mitchell's cabin—and not bribing me to go out and drop bricks on anybody in the morning.

I finished my glass in a gulp and said deliberately: 'I think I've got everything I need—except sleep.'

A small frown rippled across her forehead. 'Tomorrow, Capitan, you could become a true *liberador*.'

'Maybe. But I'm going anyway, you know.'

'A true hero of the Republica.'

'Sure. I know. They'll name an Avenida Keith Carr and have it end in the Plaza del Mitchell with the starboard induction manifold on a granite plinth and an Eternal Oil Leak dripping at the bottom. And it'll last all of five years. Until the next revolution.'

Her eyes blazed, shocked. 'There will be no more revolutions! When the generals are gone and there is a true democracy . . . You don't believe me?'

I dumped more champagne in my glass. I hadn't planned on any more drinking this evening, but it seemed my plans had stopped mattering anyway.

'My beliefs don't matter,' I said carefully, 'but just for the record, I believe democracy's simply a habit. Like smoking or drinking or driving safely. Not checks and balances, not one-man-one-vote. Just millions of people saying—instinctively—"Christ, they can't do *that*!" But it takes time to build up that sort of instinct. And meanwhile, revolution's a habit, too. Your old man isn't exactly trying to break *that* habit tomorrow, is he?'

'He has no choice!'

I shrugged and said wearily: 'Well . . . maybe he hasn't, in a way. I don't know. I don't even care. Just take it that I'm going tomorrow, if the Mitchell holds up. And that's all you want, isn't it? My reasons don't matter.'

She glared, but a little uncertainly. 'Napoleon believed that morale was three times as important as physical power.'

I grinned. 'But not tonight, Josephine.'

She stared a split second longer, slammed the champagne glass on the floor and stalked out. The slam of the door shivered the whole building.

After a while I just kicked the pieces of glass under the bed, stripped and flopped into bed.

★ 25 ★

A LIGHT, steady tapping woke me. I rolled out of bed, staggered across to the door and jerked it open without remembering to ask who it was. Luiz slid quickly inside and shut the door.

I fumbled on the bedside light and stared at him with the deep hatred of a man still half asleep for another man who is spritely, shaven and neatly dressed in a medium-brown lightweight suit.

'Why that rig?' I growled. 'The invitations didn't say fancy dress.'

'My friend, when you are going to behave illegally, I believe it is a good thing to dress respectably. It may possibly help.' He looked around, found a glass, and filled it with hot black coffee from a flask I hadn't even noticed he was carrying.

I sipped, splashed water around, and scraped a razor over my face without quite mowing off my ears. By then he'd sorted through my clothes and come up with my light-grey washable suit.

'It will have to do,' he said graciously.

Outside, the night was dead still but not quite clear: a faint haze of high cloud washed out most of the stars. It meant a no-wind take-off; better than a crosswind, but not as good as I'd hoped for.

We drove my jeep to Boscobel, and the gate was still

unlocked. So I went up to the Mitchell, left Luiz and collected the hurricane lamp, and then drove to the other end and put it back on its tree.

Then I did a careful pre-flight check of the plane with a torch and climbed aboard just after two o'clock.

Luiz was already in the right-hand seat, the Browning parked down beside him, and twiddling with a transistor radio in his lap.

'Music while we work?' I asked.

'Jiminez planned to take over the radio as the first thing.'

I sat down, remembering the pattern; obviously taking over the radio station—so that you can tell the citizenry that you've taken over everything else even if you haven't—would be top priority.

'Getting anything?'

He frowned. 'No . . .'

'Well, who else'd have a radio turned on at two in the morning?'

'I hope that is it.' But he went on tuning.

'See if you can get Miami for some weather.'

But Miami was off the air or out of range.

I turned on the master switch. 'Let's go, then.'

He watched the lights come on across the instrument panel as I began the starting sequence. 'So—it is really going to happen?'

I looked up, surprised. 'That's what we're here for, isn't it?'

'Yes, of course. One old worn-out American bomber, flown by—forgive me, my friend—by one old English pilot and a worn-out actor is going to drop a load of bricks on some aged jet fighters. Yes, that sounds very much like a Republica revolution to me. Now, I believe it.'

His voice had a bitter edge on it.

I shrugged. '*Dicho y hecho.*' And pressed the energize switch. The lights dimmed; gradually a faint whine started in the port engine as the flywheel built up energy. When the whine had reached a steady note I flicked the switch across to 'Mesh'.

The propeller grunted, groaned, turned, staggered,

coughed, spun. I stabbed the prime button and caught it with the throttle. Blue flames crackled outside the window; in the noise, I motioned Luiz to put on his headset. Now for the starboard engine.

It caught—but as I pushed up the throttle, the whole plane shuddered to a long grinding screech.

I jerked the switch back to *off*, but the grind went on.

'What is it?' Luiz asked—a crackling voice in my head-phones.

'Starter motor's jammed in mesh. Won't come declutched.'

I whanged the pitch to full revs to try and shake it out; all it did was double the racket.

'Shouldn't we start again?' Luiz called.

'That starter'll never start anything again. Just hope it chews itself to pieces soon.'

We waited. Then there was a tearing *thump* and just the engine noise. Something had bust—the flywheel probably. Spinning at a ratio of 100 to 1 with the engine itself, my burst of revs had probably thrown it to 200,000 r.p.m. Good-bye flywheel. I hope you didn't take anything with you when you went.

But the engines both ran up and settled down all right. After a few minutes testing the hydraulics and magnetos, I swung around on to the runway, pointed her just left of the distant spark of light that was the hurricane lamp, and put down full flap. With them and a bit of luck, I was going to make one of the shortest take-offs the old lady had ever lived through.

I made sure Luiz's hand was on the undercarriage lever and *not* on the flaps, shoved the throttles up to full power against the brakes, paused, then flipped off the brakes. And we ran.

But not as fast as at Barranquilla. We were heavier now, 2,000 pounds of bricks and a lot of fuel. On the windless runway we picked up speed slowly . . . slowly . . . slowly . . .

At 80 I tried a little back pressure: the nosewheel lifted slugglishly. I waited, the spark of light rushing closer, getting brighter, then hauled full back on the control column.

And yelled: 'Gear up.'

A sudden roar as the undercart doors started to close, a momentary heaviness as the wheel legs buckled before she was clear of the ground, and then we were flying—just. The light flicked away below, the tops of the trees rushed past, and we were staggering flatly towards the coast, picking up speed. And finally over the sea, retracting the flaps and pulling gently into the laden climb to our cruising height.

I throttled back carefully. After a time Luiz said: 'That was—quite exciting. I understand why you preferred to take off at night.'

'Yes.' I was busy checking everything within reach to make sure its nervous system hadn't been strained by the take-off. I was still worried by the starter motor crack-up; you don't usually bust a large piece of equipment violently without it leaving scars, but nothing was showing up on the starboard engine instruments. And is *was* only a starter motor . . .

I climbed on a heading of 098, both magnetic and true: in this area the magnetic variation was too small to bother with. Twenty minutes after take-off we passed through 8,000 feet. I took her up another 200, levelled out until I had 180 m.p.h. on the clock, then throttled back to lean cruising power and let her slide gently downhill to 8,000 exactly. Known as 'putting her on the step'; you get a little more airspeed for the same fuel, or the same speed for less fuel. Theoretically, you can't do either—but with a good theoretical knowledge of aerodynamics you can prove a bumble bee is too heavy to fly.

When I flattened out again at 8,000, the airspeed had crept up to 185—and it stayed there. I smiled, a little smugly, and started to sing.

> *I didn't want to join the Air Force;*
> *I don't want to go to war.*
> *I'd rather hang around*
> *Piccadilly Underground*
> *Living on the earnings of a high-born lady . . .*

Luiz was looking at me curiously.

'Battle hymn of the RAF,' I explained.

'Ah.' He reached into a pocket. 'You are sure you would not prefer a cigarette?'

We sat almost shoulder-to-shoulder in the cramped cockpit, cold in the high night air rushing past, dim in the faint glow of the instruments. And bracketed by the dry roar of the engines, the splatter of white flame from the exhaust stubs.

An hour after take-off I was squinting through the exhaust flames on my side, trying to make out Pointe à Gravois in Haiti, which should be our first landfall. It wasn't there, but the northern horizon was a rampart of clouds, so probably Haiti was up there somewhere. At this height we were probably getting a dying breath of north wind from sister Clara.

I decided to assume we were on time but off course to starboard. I altered the heading to due east—largely because it was easy to steer. Navigation in the Caribbean is never critical—not with islands popping up every hour to give you a definite fix.

What worried me more was that the starboard engine had missed a couple of beats in the last ten minutes. In itself nothing important, except that I had my mind on that engine after its starter troubles. And airplanes usually play fair with you: they wheeze and cough and tremble before they die—if you're awake enough to notice the signs.

Yet there weren't any other signs: the r.p.m. held steady, oil pressures and temperatures were normal. I laid a hand on the metal of the engine control pedestal. It trembled slightly, but it always had. Just the normal palsies of old age. So . . . So?

Luiz said: 'And still nothing.' He had the radio in his lap again and was twiddling.

'It's only just past three in the morning.'

'I hope you are right.' He turned it off.

The starboard engine missed another beat.

He asked: 'Where do you want me for the attack itself?'

'Better be down in the nose. You've got a good view, there; you can tell me anything you see.'

'My friend, you do not sound very impressed with my . . . usefulness.'

'You know exactly damn well why I'm not.'

The engine missed again—bad enough for him to notice, this time. He turned away, staring out at the exhaust flames.

I had caught a flicker—no more—on the r.p.m. dial, a shudder on the oil pressure. But now both were normal again. Just in the general way a doctor hands out a pill, I pushed the starboard mixture to full rich. It would cool things, if there was a hot spot the temperature gauges didn't show. It might burn off any carbon on the plugs. But mostly it would show the engine that I, the doctor, cared.

Still with his head screwed round, staring out of the window, Luiz asked: 'Do you think we will have to abort the mission?'

'Hell, no.' Or did I mean—Not yet? She'd fly on one engine, all right—it's the first thing you practise with a twin-engined airplane—but she'd be limping along at around a hundred and forty, and that engine would be drinking nearly a gallon a minute. And—damn it—there's no cross-feed on a Mitchell; each engine uses the fuel from the tanks in its own wing. We could run out of fuel on the good engine and still have 400 totally unusable gallons left in the other wing. *If* we lost an engine——

At that point we lost it for about a second; the Mitchell slewed to the right. Then, with a broadside of backfiring, she caught again. Instinctively I hauled her back on to 090 degrees. Yet the oil pressure was normal, the temperatures a bit below—but that was the effect of the rich mixture.

'I think it must be electrical,' I said, as calmly as I could. It would be, of course. If anybody could invent an aeroplane without electrics, he'd get an award from every pilot in the world, headed by the Keith Carr Medal with Crossed Beer Bottles. The nice thing about a jet engine isn't the speed; it's that the thing doesn't need continuous ignition and will keep you steaming around the sky when every blasted wire's fallen out of the airplane.

Reluctantly, I reached out and tried cutting the magnetos. With one out, I got a normal—normal for this tub—drop

186

of around two hundred revs. With the other cut——

I held her against the vicious swing, snapped the switch back to *Both* and the engine caught again in a ragged blast of thunder.

'It's a magneto, all right,' Luiz said knowledgeably. I frowned at him, then remembered he'd already flown a hundred times as many hours in this vintage of American bombers as I ever would—I hoped. And he was right, anyway. One of the magnetos was as good as dead.

Well, it happens all the time: that's why they give you two magnetos per engine. But even with electricity, there has to be a reason. I tried to remember where the magnetos were installed on a Cyclone engine . . . Then I remembered, all right: in the rear casing, right alongside the starter motor.

Now I saw the cold, thin tight-rope ahead—and behind. It's the classical pattern of flying: ignore a small thing, and it grows on you like a cancer. I'd ignored that starter motor, let it spin itself to bits—but forgotten it might not be entirely in bits. Some part was still spinning, rubbing the motor casing, building up heat and melting the magneto wiring. In a few minutes, those wires would be trickles of hot metal. Then on to the second magneto . . . already it must be affected, or the engine wouldn't be having spasms of misfiring.

Ignore a cancer and it eats you hollow; forget a jammed motor and it slowly poisons an engine. Just an ounce or two of busted metal, spinning out of control only a few feet away, and no way to stop it up here at 8,000.

'I'm going to have to feather that engine,' I announced.

Luiz said: 'We must turn back then.'

I looked at him. 'We can still reach the target. We won't get back to Jamaica on one—but we can get on to Puerto Rico. That's less than a couple of hundred miles from——'

He said calmly: 'We must not make the attack.'

'I thought,' I said, 'that you came along just to see I *didn't* turn back. To make sure I was a press-on type that Clausewitz would have been proud of.'

'Then you misunderstand, my friend. One thing a revolu-

187

tion cannot afford is a fiasco. To come in an old bomber and drop just bricks is bad enough, but to crawl in on one engine and because of that perhaps to miss ... Could a future presidente be one who employed such a feeble weapon? Jiminez would never survive the joke. It is better not to start than to fail so ludicrously.'

'I wasn't planning to fail.'

The engine missed. The second magneto was feeling the heat, all right.

I swung back on to heading. Luiz said: 'You understand? It is better to go back now.'

'If I cut her now, before she fails on her own account, she'll cool off. Then I can restart her for periods later—it'll take time for the heat to build up again. We can make the attack itself on two engines.'

'You are certain?'

'No—I'm only the pilot. But if I *can't* restart her we can reconsider the whole business then. And still make Puerto Rico on one.'

He said softly: 'You really wish to make this raid.'

'You've noticed, have you?'

When he didn't say any more, I tilted the plane into a shallow dive to keep the speed up, throttled back both engines to reduce the swing, then jabbed the starboard feathering button and cut the levers back.

As its blades twisted to meet the airflow side-on, the propeller slowed, came to a wavering stop. I twirled on rudder trim to balance the uneven pull of the port engine, and at 7,000 feet we levelled out again; slightly nose-high, slightly crabbing, the speed coming down to 150—but still heading on ogo degrees.

When I got everything balanced into the new pattern, I said: 'So that's why you killed Diego.'

He looked at me, moved his lips, but had forgotten to push his transmit switch. Then he remembered and said: 'Why should you think this thing? He was the son of my old friend Jiminez.'

'It's been worrying me—since that fuss around the plane

188

last night. *That* was the sort of secret service the generals run: a couple of down-and-outs sent just to slash the tyres. Not a tough hired killer. And you always had the best chance: you were with Diego all that evening, running around the airport. And you come from Republica originally—so you'd likely know as much about snake pistols as anybody there. You could have brought one to Jamaica—you might have thought it was snake country, too. But I never saw *why* you should have killed him.'

He waited to be sure I'd finished, then: 'But now you think you see?'

'You just told me: a revolution can't afford a fiasco. Diego flying this raid would've been the fiasco of the year. He'd've cracked up on take-off or missed or run it into the ground at that end—something, anyway. With your aircrew training you must've seen he wasn't the type. But now—he's a martyr and everybody thinks the generals are foul assassins.'

'And a true professional is flying the raid, no?'

I looked at him sharply, then realized that was right, too. 'You're a cold-hearted bastard, Luiz.'

In the faint light from the instruments I saw his face wince with pain. Then he nodded slowly. 'Perhaps . . . perhaps I am, to have done this thing. Yet—he was a playboy, but he was ready to die for his father's cause. And probably on this attack he would have died—stupidly. Perhaps. I only arranged things a little better.'

'And it—doesn't worry you?'

'About being found out? I think it unlikely, my friend.'

'That wasn't quite what I meant.'

'You have killed people yourself?'

'Yes, but——' I paused. 'I was going to say "Only in a good cause." But that's the only reason anybody ever gets killed.'

'And perhaps from a distance, in an airplane, with your own side cheering you on. That, perhaps, makes it easier.'

After a time, I asked: 'Does Whitmore know?'

'Yes: I had to tell him. He knows I have the snake gun. But for him, I had to pretend it was an affair over a girl. He would not have understood the truth.'

'And J.B.?'

189

'No.' He looked at me. 'Will you tell her?'

I shrugged. 'I doubt it'll come into the conversation.'

He went on looking. 'And you, my friend?'

'It's still film star bites dog, isn't it?—Who'd listen? But I won't tell *her*, if that's what you mean. That's your problem.'

After another time, he said quietly: 'Yes, that is what I meant. She should have been her brother, then . . .' But he left it there.

With the port engine grinding its heart out, we crabbed on across the night.

★ 26 ★

Just before we should have reached the Punta del Almirante, the southernmost tip of the Republica itself, I tried restarting the starboard engine. For an air start you don't need a starter motor: unfeathering the blades should let the airflow spin the prop to a speed at which it'll fire the engine —and it did.

I throttled back the port engine to give it a rest—that was the main object of the exercise—and kept the speed down to 160 m.p.h. We still had time to make Santo Bartolomeo at five past five. And if Clara had left most of the island still covered in cloud, first light would be a little late today.

The faint northerly wind must have backed to westerly— which made sense, if the hurricane was now about due north of us. Anyway, we reached the Punta a few minutes ahead of my revised ETA, and a bit north of track, so that we crossed the point itself for a few miles until the coastline swung sharply back north again.

I said: 'Welcome home.' Luiz peered down over the cockpit sill at the dark land until the coastline had passed beneath the wing.

'Strange,' he said quietly. 'It does not look much from here . . .'

'You should've seen some of the country we were fighting for in Korea.'

'I saw a lot of Texas, once.'

I grinned and swung left on to 045 degrees. By my guess, that should bring us past Santo Bartolomeo before we hit the coastline. And with an obvious landmark like the city, I could double back on an exact course for the air base without a lot of noisy searching around.

The starboard engine misfired again.

I looked sorrowfully at the engine instruments. I'd done everything I could: run it with full rich mixture, cowl flaps wide open—everything a father could do for an engine. And here it was in trouble again, after just twelve minutes' running.

So we tilted into another shallow dive, and stopped it again. Losing height now didn't much matter. But making the attack at ground level on two engines—that meant I'd have to escape on one. And I didn't like the idea of trying to climb on just the port engine. That could strain it a bit too much. We'd be heading for Puerto Rico low, over the sea.

I said: 'Any idea of where in Puerto Rico we might put down? You don't have any security-minded friends with private airstrips?'

He said thoughtfully: 'I have friends in the Republica. Had you considered landing at Santo Bartolomeo? The civil airport, naturally.'

I hadn't thought anything of the damn sort. 'Was Jiminez planning to grab it?'

'I think not. It is not important.'

That's what I'd thought: it was about fifteen miles out of town, and unless Jiminez had arranged an airlift of supplies, he wouldn't bother with it. Still, neither would the generals: they already had their own airfield.

But it was still walking down the tiger's throat and hoping he'd forget to swallow.

'We can't exactly hide the Mitchell,' I said. 'And as soon as the civil airport hears of the raid——'

'You remember most of the country telephone lines are down?' he reminded me. 'And if I know Santo Bartolomeo, that airport will very soon be full of senior civil servants

191

suddenly remembering a holiday they had planned in Puerto Rico. It will be one great confusion.'

He could be right there. I looked up at the VHF dial, but there wasn't a crystal for the SB civil frequency. I could check the radio beacon on the direction-finding set, but it probably wouldn't be on the air anyway at that hour: nobody in the Caribbean flies after midnight.

He had switched on his own radio and was twiddling once more—and suddenly it was hooting out martial music. Then a voice came, and he jammed the set against his ear.

Just for something to do, I tuned the DF set to Aguadilla beacon in Puerto Rico, found it working, and took a bearing. It was too close to our course to be much help navigationally, but at least it showed we couldn't be far off track.

Then Luiz put the set down in his lap.

'Well?' I asked. 'Has Jiminez moved?'

He groped for his transmit switch, and his voice was puzzled. 'I do not know. But General Bosco has moved: *he* has proclaimed himself presidente.'

When I'd digested this, I said: 'You mean the Air Force is deposing the Army?'

'It seems so. They are calling General Castillo a traitor for being too soft on the Jiminez rebels. They say Bosco has all under control.'

'Well, I suppose it adds up. The generals weren't supposed to love each other, and we know Bosco's been building up the Air Force: first the jets, then the "airfield defence units" your girl-friend told us about. He'd need ground troops to grab control of the city.'

'True—true. But why should he move *tonight*?'

'Exactly the same reason Jiminez is moving tonight: the hurricane's busted communications. And it's the *Army* that's stranded in the hills, the *Army* that's held up with blocked roads. The Air Force is still there just outside SB: tonight's Bosco's best chance. Now I see why Ned risked keeping the Vampires there through the winds.'

'Mother of God,' he whispered. 'Now we have a three-cornered revolution.'

'They say anything about Jiminez moving?'

'No . . . but they would not, anyway. They would not want to announce it.' He jammed the set back to his ear.

I flew on. It was nearly half-past four: eighty miles and thirty-five minutes to go.

What did this do to the raid? Well, it meant the Air Force would be up and about earlier than usual—but not necessarily that they'd risk flying off the Vamps before first light. In fact, they might be more inclined to keep them at home, and when it was fully light make a few low loud passes over the city to show the citizens the Air Force was really in control.

But they'd want to run a reconnaissance to see what the Army was doing; if it was turning around and heading for S.B. They might use a flight of Vamps—but it would be better to use something that could hang around the target for longer. One of their Dakotas, or—blast their eyes— my Dove.

Luiz put the radio down again. 'They are warning people to stay indoors, no matter what they hear. That means there has been shooting. Jiminez *must* have moved.'

'What does this do to his chances?'

'I do not know. He has failed to take the radio. And he must have met armed Air Force squads. There is shooting in the streets.'

Revolutions always kill somebody, a voice said.

I said: 'You must have expected that.'

'Walt and J.B. are there.'

I snapped round. 'They're *what*?'

'They went in on the Pan Am flight last night.'

I just stared. 'So Whitmore could ride in triumph behind Jiminez in the big parade? And you let J.B. go, too?'

'My friend, one does not *let* a girl like J.B. do things. And it was her idea, anyway; she thought it best to catch Jiminez at his moment of success when he would be most grateful . . . You do know why Whitmore is concerning himself in this affair?'

'I know,' I said grimly. 'But they've already been expelled

193

from there once. The Air Force probably had them under arrest straight off the plane.'

'J.B. did not think so. She thought we were not expelled officially—just a temporary whim of General Bosco's. And now we know the Air Force must have been very busy yesterday, preparing for tonight. They probably did not have time to check passenger lists.'

'You managed to stop Miss Jiminez going, I noticed.'

'My friend, the Jiminez family does not walk openly into the Republica. Not just yet. That is a very different matter.'

I looked back at the instruments and noticed I'd wandered nearly ten degrees off course. I wrenched her back angrily.

'And I suppose Whitmore insisted on staying at the Americana?' I growled. 'Bosco may not have checked the passenger lists, but he'd notice Whitmore sitting around the bar. That place is nearly Air Force headquarters.'

'I know that,' he said calmly. 'They are staying at the Colombo, on the beach front near the old town. Jiminez will control the old town, whatever happens. Now, we must consider if the move by the Air Force changes our raid.' He glanced at my meagre ten-channel VHF. 'I wish we had arranged communication with Jiminez.'

'It doesn't change the raid at all. Those Vamps are the only high card the Air Force has got. Without them . . .'

'But also they are the only things to stop the Army's tanks and artillery. If we let the Air Force and Army fight it out and exhaust themselves——'

'*Testículos*. Bosco'll play every card in the pack twice over before he starts knocking out tanks and guns. *He's* the presidente now; they're *his* tanks and guns, *his* army—he hopes. He wants it in one piece to keep Jiminez down.'

He thought this over. 'So you think perhaps he will not use the jets today?'

'He'll use them for strafing in the streets, if there's still any fighting in SB. Those twenty-millimetres could knock down a house.'

He nodded. 'But it might have a reverse effect: to swing people to Jiminez, if they see the Air Force——'

'And J.B. could be dead!'

194

After a time he said quietly: 'My friend, what war are you fighting?'

'One in which J.B. doesn't get killed.'

'Others, my friend, are fighting for somewhat larger objectives. So you will forgive me if *I* take the decisions now.'

'You take what you like. I'm going to knock out those Vamps.'

'I may decide that is best. But *I* will decide.'

'*Testi*——' but then I saw the hand and the short fat revolver glowing in the instrument lighting.

'Well, well, well,' I said slowly. 'So that's the famous snake gun. One shot, and you can try landing this old tub all by yourself—and see if that doesn't qualify for the fiasco of the year.'

'No fiasco,' he said pleasantly. 'Just two martyrs, lost in the dark sea.'

We were still over the sea.

I looked at him; his face set and unsmiling, just beside my shoulder in the narrow cockpit. And at the gun, less than an arm's grab away. Would he shoot—risk killing himself, too? Yes, he would—if I challenged him to.

I felt the cold, slow anger building inside. Always someone with a gun, saying don't fly here, saying step aside—but not any more, not to *me*, not now I'm back doing the one job I know . . .

Then I remembered that now this had become different from all the other missions I'd flown. This wasn't just because I was the best—not now. I *had* to get those Vampires before they started shooting.

'You're forgetting who you are, chum,' I said quietly. 'You're Luiz Monterrey—big star, big success symbol. I go missing and nobody'll notice. But *you* get killed, in an old bomber going to take part in a revolution—and that's really failure. That's a fiasco. It'll get more publicity than Jiminez himself.'

He frowned thoughtfully. 'I do not think there will be time for that to matter, perhaps.'

'This isn't going to be a one-day wonder—not now the Air Force has stepped in. Jiminez has got a long way to go—

and he hasn't got very far yet, has he?' I made a small gesture at the radio in his lap. 'There'll be plenty of time for the reporters to get in. They're probably on their way already—somebody else will have picked up that broadcast.'

For a long time, he didn't say anything. I eased the Mitchell back on to her proper heading again and checked the time. It was nearly a quarter to five; under fifty miles still to go. I turned the instrument lighting right down and stared carefully at the eastern sky. Was there just a hint of lightness there? Or just the distant clouds over the Republica mainland?

Then Luiz said: 'We will attack.'

* 27 *

TEN minutes later there was a faint but definite paleness in the east. Not enough yet, only enough to fool you that you might be able to identify something or judge a distance.

I let the Mitchell droop into a long descent, waited until she'd picked up a bit of speed, then eased back the port engine.

'Ten minutes,' I said. 'Better get yourself organized.'

'I can wait a bit longer.' He was staring ahead, for the first sure sight of the coastline in the dimness under the cloud that marked the land.

'Didn't they teach you how to address the aircraft captain in your air force?'

I caught the ghost of a grin. 'Of course—sir.'

'Once we cross the coast I'll start the starboard engine. After that I'll be making turns: you'll find it a sight more difficult to get into position then.'

'Sir.' He stood and carefully eased back out of his seat, picked up the Browning, and vanished into the dark cabin behind. I felt the slight tilt of his weight shift. A minute later, through one of the empty sockets in the instrument panel, I saw his shape moving against the transparent nose.

We were doing 165 m.p.h., going down through 5,000. The coast should be about fifteen miles ahead.

A crackle and hum in my headphones told me Luiz had plugged in. 'I've got the gun mounted,' he reported. 'Ready when you are.'

'Right. I'll open the bomb doors in a minute.' I didn't want the drag, but if the normal system didn't work I wanted time in hand to use the manual lever without delaying the attack. 'I hope I'll cross east of the town, then turn and pass north of the base at about a thousand feet. It'll be on our left. If the Vampires are lined up, I'll count them. *You* look around for any odd ones parked elsewhere. Got that?'

'Yes, Capitan.'

'We'll make our run from the west. Don't shoot until then. They'll see us go past the first time, but they might not guess what we're up to. Bomb doors going open.'

I leant across and held up the switch. The sudden drag and the windy roar behind me told me they were opening. The speed dropped 5 m.p.h.

Luiz said: 'Coast ahead.'

I looked up from the instruments, and there it was: a faint ragged greyness on the horizon with a thin, flickering line of breaking surf. I stared at it. 'Christ, we've missed the city entirely. There should be lights——'

'One does not switch on one's light's when there is shooting in the streets, my friend.'

I should have thought of that. The Santo Bartolomeans would be old hands at how to behave in revolutions by now.

But I still couldn't see the city.

Then a faint flick of light, brief as a flashbulb, over to port. I stared at where it had been, wondering about it, and if I was imagining a shapeless darker shape around it.

'A grenade,' Luiz said sombrely. 'There is still fighting.'

I was two or three miles starboard of track. I turned gently due north to skim the edge of the city. Still about eight miles out, down to 3,500 feet.

Gradually the coastline hardened ahead. The paleness of beaches, the darker cliffs, the still darker shapes of trees above. Then slowly filling with dim colour in the greyness.

And over to the left the city, the dark mass separating into a jumble of little blocks with light and shadow sides, like a child's building bricks.

Still with the occasional flash of a grenade.

When the coastline was on the nose, I reached for the starboard engine controls. The prop blades twisted to catch the wind, turned, vanished. The engine coughed, and caught in a clattering howl.

Luiz, with his clear view downwards from the bomb-aiming window in the nose, said: 'Passing over coast . . . now.'

I swung into the wide flat turn that should bring me to the road bridge west of the city—a good big landmark—and from there an exact course to the air base ten miles east.

I'd been half expecting, more than half fearing, runway lights. Which would show they had started flying already. But from about three miles out, there was just the sparkle of lit windows in the base offices. No shooting out here; they knew Jiminez wouldn't be fool enough to attack a wakeful and well-defended base head on. Not in person.

As we closed I saw the dark hulks of the two hangars, the thin pale line of the runway, seen side-on—and definitely no flarepath. And searching desperately for the dim silvery patch that would be the parked Vampires.

Then, as the angle widened, they came into view just beyond the second hangar.

Luiz called: 'Target in sight!'

'Shut up! I'm counting!'

We skimmed the northern edge of the field, the Vamps half a mile to port, almost parallel . . . one, two, three . . . spaced about three-quarters of a wingspan apart, say thirty feet between each . . . four, five, six . . . the line bearing about 120 degrees from the front of the second hangar . . . seven, eight. Full stop. *Eight.*

'There's two missing!' I yelled. I looked forward, at the west end of the runway, at the taxi track leading to it—but nothing. In the hangars, under maintenance? Normally, yes —but today of all days Bosco would want one hundred per cent strength, and Ned must have had well over a day's warning to reach that.

Then we were past the field, heading into the dark west and I was counting the seconds before the turn back.

Luiz reported soberly: 'I could not see them.'

'We'll get the eight, anyway.' I was trying to work out the length of my target. A Vampire has about a forty-foot span, so eight times forty—plus the space in between, say seven times thirty, which is . . . call it 500 feet. A bit over a two-second run.

Then it was time to turn, gentle and slow, both engines throttled back and sliding down to attack height. The dull silver of the Vampires vanished behind trees, but the tall black hangars stood up clear. I levelled out at a hundred feet, aiming for the nearest hangar on a course of 120, waiting for the speed to settle at 150 before pushing up the throttles.

And I could taste it again: the old savage hunger of the hunter, still familiar after twelve years because I was still Keith Carr. The same hunger to reach out and kill, and the same certainty that makes you wait for exactly the instant, time flowing slow as a glacier, because you know you're *going* to kill . . . And I knew I was going to get this attack right.

Then, suddenly—fear. Because I *had* to get it right, I *had* to kill—every Vampire on the field and two I hadn't even found yet. Because this wasn't a private war any more, because if I let one escape, it could fire the lucky shot that was all that mattered to me now.

The cold sick fear of failure. And the Mitchell and her bricks seemed an old, frail, absurd weapon to throw against ten jets. She trembled under my trembling hands.

God, just let me forget that this time it *matters!*

Then we skimmed a line of palms and were over the open airfield, the Vampires not quite dead ahead. A quick, skidding S-turn to line up with them and I grabbed for the release panel. A glance at the instruments: 100 feet and just over 150 m.p.h.—and now 1,000 feet ahead . . . now 800 . . . and—*Now!*

The Mitchell reared as the weight poured out, pitched as the dragging net clutched at the airflow. I stabbed the second button . . . and the third—then didn't touch the fourth. The line of Vampires flickered beneath and we were over the hangars, throttles going up to hold the speed against the trailing nets.

Luiz hadn't fired. Then he did—and shouted: 'I see them!'

I saw them myself: two Vamps taxiing sedately around the perimeter track towards the east end of the runway, hidden from us by the control tower on our approach. And we were too far right to pass over them.

Dust puffs spat up around them; Luiz was good, all right, shooting part-sideways at close range—but twenty rounds of ·30 fire wouldn't stop two Vamps. Then we were past, and I hauled into a left-hand turn over the middle of the airfield.

'I think I hit them,' Luiz reported soberly. But over my shoulder I could still see them moving, one just ahead of the other. And I knew who would—who must—be leading the first strike of the Air Force's big day.

As we curled back, the line of eight Vampires came in sight again; a jagged line now, in a drifting mist of yellow brick dust. Two—no, three collapsed, part of the undercarriage gone; another with a broken tail boom, another——

But it only needed one, just one, left untouched . . .

I lined up on the perimeter track, the taxiing Vamps several hundred yards ahead. Suddenly there was the silent *tick-tick-tick* of tracers slanting across below. Somebody had reached a mounted machine-gun.

'Never mind that!' I yelled. But he hadn't fired anyway.

I straightened, reached for the last button and the last net. Luiz fired, and again dust spattered the Vamps. I felt the net go—but saw the leading Vampire swerving suddenly on to the grass.

We swung away in a tight S and I looked back. One Vamp lay slewed across the track, wingtip on the ground. But the other—Ned—was bouncing across the grass towards the runway.

I had one pass: just the one. Ned couldn't take off on the grass, the field wasn't wide enough; he'd have to turn on to

the runway. And when he did I had to be behind him.
'Reloaded?' I asked.

After a pause, Luiz said: 'Ready to fire.'

'I'll bring you in behind him.'

I throttled back, losing speed in a gentle upward curve
that I could change into a fast, diving turn at any moment,
waiting and judging . . . Another burst of tracer arched
towards us, but fell low. Nobody had seriously trained for
A.A. defence.

He was almost on the runway, but I had to wait, daren't
commit myself—then the starboard engine misfired. *Damn
it, live, you old bitch! Just a few seconds longer, just that* . . .

Then Ned was swinging smoothly on to the runway and
I had the throttles wide open and diving in behind him.
More tracers—and a rattle in the tail this time, but nothing
seemed to break. I was pulling up on the accelerating
Vampire. Two hundred yards. Down to one, and down to
less . . . Luiz fired and dust puffs spurted behind. Another
burst and I thought I saw holes open on the Vampire's wings.
And another and more holes—but now the gun was empty
and the Vampire ran on.

Luiz started to say something. We were overtaking the jet,
pulling just over and ahead. I snatched back the throttles,
pushed down the nose, and sat down right on top of it.

A shattering *clang*, the Mitchell wrenched and swerving
wildly, and then racing away a few feet above the grass,
filled with a terrible tearing shudder that wouldn't go away.
We just lifted over the line of palms at the edge of the field.

Luiz was shouting, but so was I. The airspeed was down
to 100—or something: the needles on every instrument were
shaking wildly with the shudder. Whatever it was, it was
the Mitchell's death-rattle.

I over-rode Luiz's voice. 'Get out of the nose!'

We skimmed a small rise and then the ground fell away
and ahead was the grey glitter of the sea. Luiz appeared at
my elbow, scrambled into the co-pilot seat and plugged in
his headset.

'What happened?' he yelled.

'Bust or bent the port prop—hit the Vamp or something.

201

Come off the wing in a moment. Strap yourself in. What happened to the Vamp?'

'It ran through the boundary fence.'

I was fighting the shuddering controls, and should have cut the port engine by now—but with the starboard engine likely to cut itself at any time . . . Then we were over the sea and out to starboard, half a mile away, a long white beach.

Holding my breath, I edged into a turn, and we didn't quite fall out of the sky. Then pushed down full flap, cut the throttles and ignition and held her off as long as possible—and she flopped on the beach in a long tearing hiss of flying sand.

★ 28 ★

'SHE did all right, in the end,' I said. And I patted the silver paint below the cockpit window which hid the faded *Beautiful Dreamer*. Perhaps I should have painted that on again before the raid. She might have liked it.

She would never fly again. She lay on—and in—the sand at the end of a 100-yard trench she'd dug for herself. The propellers were folded right back over the engines, and buried to the hubs in the sand they'd piled up in front. The bomb doors had torn off and lay halfway back down the trench, and for the first time I discovered I'd lost the port wingtip. It must have hit the ground when the prop hit the Vampire.

But she looked oddly restful lying there. Without the hunched, alert look she had had sitting on her wheels. An old lady who had finally got her feet up.

I looked round for Luiz. He was standing beside the nose and lighting a cigarette with hands that shivered just a little. He caught my eye and said: 'You professionals play rough.'

'Aren't you the man who talked about dumping us both in the sea?'

'Ah, I was younger then.'

I started to work out where we were. About six or seven

miles west of Santo Bartolomeo, I guessed, with the air base just a little way inland. The beach itself was about six hundred yards long, littered along the tideline with logs and planks tossed up by the waves behind Hurricane Clara. Above were low, broken cliffs topped by an uncombed tangle of bushes and palms. No buildings in sight.

Luiz asked: 'How far are we from the air base?'

'Couple of miles.'

'Will they come looking for us?'

'They don't necessarily know we're down. They just saw us going away low. We'd have done that anyway.'

'If they get an airplane up, they will see us.'

True: we were probably on one of the approaches to the airfield, and the Mitchell would stand out like a coffin at a cocktail party on that white sand.

Luiz said: 'So we had better move.'

'Yes.' I was watching the sky. We'd been down nearly five minutes. A wide-awake base—and that one certainly was, by now—should have had a flight of Vamps up already. If any were still serviceable.

Or was I fooling myself? Should we take the BAR and park just outside at the end of the runway in case anything tried to take off? Or was there a better way still, now I was on the ground?

'The Hotel Colombo,' I said firmly. 'Then the civil airport.'

Luiz thought about it, then nodded. 'But of course, we are on the wrong side of town. Jiminez is in the old town, the east.'

'So let's get started.'

'Yes. You see now what I mean about being respectably dressed? We do not look like rebel airmen, I think.' Then he spoiled it by adding: 'But I will take the rifle—just in case the disguise does not work.'

He yanked off the emergency escape hatch in the side of the nose and climbed in for the Browning. I patted the side again—then took out a pencil and scrawled ten quick little airplane symbols just below the cockpit. If she hadn't got all ten, it had been my fault, not hers. She'd done all right.

Then we walked away from her.

By six, when the sun finally rose above the clouds over the eastern hills, we'd come perhaps a mile and a half. Along the beach, up the cliffs, then threading through overgrown palm plantations. It was heavy going, still soaked from the rain and scattered with uprooted bushes and blown-down palm fronds. By now we were probably out of danger from any ground patrols sent out from the base, and I hadn't heard any aircraft. But we weren't making much progress.

'At this rate we won't be in town until about nine,' I said.

Luiz stopped, and delicately patted his brow with a handkerchief. He'd taken the hurried going over rough ground well—he must have been nearly fifty, after all—but from now on the day was going to start hotting up, and he was humping a 15-pound automatic rifle. I had the snake pistol; I had it in my hand, too, but only for snakes.

He said: 'What do you suggest, my friend? That we run?'

'We can go up to the road, or back down to the beach; walking on sand'll be easier than this.'

He looked reproachful. 'Another plot to get my feet wet. On the beach we will be a little obvious—and with no retreat.'

'All right: the road.'

'There, we may be able to borrow a car.' He hefted the Browning expectantly.

'That's not exactly helping the formal dress image,' I growled. 'Throw the damn thing away.'

He frowned. 'When we reach the road, perhaps. But Jiminez could use it.'

'If you're expecting to walk down the *avenidas* of the west town with *that*——'

'It would be quite fashionable, today.'

'One day a year, pheasants suddenly get fashionable, too.'

It took us about a quarter of an hour to zigzag inland and find a road: a straightish, narrowish, newish concrete affair.

I looked up and down it, saw nothing, and asked: 'D'you

know where this road leads *that* way?' I nodded west, away from the city.

Luiz just shrugged.

I said: 'It's your country, isn't it?'

'I do not remember every road, my friend. Anyway—' he tapped a neat brown Chelsea boot on the concrete '—it is new.'

I scowled at the road, then the map. But air maps don't bother much with roads: they aren't usually much use navigationally. 'If it's the usual route from the air base to town,' I said, 'it's not going to be healthy for us. But if it's just the coast road . . .'

He shrugged again. 'We can sit behind a bush and see.'

'We aren't making much progress sitting behind a bush.'

'Quite true.' He lit a cigarette and waited for me to make a decision.

'Ah, hell,' I decided finally, 'we'll risk walking. Throw away that blasted field gun.' I offered him the snake pistol.

Reluctantly, he laid the Browning and two spare magazines down behind a tree, studied the place carefully, then took the pistol and shoved it in his hip pocket. We started walking.

For five minutes nothing happened. Then a car appeared, coming from the city. We hopped behind a bush, but it went past like a scared rabbit. All I could see was the orange roof that labelled it a taxi.

Luiz said thoughtfully: 'The taxi-riding classes are leaving town. That is a good sign.'

We walked on. Ten minutes later I heard another car, coming slower, behind us.

Luiz looked at me. 'Shall we try to beg a ride? Or borrow the car?'

I glanced at my watch. It was nearly half-past six. 'I suppose we'll have to.'

He pulled out the snake gun and held it behind his back. 'If I still had the Browning, it would be much simpler.'

'If you had that thing, you'd have had to shoot anybody who saw you with it.'

The car swung into sight; a white Mercedes saloon. Not

205

likely to be one of Jiminez's supporters, but not an official Air Force car either.

Luiz stepped forward and waved a hand in gesture that was friendly but commanding. The car slowed, then suddenly stopped a good twenty yards off. The front doors jumped open.

An airman with a sub-machine gun piled out of one; Ned, in flying overalls, with a streak of dried blood on his face, and the stubby revolver in his hand, out of the other.

Twenty yards was much too far for the snake gun; the machine-gun made it even farther. Luiz sighed and I heard the pistol clatter on the concrete behind him.

Ned walked slowly forward and there was a grim, satisfied smile on his face. 'The gallant aviators themselves,' he said quietly. 'I'm *so* glad to meet you.'

Then he swung the gun.

★ 29 ★

I DIDN'T go out, but I didn't bother to notice much of what was happening until I was seated in Ned's suite at the Americana with a tall glass of Scotch in my hand. Seven in the morning is a little early for the first drink of the day usually, but usually I don't seem to have toothache in every tooth I own and several sets borrowed for the purpose. The gun barrel had clipped me just on the left jawbone.

Ned was on the telephone; Luiz was standing by the window staring out over what he could see of the city. The guard was just inside the door, still with his sub-machine gun.

Ned put down the phone and said: 'A short delay before we meet the General. Better think up something good.'

Luiz turned round. 'Ah, we are to meet the new presidente?'

'I came in to report to him personally. It's nice to have you two on the credit side of the sheet.'

'Tell me something, Ned,' I said out of the corner of my

206

mouth, just like any amateur George Raft down in the casino, 'was that the usual road from the base?'

He looked at me. 'No. You were lucky to meet me. Your pal Jiminez started shooting up our people on the normal road just before first light. That's what I was taking off so early for: clear the road-block. And why I had to come into town on the coast road.'

Luiz sighed. 'Just lucky. I understand.'

'How many did we get, Ned?'

He looked at me hard for a while before answering. 'All bloody ten,' he said slowly. 'Three need engine changes. Three, maybe four, are complete write-offs—that includes mine.'

'Glad it didn't include you,' I said politely.

'Yeh—I noticed how bloody careful you were. Just tried to chop me up with the prop.' He shook his head disbelievingly. 'I never thought I'd see a man like you take a risk like that, Keith.'

Luiz murmured: 'I also found it somewhat surprising.'

Ned came over to the refrigerator and pulled out a bottle of Swan beer. 'It don't look like I'm going to be flying today, so . . .' He started pouring. 'Bricks. Bleeding *bricks*. You should've been in jail, Keith. I knew you'd be coming back, but I knew you hadn't got any bombs. Them bricks was all your own idea.'

He turned away, then back again, and said quietly: 'In case it interests you, I was just off the ground when you hit me. So you can count me. That makes five, don't it? You're finally an ace, Keith. But round here, aces count low. Bosco'll tell you just how low.'

I shrugged. 'It's over now, anyway.' I glanced as casually as I could at the guard by the door. He was propping up a wall, the sub-machine gun still in his hands, but gazing at the carpet with an expression left over from the Stone Age. If he understood English, I was going to lose an expensive bet, but I was prepared to have a side bet that understanding wasn't something he specialized in anyway.

I said: 'So where's the Dove, Ned? Still at the airport or over at your base?'

He stared at me. 'What the hell are you worrying about *that* for?'

'You've got a car downstairs; we could be airborne in half an hour. I'll give you a free ride to Kingston or PR—whichever you like. What d'you say?'

There was a crackle of gunfire from the old town, a couple of miles away. The snap of a grenade, the buzz of a machine gun. It lifted quickly to a crescendo, then died away.

Ned was still staring, now incredulously. Then he said slowly: 'You really think because we was once Dear Old Pals, that——'

'You need a pal right now, Ned.'

'*I* need one? What about yourself?'

'Oh, I've got friends in this town.' I waved at the window. 'They're not too close just yet, but they're there. What about you?'

'What about me?'

'Suppose Castillo and the Army come back in: they'll cut your throat because you're Bosco's right-hand man. Right? Or suppose Jiminez takes over: *he'll* cut your throat, too, except with the personal touch because you've actually been shooting at his people. Right? So that leaves Bosco.'

'I've got news for you, Keith: I'm already on Bosco's side.'

'That might be news to Bosco, too. He had just one weapon, Ned, one: the Vamps. And *you* lost them for him, every damn one. You've probably lost him the revolt. I wonder if Bosco *is* your pal any more.'

Luiz had turned away from the window. Now he nodded with grave approval.

Ned said softly: 'I wish I'd killed you, Keith. I wish I'd got her up.'

'It wouldn't have made any odds by then. You weren't hired as just a pilot, Ned: you were the coronel, the boss, the thousand-a-week man. You were in *command*—and by then you'd lost nine-tenths of your command. Because you left 'em neatly lined up for me to hit them on one run.'

'Hell, I didn't think you'd be coming *today*: we didn't

think Jiminez was ready. And we'd sent a couple of——'
Then he stopped.

I nodded. 'I know: I met them. I was sleeping in the plane
that night. But don't make your excuses to me, chum, make
'em to Bosco. He'd hired *you* to do the thinking about those
Vamps.'

After a while he said again: 'I still wish I'd killed you,
Keith. Just personal reasons.'

One of the phones buzzed.

Ned walked across, studied them, and said: 'That's
Bosco. Here we go.' He picked up the green one, listened,
said: 'Yes,' several times, put it down and turned round.
'On your feet, boys. Sorry there hasn't been time for a hearty
breakfast.'

We filed out, Ned leading, the airman with the sub-
machine gun bringing up the rear. We went along the
soft-lit, thick-carpeted corridor, up a wide staircase, and out
in front of the double doors of the pent-house suite—with
a double armed guard outside.

Ned knocked on the door, opened it, and we marched in.

It was a wide room—and dark, except for pools of light
around a jumble of radio and telephone equipment in one
corner and a big desk in the centre. Then I saw the steel
shutters over the windows on two sides; the General wasn't
taking any chances with stray snipers.

There were two men at the radio, three at the desk. Bosco
was behind it, an officer with a telephone at each end. One
of them was Capitan Miranda.

Bosco said: 'Make your report, Coronel.'

Ned took a breath and started. All aircraft had been
serviceable, fuelled and armed, by four o'clock. At five he'd
got a call to clear an ambush on the road, started taxiing a
couple of minutes later. He hadn't seen me make my scout-
ing pass, hadn't heard me because of his own engine noise.
The tower had warned him by radio in time to watch my
bomb run . . .

Bosco listened silently, his meaty near-handsome face
expressionless. He was dressed very simply: khaki trousers
and a shaped shirt of the sort American sergeants go for,

fitting as tight as a tee-shirt; black tie tucked in below the second shirt button, webbing belt and holster. But all very clean and crisp; knife-edged creases on the shirt arms, medal ribbons in exact parade rows. The perfect soldier: tough but tidy, efficient but elegant. Just what you'd want your new dictator to be.

I almost felt sorry I'd wrecked the background to the picture.

Ned wound up: he'd spent an hour examining the Vamps, giving orders about repair. They were working flat out on the two least damaged, cannibalizing parts from the total wrecks—but both had brick holes in fuselage and wings, which had to be patched, not replaced. One might fly tomorrow evening. Might.

Bosco swivelled his eyes at me. 'Now *your* report, Señor Carr.'

I shrugged, but there didn't seem to be any secrets to be kept. I'd dropped around 360 bricks from four fishing nets, attached to shackles . . .

When I'd finished, he said: 'It was Señor Whitmore's airplane?'

I shook my head. 'Mine. I'd taken it as a payment for the film work, and because he felt a little guilty about my losing the Dove. You remember that?'

Just a quick flick of a smile under the neat moustache. 'I remember. Also I remember telling you to stay away from the Republica.' Then he shrugged. 'I am sorry you did not accept our offer to work for us: you were clearly not over-rated. Now——'

He looked back at Ned. 'Coronel, you are reduced to *teniente*. Capitan Miranda will take command of what you have left of the squadron. You will go back and work on the airplanes and if the Capitan needs you, you will fly one of them when it is ready.'

Even in the dim edge of the desk pool of light, Ned seemed pale. 'I was hired at a rate and a rank. I quit.'

'You are in a military service, Teniente,' Bosco said calmly. 'One does not resign in a war. When it is over, we will consider.'

210

I glanced at Miranda. He was leaning back in his chair, looking at Ned with a satisfied, thoughtful smile.

Bosco had been studying Luiz and me carefully. Finally he said: 'I think you forgot something in your report, Señor. Clearly, you had decided when your mission was finished that you would land and enter the city to discover its results. Therefore, you are spies. You will be shot.'

I hadn't exactly expected *not* to be shot, but I didn't understand this 'spy' business. 'If you think I *intended* to hang around here afterwards——'

'Señor?' He smiled. 'So why are you wearing these clothes? I believe one flies a military operation in military uniform —no? You make things easier for me.' He turned to the officer. 'Make sure photographs are taken—to prove they were in civilian clothes.'

'Presidente,' Luiz said quietly, 'may I be permitted to point out your mistake?'

'That you are Luiz Monterrey, the great famous film star, the American citizen? No—' he tossed the thought aside with an elegant flick of his hand. 'Since we met last time, I have had you investigated. I know now why you are so interested in Señor Jiminez—I know you were born here. *That* is not something you have much publicized; your American newspapermen will be as much interested in that as that you are dead. And the *norteamericanos* all know we . . . *dagoes* are fanatics about our homelands. They will understand.' And when he smiled this time, it was like the slow opening of a knife cut.

'No, Presidente—' Luiz waved a hand just as elegant—'I just wish to point out that publicizing our fate—and there are those in Jamaica who will know we have not returned, so the publicity is not entirely in your hands—will mean publicizing our success. Did you *plan* to announce that General Bosco's teeth have all been pulled?'

There was a long time with just the hum and distant gabble from the bank of radio equipment in the corner. A phone buzzed; Miranda picked it up, listened, put it down again.

Then the General said: 'Jiminez must know already.'

Luiz made the slightest of slight bows. 'I think so. He knew we were coming, he knows there have been no jets overhead today, and it has been light enough for—' he consulted his watch '—for two hours now.'

'So?' Bosco snapped.

'But General Castillo—*he* does not know his tanks and guns are in no danger; *he* does not know the Army could walk into the city as soon as it could get here. Not yet, anyway.'

After a moment, Bosco lifted both hands in a brief shrug. 'And so? How do you propose to tell Castillo? Or stop him knowing?'

'I know nothing of Castillo—except that he will be trying very hard to find what is happening in the city. If an execution happens, can you be sure he will not know?'

Bosco eyed him, then smiled thinly. 'I could arrange a most *quiet* execution.'

'Señor Presidente,' Luiz shook his head sadly and patiently as if Bosco were a particularly dim pupil, 'to execute me as a spy is one affair. Murder me quietly in an hotel bedroom and what *norteamericano* reporter is even going to *ask* if I were guilty of anything?'

Bosco glared silently. Then one of the men at the radio called something and turned the radio full blast. We caught a roar of tape-recorded trumpets, a click, an amateurish heavy breath—and a sonorous shout: '*Viva el liberador—Jiminez!*'

Miranda and Bosco were both shouting. The radio got turned down hastily. Luiz said softly, 'He has captured the radio station, finally.'

Miranda and the other officer snatched up phones and started yelling. Bosco just looked at me. 'With the jets, we would have held it.' Then he cocked an ear to the muttering radio. 'Jiminez will speak in five minutes.'

I felt Luiz stiffen beside me. It needed just one sentence from Jiminez; if he couldn't resist announcing that the Air Force was crippled, if he forgot it would be an open invitation to the listening Army to walk back in . . .

Bosco said drily: 'It would seem your lives are not in my hands any more, Señores.' He started rattling out orders to Miranda and the other officer; both grabbed their phones and passed them on. Then Bosco seemed to think of something else, called a question to the man at the switchboard and lifted his own phone. 'It seems the line to the radio station is not yet cut.' He held the phone out to Luiz. 'Perhaps you would care to discuss with your old friend.'

Luiz reached for it, reluctantly. 'I will remind him that it is damaging to his cause. That is all. And he will decide.'

'Of course. I shall not blame you; I shall only shoot you.'

Luiz smiled crookedly and put the phone to his face. 'Señor Jiminez, con permiso ... qué? ... Ah, si—' he looked at Bosco and twitched a quick grin '—Presidente Jiminez ... Luiz Monterrey ...'

Miranda was starting to say something, but Bosco waved him down. Then Luiz must have got to Jiminez, because his Spanish went into top gear and I was left behind. I just picked out the word 'Americana'.

Finally he handed the phone back to Bosco, and turned to me. 'It will not be mentioned—this time. Later, or if he hears we are dead . . .' he shrugged.

Bosco said: 'You told him where you are. Did you hope he would lead a gallant rescue party? I much hope so myself.' He banged both hands flat on the desk. 'So—we wait. I am sorry we cannot offer you rooms in the Hall of Justice, but your friends blew down one of its walls in order to do some recruiting there.'

Luiz nodded approvingly: busting into the town jail to free your pals would be the proper opening gambit of any revolution.

Bosco looked around and saw Ned, still standing there, silent and sullen. 'Teniente—take them to your room and guard them properly.'

Ned said: 'Thought I was supposed to be repairing Vamps.'

'That can wait. You may—' Miranda leaned across and said something quietly. Bosco listened, nodded, looked up

213

at me. 'Capitan Miranda reminds me of an unfinished conversation the last time you met.'

I knew what was coming, now. Miranda stood up, quick and smooth, and stalked around the desk, his eyes on my face.

There was nothing to do but wait for him.

He stopped in front of me, studying me with a small, hungry smile. Then suddenly his left shoulder dropped as for a stomach punch; as my hands came up to guard it, he lashed out with his right. I rolled with it, but not enough, not nearly enough. He'd aimed at my bruised jaw and I went down with pain screaming through my head.

As I climbed slowly on to my feet, Bosco said calmly: 'That is all. You may go.'

I dabbed an already bloody handkerchief at the fresh blood on my lips. 'General,' I said thickly, 'don't ever wonder why people like me turn up on the other side to people like you.'

He watched us file out with a still, calm, expression.

★ 30 ★

I was sitting in a deep square Scandinavian chair in Ned's room. Half an hour of cold water on the outside, and neat Scotch on the inside, had got my face back into limited conversational use.

'Just what's Bosco waiting for now?' I asked Luiz. He was sitting at the card table, where he could keep watch out of the window, absently dealing himself a series of poker hands. Ned was sitting and brooding, a glass of beer in his hand, in another deep chair. The guard was leaning beside the door.

And still the occasional distant crackle of shots from the old town.

Luiz shrugged and scooped up the cards. 'For the reaction from the Army officers. If they shout Viva Bosco he invites them to bring their tanks to join the fight for liberty, the fatherland and a Swiss bank account for all above the rank of major. Once they are committed to him, they cannot go back to Castillo, so the news that his jets are all kaput does not matter.' He shuffled with a quick snap of his long fingers. 'On the other hand, if they cry *Viva Castillo* he says keep your distance or my jets will plast you to pieces, and goes on fighting with Jiminez alone.' He glanced at Ned. 'Always keeping the road to the air base open and a transport airplane warmed up and his bank-book packed.'

Ned just grunted.

I swilled more Scotch around inside my cheek and asked: 'How does Jiminez getting the radio station affect this?'

Luiz stretched a hand and rocked it delicately. 'How you like. It convinces some that the situation is as serious as Bosco claims, others that Bosco has failed already.' He smiled suddenly. 'That is my guess.'

I looked casually round at the guard: he was the same one as before, still staring vacantly across the room, with both his brain cells obviously resting hard.

I said to Ned: 'So where's the Dove, *Teniente*?'

He raised his head slowly and his face was hard. 'Don't you worry, matey. I won't be *teniente* long; just as soon as we got something serviceable—Miranda couldn't lead a cat to cat-mint.'

'He belongs here,' Luiz said quietly.

Ned turned. 'What does that mean?'

Luiz started dealing. 'I believe your reputation reaches from Korea to the Congo; you could find a new flying job anywhere. But I think you would agree that Capitan Miranda's reputation is—perhaps a little limited?'

'Nobody's heard of him,' Ned growled. 'And anybody who has, wouldn't hire him to wipe his own nose.'

'Exactly. So we might assume that his future depends on the one man who *has* hired him: General Bosco. And they both know it, and both know the other knows it. That is what is called, in some circles, loyalty.' He paused with a card frozen in his hand, looking at Ned. 'You made a bad mistake up there, my friend. You said, "I quit." One does not say that to dictators; above all things they prize loyalty.

215

They hire the best men at the highest prices—and then dream that such men truly believe in them and love them and that when the power and money are gone, those men will still be there to bleed and die and hold back the fall of night.'

He turned the card in his hand, scowled at it and snorted: 'Sonofabitch! I never learn not to draw to an inside straight.'

I said: 'So how about that Dove, Ned? Or are you waiting until you're chopped down to corporal?'

He drained his glass and walked slowly across and looked down at me. 'Or perhaps I'm waiting until I forget who got me cut down—had you thought of that? Keith—if I thought you'd done it for money, I might let you go. If I thought you was a God-and-Liberty patriot for Jiminez—then maybe I'd let you go. But *I* know you don't believe in Jiminez any more'n in Father Christmas. You did it just as a private war against me—because you're the great bloody Keith Carr. All right. But you never stopped to think how that'd make *me* feel. Keith—I'm going to *enjoy* watching you shot.'

He jerked the refrigerator angrily and snatched out a bottle.

I said wearily: 'You're right in a way, Ned—but it wasn't anything personal against your career.'

'God help me when you have a crack at me career, then.'

I got up and walked to the window and stared out across the city. Far off, down by the docks along the river in the old town, a column of thick black smoke crawled sluggishly up the quiet sky. And nearer, but to the north, a haze of whitish smoke—perhaps over the radio station. But that was all. From up here, in the cool hushed hotel suite, you couldn't see much but the tops of the royal palms along the drive, the top storeys of the houses down the broad *avenidas*.

About the view you'd get from a jet on its firing pass. From here—or there—you wouldn't see anybody move: wouldn't see anybody die.

'People like us, Ned,' I said. 'We're damn useful in the Battle of Britain or Mig Alley or something . . . But between wars, they ought to lock us up in cages. We've no damn business in places like this, times like this. That's why I took you out. In the end, there was another reason—but that was the real one. Pros like us don't belong here.'

'It's my *job*, matey.'

'Yes. But I don't have to like your job, Ned.'

He sneered. 'You've got bloody righteous since you started flying charter.'

I shrugged. 'Or since I stopped knocking down towns.'

'We weren't going to take out the town——'

'Weren't you?' I jerked around. 'Weren't you? You were damn well going to do what the man upstairs told you. If he'd said knock down the old town, you'd have knocked it down. *That's* your job.'

We stared at each other.

There was a soft tap on the door.

Ned swung round, patted the revolver in his shoulder-harness, then nodded. The guard swung open the door, clamped his hand quickly back on the sub-machine gun.

An urgent, pleading female voice muttered fast Spanish and sounded familiar. I glanced at Luiz; he was frozen in his chair.

Then the guard stepped forward, out of sight. There was a *thud*—and Whitmore walked in, carrying the limp guard in one hand.

Ned grabbed for his gun. Whitmore's free hand made one flickering movement and was pointing a big automatic at Ned's middle.

'Thirty years I've played this scene,' he drawled, 'and you don't think I've learned it *yet*?'

Luiz said: 'What the hell kept you?'

J.B., with the guard's sub-machine gun, came in and closed the door. Whitmore took Ned's revolver, waved him back into a chair, then saw the glass of beer.

He finished it in one gulp. 'You realize I been awake since damn near midnight?—when they blew in the Hall of Justice. Just up the road from us.' He turned to Luiz. 'What for Chrissake d'you mean, what kept us? Only three-quarters of an hour since you told Jiminez where you was. Took us all that time to borrow a bunch of luggage and get a cab and

217

make like we were tourists rushing for the best hotel in time of crisis.'

For once, he was fairly smartly dressed: light fawn trousers, a darker fawn jacket, white shirt, even a tie. Clearly a *norte-americano* and if you didn't recognize him he might well have been a stranded tourist.

'Anyhow,' he added, 'you don't think we came to rescue *you*, huh? We just figured Carr might be running out of your cigarettes.' He lifted his left hand, found the guard was still dangling from it, and tossed him on the sofa. Then took out a pack of cigarettes and threw them at me.

J.B. came forward and dumped the machine gun on top of the refrigerator. She was wearing a slim white skirt and a blue-and-green impressionist jungle of a blouse. She lifted a hand: 'Hi, Keith.'

I waved dazedly back. I was just beginning to catch up on Luiz's plotting.

Then she saw the dark bruise on my chin. 'Did that happen when you crashed?'

'No. Just a couple of short conversations with the Air Force.'

She spun round on Ned. 'Where's a first-aid box?'

He shrugged. 'He doesn't need one. It'll get better with time. If he has any time.' Then something clicked and he sat up straight. 'Christ—*she* was why . . . you knew *she* was here. You didn't want to leave a single Vamp alive and shooting.' He leant back in his chair. 'I never thought I'd see *you* take a risk for anybody else, Keith.'

J.B. was looking puzzled. 'What's this all about?'

Luiz said sadly: 'In order to stop the last jet taking off, we had to collide with it. Carr was most brave. He totally forgot I was also on board.'

Whitmore whistled softly. 'So that's how come you lost the ship, huh? Well, we can get another.'

'*Another?*' Ned was sitting up straight again.

'Hell, yes. I got a picture to make.' He frowned and poured himself more beer. 'But would've been better to use the same one that took part in a revolution. Great publicity angle.'

Ned was staring at him as if he'd turned green and bug-

218

eyed. Then he leaned back again, shaking his head in bewilderment. Finally, he said: 'Well, all your actors are here. Did any of you remember to bring a script?'

Whitmore waved the pistol. But I said: 'It's a fair question: where *do* we go from here?'

'Hell, we just bust through the Jiminez downtown. It ain't cordoned off except up around the radio station.'

I shook my head. 'You can do what you damn like—but I'm getting J.B. out of the country. There's a lot of shooting yet to come.'

She smiled, frowned, grinned, scowled—a fast flip through the whole expressions catalogue. 'It's a nice thought, Keith, but——'

Luiz said firmly: 'The old town *is* cordoned off, by now. Bosco gave the orders upstairs, when he heard Jiminez had taken the radio. That is his tactic now: to pin Jiminez down—and to wait. For some jets to become serviceable, to see which way the Army jumps. And the longer he makes Jiminez wait, the less chance Jiminez has of a popular uprising. People do not jump on a bandwagon that is not moving.' And his face was suddenly old, tired; the face of a man who has heard the chariot pass him by. 'It will take time, now. Better get out, Walt.'

Whitmore frowned. 'Yeah? Hell—and we got to be back on the picture day after tomorrow.'

Luiz smiled a little crookedly. 'And of course, there is that.'

Ned was looking at Whitmore, still not quite believing in him. 'This is just a couple of days' holiday from moviemaking—that right, matey?'

'Button up. I got an investment to protect.'

'An *investment*?'

I said: 'He means he's in it for the money, same as you.'

That got me stiff looks from both—but I was still right. It was just cash that had put them on opposite sides. If it had brought them together, they'd have had a perfect understanding.

Whitmore rubbed the slight bristle on his chin with the

219

pistol. 'Well, I guess if it ain't going to finish today, we better pull out.' He sounded honestly reluctant. There must have been bars and brothels he'd hated to leave before closing time, just because he had a picture to make in the morning. But he'd always left. He was a pro—in his own way. 'So, how do we do it?—If the old town's sealed off?'

'You don't,' Ned said. 'You're stuck.' He stood up and held out a hand. 'Like me to take over now—or you want to wait for the shooting?'

Whitmore looked at him. J.B. said quickly: 'There's still the civil airport. Jiminez said there wasn't any fighting up there—and there's a Pan Am flight for Kingston due just after eleven.'

I said: '*If* Pan Am knows there isn't any fighting there. They'll probably overfly us.'

'Anyway,' Luiz said, 'it will be booked five times over already. And it would not be a good place to be stranded. It is just a little obvious.'

There was a short, thoughtful silence.

I said: 'That brings us back to the Dove—wherever it may be.'

Ned said: 'Get stuffed.'

'In case you hadn't noticed, you're down to corporal already, Ned. You haven't been exactly a ball of fire even as a jailer, have you? You could be up against the wall with us. Now let's get to hell out of this country.'

He considered me carefully. 'Keith—you don't understand, do you? It ain't just getting me throat cut—but I had a reputation, too. I was a damn good war pilot. You busted that. But we'll have two Vamps serviceable in forty-eight hours. I've *got* to stay for that. I've *got* to pick up the pieces. Or I'm finished. I'll never get another job again.'

In the silence, J.B. said: 'Are we talking about your airplane, Keith? Jiminez told us it had been moved over to the air base.'

I nodded. 'So now we know.'

Ned smiled faintly. 'The old man liked it: had it done up and's been using it as his personal plane.' He nodded at Whitmore. 'Now let's see him act the scene where he breaks into the big well-defended air base and swipes the General's private airplane.'

A phone buzzed.

'Or,' he added, 'ask Bosco for permission. Now's your chance.'

I was on my feet, holding out a hand at Whitmore. 'Give me a gun. He'll believe *I'll* kill him.' Then I swung Ned's own revolver at him. 'All right—dear old pal. Talk us out of this.'

He eyed the squat, heavy Magnum. 'You never *could* hit a hangar at five paces, Keith.'

I clamped both hands on the gun. 'I'll come as close as it needs and shoot as often as it takes—if you're the man who gets *her* caught in this town.'

The phone buzzed again—longer.

He waved his hands and his head. 'I didn't think I'd see a pro like you become so bloody amateur.'

Then he stood up, took a deep breath, and snatched up the phone. 'Hello—General? . . . Sorry, I had been in the bathroom . . .' Luiz leant in cautiously, listening hard.

I kept the revolver pointed at Ned.

He didn't say much, just grunts and a 'yes' and a 'no'. A few geological eras passed. Then he banged the phone down again, glanced contemptuously at Luiz, and said: 'You tell 'em.'

Luiz said evenly: 'The General is going with Capitan Miranda to the base. Señor Rafter is to wait here with his prisoners. A firing squad is on call downstairs in case . . .' He shrugged delicately.

Whitmore said: 'So, what now?'

'We wait,' I said. 'Just long enough to let Bosco get settled in his office out there. Then we take Ned's car out, Ned helps us bluff past the guards on the gate, we find the Dove, we climb in—*zoom*.'

Ned stared incredulously. 'You're barmy.'

'Ned—what have you got to stay for? When Bosco finds out you faked that phone call, you'll be ten ranks below corporal and six feet under ground.'

'No-o.' He shook his head slowly. 'I can bluff that out. Your Hollywood pals could've come in *after* the call. One way or another, you won't be around to say they didn't. And Bosco ain't going to believe *him*.' He jerked his head at the guard, squirming around on the sofa and trying to remember which end of the sky had fallen on him. 'So what's your script say now, Keith? Stick a gun in me guts and tell me to drive you through the gate or else . . . ? It always works in the movies.'

★ 3I ★

WHITMORE took the heavy automatic from his belt, whacked it against his other hand. 'That's exactly dead right, fella. Get moving.'

Ned looked at the gun, expressionlessly, then shrugged. 'You're the dealer.' He took a step towards the door.

I said: 'Hold on.'

Everybody turned. I said: 'Ned—you *do* realize we've got a pretty limited choice, don't you? If we can't get to the Dove, we've got to try and break through to Jiminez. With your car, and the firepower we seem to have collected, we might do it.'

'But first you'll put a bullet in me head?' Still expressionless.

I looked down at the gun in my hand. 'No-o. I don't think I could do that. We'll just take you along—and if we get through, turn you over to Jiminez for safe-keeping. How safe he'd keep you, I wouldn't know—but then, I wouldn't have to watch, either.'

His face may have got a little stiff. Then he nodded briefly. 'So I'll get you through the gate.'

'Right,' Whitmore said impatiently. 'So let's get moving.'

I said again: 'Hold on.'

He spun round and his voice was up to cow-punching level. 'So *now* what in hell's bothering you?'

'It didn't work,' I said wearily. 'If he takes us through

that gate, he's turning traitor. And I know Ned: he doesn't do things like that, not that easily—not when he's getting a thousand a week to stay loyal. He'll ditch us—somehow. Forget a password, tip them the wink. Something. And whatever happens, he stands a better chance than with Jiminez.'

Whitmore looked at Ned thoughtfully, carefully. Ned stayed completely blank. Whitmore turned back to me. 'So—what now?'

I was looking at Ned myself. Now was the time to think of something that meant more to him than his loyalty to Bosco, more than $1,000 a week. As easy as that.

'You're sure you don't want to cut your losses and come out with us, Ned? There'll be another job waiting, in Africa or somewhere.'

'At the same price? And when they hear I walked out on this job when things got rough?' He smiled faintly.

'You're ready to bet we'll let you live, Jiminez'll let you live, Bosco'll let you live—and you'll redeem yourself when a Vamp gets serviceable again?'

'Keith, I just don't have even a limited choice.'

I nodded, then said quietly: 'It's one hell of a gamble, Ned.'

He smiled again. 'I'm a gambling man—remember?'

'I remember. So I'll roll you dice for it.'

There was a long stunned moment—then everybody was saying something. I waved the Magnum. 'Shut up! I'm handling this.' Then, to Ned: 'Well?'

He stared curiously. 'You're betting I'll get you through that gate, without tricks—against what?'

'We leave you here when we make a run for Jiminez. Tied up, locked in—but here. In one piece.'

He thought it over. 'You're crazy, rolling dice with me. But——'

'I'll say he is!' Whitmore exploded.

'Then think of something better.'

'Christ, I can think of a stack of things better'n shooting craps when you got a revolution going on downstairs——'

'Like going downstairs and starting shooting people?' I

sneered. 'Look, Mr Whitmore, this is the one chance we've got of getting through that gate: getting Ned on our side. Nothing else'll work, not with that base as nervy as it'll be now. It's been attacked once today already—you remember *that*?'

He lifted the automatic. 'Hell, we could still do it by——'

'Walt,' Luiz said warningly, 'quiet down.' Without anyone noticing, he'd reached the sub-machine gun. Now it pointed, just casually, at Whitmore. 'Put down the gun, Walt,' he said pleasantly. 'Don't tempt yourself. This is Carr's play.'

Whitmore stared, totally disbelieving. Then, as the idea sank slowly in, he bent down and flicked the automatic across the carpet. Luiz kicked it under the sofa. 'Thank you. Proceed, gentlemen.'

J.B. said quietly: 'Even if your friend loses'—and I liked that 'even if'—'why should we believe he'll keep his word?'

'Because I know him. He'll cheat us blind, deaf and dumb —he's a fighter pilot. I told you something about that. But he's also a gambling man—and one thing he'll never do is welsh on a bet. Never. That's the one thing he believes in.'

'*Todo hombre tien algún aspecto de honor,*' Luiz murmured. Every man has some aspect of honour.

Ned glanced sharply at him—he must have known enough Spanish to follow that—then back at me. 'You're pretty crafty, Keith. But I'm not just a gambler, sport, I'm a winner.' And there was just a shade of suspicion behind his voice.

I shrugged. 'All right, so we'll even it up for me a bit. Cut out all the fancy betting and the long odds. Just one play of the dice; one shooter rolls until he wins or loses. That's all there is to it.'

He frowned. My idea wasn't quite what gambling means to a gambling man. He works on a superior knowledge of long-term odds, of balancing winning and losing bets. I was suggesting a straight toss-of-the-coin situation.

I said: 'But I'll shoot if you like. It was my idea.' Somewhere, I'd read that the odds are slightly—about one per cent—against the shooter.

He went on frowning.

I said: 'I just want to get something *settled*. But if you're scared to take a bet——'

His face snapped shut. 'You've bet, matey.'

The drawer below the telephones was stacked with cards and dice, some still in cellophane wrappers. I took out a pair and clinked them in my hand. They were normal casino dice, the same as they used downstairs—which would be where Ned had got them. 'Where do we play?'

'Up against the wall there. The carpet's smooth enough; we've shot dice there before.'

I looked around the room. At Whitmore, staring grimly back at me; at J.B., arms folded, hugging herself slightly, puzzled; at Luiz, cradling the sub-machine gun easily and comfortably because he knew about machine guns.

Ned said: 'So—shoot.'

I knelt down on the carpet, then nodded back at the guard on the sofa. 'And keep an eye on him.'

Everybody glanced at him. Luiz smiled, nodded, then moved so he could cover the sofa as well as Whitmore.

Ned said: 'I bet I get you through the gate, you bet you leave me here—right?'

I said 'Right' and threw the dice.

The carpet slowed them more than the baize of a craps table would have done; they didn't even reach the wall.

I'd thrown a 6—no win, no loss.

I looked up. 'You accept that—or do I throw again?'

He shrugged. 'She'll do.' In the thirty-six combinations a pair of dice can show, there are five ways of throwing a 6—but six ways of throwing a 7. And I had to throw another 6 before a 7.

I reached for the dice, shook them, rolled them.

An 8. Nothing.

I reached, shook—and far away, through the double windows, the crack of a grenade, the patter of rifle fire. But not my business. No Republica politics for me. I rolled the dice.

A 4. Nothing.

I collected the dice, looked up at Ned. His face was quite

still, but his eyes were bright and hungry. Locked in the private cockpit of his head, willing the dice, guiding them —with a control column and rudder pedals and throttle that he didn't have. Gambling man.

Then he caught my eye and relaxed instantly. 'The odds're against you, matey.'

Behind me, Whitmore took a rasping breath. 'Christ, we should've done this on the end of a gun, not——'

'Ned's not as impressed with guns as you are,' I snapped. 'He's spent his life being shot at—and not with blanks.'

Ned just smiled quietly.

I threw another 8. Another nothing. And my hand was damp as I picked the dice up.

Ned said: 'Getting time for a seven, I'd say.'

I threw. One showed a 4, the other spun on a corner, rocked, settled—a 2.

And after a long time, Ned said quietly: 'I'll get you through the gate.' The light was gone from his eyes.

We stripped off the guard's uniform and left him tied up with a mixture of telephone cable and Ned's ties and belts. Luiz climbed into the uniform—wearing the expression he usually kept for getting his feet wet. In the end, it didn't fit him, but that was fairly normal in the Republica forces. What worried me more was the casual elegance he carried into any clothes; he looked like a general dressed as a private.

But the way he handled the sub-machine gun was still convincing.

Ned led the way down the corridor; Luiz and I were the last out. As we went through the door, he murmured: 'The next time you play with loaded dice, my friend, please remember they are only *certain* to work over a period of time. Not on just one play.'

He'd known what I was doing all along, of course, even if he hadn't seen me switch Ned's dice for Bosco's when everybody glanced at the guard on the sofa.

I shrugged. 'He was pretty suspicious of the idea anyway. If I'd beaten him over a long game . . . Anyway, the odds were three to two on my side, so I *ought* to have won.'

He looked at me. 'Ye-es. But next time, play only for money—please?'

THE hotel lobby was crowded with tourists; sitting on their luggage, swearing at a deserted desk, shouting down phones that didn't answer. A few of them looked at us hopefully—until they saw Luiz's uniform and gun, Ned's flying suit.

At the back, on a table flanked with potted palms, a radio loudspeaker was making a triumphant, but possibly rather weary speech. It said 'Jiminez' several times, so it sounded as if he was still in business down there. The only people listening were three locals—senior civil servants, judging by the size of the pistols in their belts. Probably they'd decided the Americana, under Bosco's wing, was the safest place for them that morning.

There were no Air Force men around apart from a couple of guards outside the glass front door. We arranged ourselves carefully—Ned led the way, J.B., Whitmore and I followed, and Luiz—still looking like a general dressed as a private—escorting us. We aimed for the back door.

Whitmore said: 'I need a gun.' We'd left his pistol up in the room; now he was staring hard at the pocket where I still had Ned's Magnum.

I shook my head. 'You could have it rather than me, but Ned's got to carry it through the air base gate. He'd look damn suspicious with an empty holster.'

'Yeah.' He saw the sense of it—reluctantly. 'Hell, though.'

Then he saw the civil servants.

He half-turned his head to Luiz and said out of the side of his mouth: 'Get one of those guys with us.'

Luiz frowned, then looked resigned, and took a diversion past the group. 'Señor, por favore. Presidente-Generalissimo Bosco . . .' Then we were round a corner and I couldn't hear any more.

As we came out into the open by the deserted patio bar,

227

Whitmore hung back. I heard footsteps in the corridor behind, then the whack of a fist. Ned, who hadn't noticed anything before, stopped. 'What the hell are you——?'

Luiz and Whitmore came out behind us, Whitmore carrying a fancy gunbelt covered in cartridge loops and silver studs and examining a big, long cowboy-type revolver.

'A real Colt forty-five,' he said happily. 'Hell, that's great.'

Luiz said wearily: 'Why did you think I chose *him*, Walt?'

'Thanks, fella.' He twirled the revolver expertly.

'Put the bloody thing away,' I snarled. 'You're a prisoner under escort.'

He looked down at his loose, one-button jacket, realized how obvious the belt would be, and sadly threw it into a bush. He jammed the Colt down the back of his trousers.

Ned shook his head in disbelief. 'You never stop playing, do you?'

Luiz said: 'My friend, he is not playing. He's real.'

We climbed into the white Mercedes.

After about ten minutes, Luiz said suddenly: 'Just here,' and Ned stopped the car. Luiz climbed out, went over to a tree at the roadside, and came back carrying the Browning Automatic Rifle.

Assuming that by now the ambush would have been cleared off the direct route, we were using the coast road again. I didn't want to run into Air Force traffic.

Ned looked at the rifle curiously. 'That the thing you was shooting at me with? You stuck one about five inches in front of me nose.'

Luiz smiled apologetically. 'I am sorry. Carr was not holding our plane completely steady.'

Ned gave him a look, banged the Mercedes into drive and growled: 'Well, you're kidding yourself anyway. You won't get past the gate carrying that. Nobody in our lot carries BARS—can't afford 'em.'

'They are expensive,' Luiz agreed, 'compared with these unfortunate little tin things.' He held up the sub-machine gun and sneered at it. Then sighed and handed the rifle to the back seat. 'Hide it somewhere. I will carry the tin thing through the gate.'

Ned said: 'We've about a couple of miles to go. What d'you want me to do?'

'Where's the Dove parked?' I asked, shaking cartridges out of his Magnum.

'Second hangar. Past the tower.'

'Guarded?'

'You don't guard planes on a guarded base, matey. But it could be crowded. They might've hauled in a couple of Vamps to work on 'em there.'

I handed forward the empty revolver and said: 'But it wouldn't be odd if you drove your car right up there?'

'No-o.' He sounded a little reluctant. He was committed to helping us, but that didn't stop him hoping he'd fail. 'So what's your plan for the gate?'

'What's the normal procedure?'

'Him'—he nodded at Luiz—'he hands over his own pass and mine. I explain who the hell you are——'

'Prisoners Bosco wants to interrogate, fast,' I said.

J.B. said: 'A delegation from the American Embassy.'

'Make up your minds.'

Luiz said: 'I fear that will not work anyway.' He was examining the pass he'd pulled out of a pocket in his uniform. 'This photograph looks most unlike me—I am happy to say.'

'Then you're stuck again,' Ned said calmly. 'Anywhere else I can drop you?'

I leaned forward and tapped him on the shoulder. 'Gambling man—you lost a bet, remember? Now get us through the gate.'

Just the purr of the Mercedes at half speed, the thrum of the tyres on the jointed concrete road.

Then Ned said quietly: 'All right. Just sit tight and look proud and hope they haven't heard I'm down from coronel.'

The base swung into sight as the trees thinned out.

It was wrapped in a nine-foot barbed-wire fence, which was a lot more protection than I'd ever seen on any other airfield. But perhaps I just hadn't been in any other country where the most likely trouble was civil war—war without a front line.

The gate was just a gap, blocked by a thin red-and-white striped pole, but with a wooden trestle wrapped in more barbed wire that could be shoved into place in a few seconds. On one side was a small wooden guard hut. On the other, a concrete pit with a man leaning on a light machine gun. Two other guards, both with rifles.

Just before we reached it, Ned trod on the accelerator, then the brake, so we arrived on locked wheels, scattering gravel. Before we were even stopped, he had his head out of the window and shouting.

'Don't you know this bloody car by now? Get out the bloody road!'

The guard on his side stiffened nervously. '*Si, Coronel. Excepto General Bosco*——

'*PRESIDENTE Bosco, idiota!*' Ned screamed.

The guard got even stiffer. By now he was standing so tall he could hardly see into the car at all. '*Si, Coronel, si. Excepto*——'

'What's a matter? You know me, you know *him*'—a jerk of the hand at Luiz—'and them's *norteamericanos* the Presidente wants to see. All right?'

The guard looked unhappy.

'*Telefono,*' Ned said decisively. He shoved open his door.

'*No, no, Coronel.*' The guard spun around and yelled at his companion. The striped pole swung up. The guard whipped his rifle to the 'present' and we were through.

I said quietly: 'Thank you, Ned.'

There isn't a military organization in the world where a loud enough shout from a high enough rank can't bypass the most elaborate security arrangements. You can spend as long as you like telling sentries to demand passes, authorizations, identifications—but you'll always have spent longer telling them to jump when a colonel says jump.

And people still wonder why the military is so damn bad at keeping military secrets.

After a hundred yards, we swung left and were cruising

around the wide perimeter track itself. And ahead of us, the collapsed shape of a Vampire, the one that had been Ned's Number Two that morning. Nobody was working on it, and as we pulled off on to the grass to pass it, I saw why. It looked as if it had been hit by a gigantic shotgun: there were a dozen and more jagged holes the size of a spread hand punched through it; one rudder assembly was wiped clean off; a main undercarriage leg was gone. And the concrete a hundred yards all around it was littered with scattered and smashed bricks.

We'd got that one, all right. The Mitchell and me.

Ned said: 'Thank you, Keith.'

Then we were back on the track and coming up across the front of the first hangar on our left. A shabby old C-47 transport parked beside it, and tucked away inside, rusty and rotting, a couple of propeller fighters without propellers.

We passed the control tower on our right; a big office block, set well back, on our left. The second hangar came up ahead.

So far, the base had the tense, creepy feeling of being quiet—but not empty. Quiet because there were a lot of people all working hard and silently in their proper places, not walking around borrowing cigarettes and taking a coffee break. But all awake and alert.

Just one shot—maybe just one move that made us no longer fit into the pattern—and we'd have a hundred men on our necks.

'Exactly where's the Dove?' I asked—and found myself whispering.

'Far side.'

'Nothing blocking it?'

'Shouldn't be.' But reluctantly. 'Standing orders that it's always kept clear.'

'Drive up. Not fast, not slow.'

Luiz turned and handed the sub-machine gun over the seat back; I hoisted the rifle from under our feet and passed it awkwardly forward.

Then we were crossing the front of the hangar and the

base certainly wasn't empty and not even silent any more.

Despite the daylight, neon lights flared across the metal rafters. They'd hauled three Vamps inside there, and men—maybe fifty in all—were swarming over them like bees. The screaming, whining, rattling of electric tools swamped the car. I nearly panicked, nearly shouted to drive on. But there, against the far wall, just a few yards inside the hangar and facing out across the field, was the Dove.

Ned curled in towards it.

'Not right in front, chum,' I said. But he swung wide and stopped in line with the hangar wall.

The silence was a sudden, shocking thing. Everybody in the hangar had stopped to watch us—us, the men from the outside, who knew how things were going in town.

Ned pulled on the handbrake with a loud rasp and said: 'It's your party, matey. Introduce your guests.'

'Get out and show yourself.'

But Luiz was the first out, with an exaggerated military leap ending in a rigid at-attention, the rifle stiff across his chest. I shuffled past him and muttered: 'Wrong air force, chum.'

Then I turned to look around the hangar, as a visitor would, making it slow and deliberate. Fifty men stared back. But there was safety in numbers. One man will come and ask questions just because there's nobody else to ask them; with fifty, each reckons there's forty-nine others to make the first move.

I hoped. Repeat, hoped.

Then, slowly, the noise built again as man after man turned back to his work.

Whitmore had to lean in over my shoulder to make himself heard.

'We'll never get away with this, fella. The second you press the button, we'll have every goddamn man in the shop on our necks.'

'They're mechanics. You don't carry a gun to repair a plane.'

He cocked a slow eyebrow. 'Or she may not even be fuelled. Or the batteries——'

'She's the General's getaway plane. She'll be ready to get away.'

Logical—but with a lot of hope sprinkled on top. I turned and strolled back towards the Dove.

Luiz was still standing guard by the car, Ned near him. J.B. was leaning inside the open door, her hands out of sight behind it: she must have had the sub-machine gun there. And Whitmore had his Colt, Luiz the rifle—but Ned still had the Magnum. Well, if it came to a gunfight, my job was throwing rocks.

As I rounded the little airplane's nose I casually kicked the chock away from the nosewheel, then ducked under the wingtip down to the door on the left side. That put the Dove between me and the honest workmen.

After the Mitchell, she seemed abruptly unfamiliar; lower, a little wider, and clean, neat, modern. I smiled to myself: I'd never expected to think *that* of her. Then the familiar Dove smell hit me, and I knew her perfectly again. I dipped my head just the right amount, angled myself sideways just enough to pass between the passenger seats, and walked quickly up to the cockpit.

I didn't need to sit down. I just leant in over the seats and ran my hands across the controls and switches. Quietly, she woke up. Lights came on across the panel, instrument needles jumped off their stops, swayed, settled down. The fuel was there, the power was there, the air pressures were there— more than I'd ever seen on her. The General must really have had some work done. I shifted the fuel, throttle and pitch levers to where I wanted them; but that was all I could do. The next stage was the noisy one.

I hurried back and out of the door. The group had drifted in beside the Dove's nose, out of sight of the hangar. Except for Luiz, still stiffly at attention in a way the Republica Air Force had never achieved.

'All aboard that's coming aboard,' I said.

J.B. and Whitmore moved. Luiz stayed. Out of the side of his mouth, he said: 'I think, my friends, that I will stay.'

Everybody turned. Whitmore said: 'You're doing what?'

'Jiminez can use this gun. Perhaps me also.'

Whitmore blew up like a 500-pounder. 'Christ, you got a picture to finish!'

Luiz smiled very slightly. 'Perhaps in a week or so, Walt. When things are settled—one way or another.'

I said: 'You could've picked a better place to stay; not the middle of a fortified base.'

'I shall take the car.'

'You won't get it through the gate.'

'I think there is a hole in the wire—where Señor Rafter crashed. I can take the car that far.'

'It'll be guarded.'

He hefted the rifle in his hands. 'They will not be quick to shoot at this uniform.'

Whitmore said: 'You're still crazy.'

This time Luiz turned. 'Walt—I also have an investment to protect. Not as big as yours, perhaps—but I have it.'

I said softly: 'Just one life.'

But nobody else knew what we were talking about.

I said: 'All right—if anybody's going, let's go.'

Ned said: 'Nobody's going.'

* 33 *

WE hadn't been looking at him—not for far too long. The Magnum was in his hand.

Whitmore frowned at it, then me. 'You emptied it, didn't you?'

Ned said: 'But I filled it. Always carry a few loose rounds. Never know when you might need 'em.'

I said bitterly: 'And I thought you were paying a bet.'

He nodded. 'All paid. Said I'd get you through the gate. Well, you're through. Now let's go and talk to Bosco.'

Luiz, still watching the hangar with his back to Ned, said: 'Honour does not end as the clock strikes, my friend.'

'I'll bet it sounds even better in Spanish. Put down your gun and turn around.'

Slowly Luiz laid it down, stood up, turned. The Magnum

234

flicked to J.B. She brought the sub-machine gun from behind her back and put it down.

'Fine.' Ned let the Magnum hang loose, pointing towards the floor. 'I know Mr Walt bloody Whitmore's got one, but I think we'll leave it there. Unless he wants to try another fast draw?'

Whitmore just looked at him.

Ned grinned. 'Right. Now lets——'

Miranda came around the hangar wall, pistol in his hand.

Ned glanced at him, sighed. 'Your timing never was much good, was it, matey?'

Miranda frowned, the pistol poking around suspiciously. 'I saw your car arrive, Teniente. You were told to stay at the Americana. Why is *this*?'

He looked carefully around us. He saw Whitmore and J B, and me, just standing; he saw Ned, the Magnum not pointing at anything; he saw the Dove behind us . . .

Luiz said: 'Just a short trip to Puerto Rico.'

Miranda stared, then recognized Luiz's face above the uniform. And he got the idea. Almost the right one.

'*Traidor!*' He screamed at Ned.

'Now, look——' Ned started.

Miranda shot him.

The hangar was suddenly silent. Then Whitmore grabbed behind him and the big Colt was blasting. Miranda was flicked away as if by a gust of wind.

Then just the echoes in the metal rafters.

Luiz snatched up the Browning, ran out in front of the Dove and threw a burst at the roof. There was a rush and clatter as the mechanics dived off the Vampires for cover.

Luiz yelled: 'Get going!'

But I was bending over Ned. His eyes opened, and he grinned a bit crookedly. 'He's no better'n you are, Keith . . . should've blown me apart at that range.'

But there was already a wide bloodstain spreading through his flying suit, just below his left ribs.

I said: 'I'll get you out of here.'

'Go to hell . . .' His voice was a series of grunts. 'You was right . . . I'm in command here . . . specially now Miranda's finished . . .'

'Ned, don't be a damn fool.'

Luiz shouted: 'Get *started*!'

Ned managed another grin. 'You heard him.'

I waited uncertain for a moment—then lifted a hand, waved, and ran for the Dove.

Thirty seconds later she started to move, both engines turning, but spitting and coughing as I pushed them from cold to full boost.

Luiz fired a last burst across the hangar, threw himself into the Mercedes, and backed away in one tearing sweep. As we bumped on to the grass, I saw him straightening out and accelerating on the perimeter track.

There was hardly any wind—but there was that mounted machine-gun. I pushed down twenty degrees of flap and just held her straight across the grass, across the runway—and into the air two hundred yards short of the far boundary fence.

A few minutes later, as I climbed out over the sea heading for the Punta del Almirante, J.B. came forward into the cockpit. 'I think Luiz made it. I saw the car by the fence. If he got that far, he'd get the rest.'

She eased herself carefully into the co-pilot's seat. 'Well, it's been quite a day for a boy who doesn't take risks and doesn't gamble. You really are slipping, Keith. Better retire now.'

I nodded. 'How's Whitmore?'

'Busy figuring out how he can write Luiz out of the script if he gets killed or elected Minister of Culture or something.'

We passed through 8,000 and I took her up another 200, throttled back and put her on the step. The General really had done some work on her; she was in a lot better shape than when he'd first pinched her. And now even a check four wouldn't come too expensive.

I trimmed the Dove precisely and loosed the wheel to prove it. J.B. reached across and took my hand.

'Jamaica?' she asked.

'First stop.'

'And second stop?'

I considered. 'Tell me—d'you happen to know a place the FBI not only doesn't have an office but doesn't go on holiday, either?'